Disciple's Quest III
Esther & Overcomer
Women of God

Walter F. Cantrell

ISBN-13:978-0692702970

ISBN-10:0692702970

Cover Design by Tyson Roberts

Editing by Rebecca LuElla Miller

All Scripture verses are the Author's own wording or taken from the King James Version or the New King James Version. All Scripture quotes are listed at the back of the book.

Scripture taken from the New King James Version®. Copyright © 1982 by Thomas Nelson. Used by permission. All rights reserved.

Published in the United States by Grace and Truth Publishing

:

DEDICATION

I would like to dedicate this book to my lovely daughter,
Tori Cantrell. She is the first one to read through my rough drafts
and gives me valuable input. I'm thankful for her as my daughter, and
as my partner in this writing endeavor.

Table of Contents

1

THE ADVENTURE BEGINS

Esther was in the fight of her life. She struck one of the creatures with her Sword, sending it squealing into the forest. Loud grunting noises emanated all around, signaling that others would attack soon. She leaned against her Sword to catch her breath. "God," she prayed, "give me the strength and the wisdom to prevail." The ground began to rumble as if a herd of wild animals was stampeding. Suddenly her enemies darted out of the woods and shot straight toward her.

Each creature—dark black and weighing at least two hundred pounds—looked like a wild boar with large sharp teeth. One stood in front of her, thrusting its head upward and digging into the dirt with its hoofs. Suddenly the creature lowered its head and charged. Esther slammed her Shield into its face, knocking the creature off balance and sending it rolling toward the edge of the trail. Another wild boar-like creature rushed her from behind, but she quickly turned and brought her Sword down on top of its neck. The creature crumpled to the ground and lay still. Another one charged toward her and jumped up into the air. Esther took cover behind her Shield, and the creature bounced off then ran away.

Two more of the wild boar creatures emerged from the woods on opposite sides, squealing and lowering their heads. They then both charged Esther at the same time. She thrust out her Shield toward the one on the left while striking with her Sword at the one coming from her right. Both fell to the ground and squealed in pain. Suddenly, a much larger wild boar-like creature stepped out of the woods and stalked her. It sniffed at one of the creatures that lay wounded on the ground, then circled her as it snorted loudly.

The creature drew closer and let out an awful grunting sound. Without warning, it rushed at her full speed. Esther raised her Shield just in time to repel the assault. The wild boar retreated a few steps and snorted defiantly. Hearing a rustling sound behind her, Esther glanced over her shoulder. Her other enemies were starting to recover from the blows she'd inflicted. Soon they'd have her surrounded.

The larger boar-like creature started to circle her again, but Esther moved before it could attack. With her outstretched Shield protecting her, she charged toward her enemy. The boar jumped at her throat, but Esther dodged to the left and smashed her Shield into the side of its head. The creature landed on the ground with a thud and rolled over on its back. As it struggled to stand up, Esther plunged her Sword deep into its neck. The boar-like creature squealed in pain, then collapsed and lay lifeless on the ground.

When the other beasts saw that their champion had been vanquished, they ran toward the woods and disappeared. Esther knelt to catch her breath, while still keeping a constant watch for any more enemies. She'd been up since early dawn, and this battle had been exhausting. These wild boar-like creatures had been tracking her ever since she started on this trail, and she'd heard them making terrible grunting noises all along the way. She had to stay constantly on guard because she didn't know how many there were, or when they might attack.

The constant anticipation of the battle had been almost as grueling as the attack itself. A dense thicket of trees lined each side of the trail Esther had been traveling, and while she could see what was on the narrow path in front of her, she never knew what was just off the trail and lurking in those woods.

The fight with these creatures and the events leading up to it taught Esther that she had to walk forward on her path trusting in God, even when she wasn't able to see everything clearly around her. If she used up all her strength worrying about the battle that might be ahead, she would not have the strength that was needed when the battle occurred.

After spending some time recovering from her exhaustion, Esther continued on. A short while later, the trail opened up into a meadow, leaving the dense woods behind. A sign planted in the ground announced that an inn was just up ahead. Seeing that her path was heading straight toward it, Esther picked up her pace.

When she arrived, she knocked on the door, and an older woman greeted her and checked her into a room. Esther had been hiking and camping for days, so she was glad to finally be able to relax and get cleaned up.

First, she took a nice warm bath, then slipped into some comfortable clothes. She sat down in front of a dresser and peered into the mirror. Esther had long blonde hair that looked like silk. Her skin was soft, and her kind blue eyes gleamed with innocence. She had a sweet, gentle smile that made everyone she met feel accepted and important. Her face had a peaceful glow which some of her friends described as the appearance of an angel.

Esther picked up a brush from the dresser and began to work the snarls from her newly washed hair. Staring into the mirror, her thoughts drifted to the events that brought her here. It was only two weeks ago that she began traveling on her own for the first time. She had just graduated from a House of Knowledge and was excited to explore the world and embark on new adventures.

She had attended the House of Knowledge for four years, and while there she became close friends with her roommate, Melissa. After their second year in attendance, they began to go on adventures. None turned out to be dangerous, but even through minor skirmishes with different enemies, Esther learned to use her Sword and her armor well. She and Melissa often talked about traveling together after they graduated, but in their last year at the House of Knowledge, Melissa became very close to a young man named Collins. By the second semester, they started making plans to be married soon after graduation.

The last few weeks at the House of Knowledge went by quickly, and the day of graduation arrived. The commencement ceremony was inspiring, and Esther's parents were so proud of her. She had graduated with honors and was near the top of her class. A celebration dinner followed the ceremony, and all of her instructors wished her great success. That evening she told her parents that she believed God was calling her to travel on her own. The idea concerned them, but Esther agreed to stay with them a few days to discuss it further before heading out.

Her parents left to go back home, but Esther stayed because Collins and Melissa were getting married the next day in the campus chapel. Esther was the maid of honor, and she helped Melissa with the preparations. The wedding was beautiful, and many of their friends at the House of Knowledge attended. During the reception, it hit Esther that she was twenty-two and had yet to be in a serious relationship. She observed Collins and Melissa together and wondered when it would be her time to meet someone special. She had met a few interesting and eligible classmates during the last four years, but none of the relationships went beyond friendship.

Around the same time that Melissa had announced her engagement, many of Esther's other fellow students became involved in serious relationships. She had assumed her turn would come soon, but with graduation now over, Esther realized it wasn't to be. Seeing Melissa with her new husband drove home the reality that she remained single. Her relationship status weighed on her as if a giant sign hung above her head that read, "Destined to be old and unmarried."

The day after the wedding, she left to go stay with her parents for a few days. At first, they were concerned about Esther being on her own, but after a long discussion during that first evening, they felt reassured. The next morning they all discovered that Esther's path was moving away. After a time of prayer and eating breakfast together, she set out on her journey.

Initially, everything had been quiet and uneventful. Esther spent some nights camping and some staying at different inns. Even when she camped, there were always others nearby. However, yesterday, her path veered off toward a small forest. A narrow trail ran through the middle, and at first, the trees on each side were spaced far enough apart so she could easily see all around her. But as she went further, the forest became more dense, and she could hardly see into the woods at all. Then she started hearing loud snorting and grunting, as if unseen creatures were taunting her. The constant fear and dread of the unknown wore her down so that she had little resources to fight back when the creatures had begun darting out to attack her.

Esther stretched out on her bed at the inn and reflected on all the events of her day. The Holy Spirit impressed upon her that He'd led her to a place that was beyond her comfort zone. Yes, there were enemies in the forest, but God had never left or forsaken her. She needed only to place her trust in Him.

Esther took out her Book and turned to a comforting passage that she'd learned during the past year. "Do not fret or worry about anything, but in everything, continue to make your desires known to God, praying with definite requests and an attitude of thanksgiving. And God's peace, which transcends all understanding, will place a guard around your heart and mind in Christ Jesus."

Esther asked God to forgive her for allowing worry and fear to dominate her thoughts. She had spent far too long dwelling on her fears and so very little time reflecting on the words from her Book. She thanked God for His guidance and protection. She then read the Twenty-third Psalm. A couple of lines, in particular, stood out:

"He leads me in the paths of righteousness for His name's sake."

God was the One that would lead her in the path she was to go, and she could always trust it would be a path of righteousness to bring glory to His name.

"Yes, even though I walk through the valley of the shadow of death, I will fear no evil, for You are with me. Your rod and Your staff, they comfort me."

It was God that would be with her even during those times when there was danger all around. She could be comforted knowing that His rod was there to protect her and His staff to guide her.

As she prepared to go to sleep, the refreshing power of God's words soothed her soul. Soon she drifted off.

The next morning she wrote a letter to her parents, letting them know she was safe and doing well. She didn't mention her battle yesterday because something like that would be better shared in person. She finished the letter and then went downstairs for breakfast.

After eating, Esther packed up and started on her way. She traveled for a little while, then came upon a House of Instruction where a lady with thick gray hair was outside weeding the flower beds lining the walkway. She wore a pleasant and kind expression, and despite her apparent age, her face didn't have a wrinkle on it.

Esther strolled up and stopped a few feet from her. "I love those flowers. They're so pretty."

"Why thank you. I believe it's important that a place of worship should have the beauty of God's creation all around it. I'm Mrs. Peterson."

"I'm Esther."

Mrs. Peterson took off her gloves. "I see that you're traveling alone."

"Yes ma'am, I graduated from a House of Knowledge a few weeks ago, and I've been traveling ever since."

Mrs. Peterson pointed toward her home, which was the next house over. "If you'd like, you're welcome to join us for lunch. My husband is the leader of this House of Instruction. We'd be glad to have you."

Esther set down her backpack. "Thank you so much, but you must let me help you with your flowers."

Mrs. Peterson welcomed the offer, and Esther spent the rest of the morning helping her weed the flowerbed. They had a quick lunch together, then Mrs. Peterson gave her a tour of the community. When they came back, Esther helped her prepare dinner.

When everything was almost ready, Mr. Peterson walked in the door. He was a stout man who looked to be quite strong even in his older age, and he carried himself as a man who wouldn't tolerate foolishness. As soon as he smiled though, he showed that his heart was full of grace and mercy. He headed into the kitchen and greeted his wife with a kiss on the cheek.

Mrs. Peterson put her arm around her husband's waist. "This lovely young lady is Esther. She just recently graduated from a House of Knowledge and has been traveling on her own. She's been so helpful today."

Mr. Peterson smiled at Esther. "My wife always has a lot to do, so I'm sure she appreciated your help."

Esther nodded. "I've enjoyed spending time with her, and helping was the least I could do to repay her hospitality."

Mrs. Peterson and Esther finished the dinner preparations, and they all sat down at the table.

Mr. Peterson glanced toward Esther. "This reminds me of when we used to have dinners with our daughter, Stacy. Several years ago she left to attend a House of Knowledge, and when she graduated, she also traveled by herself for awhile. She eventually met a nice young man, and they married. They live about four hours from here, and we visit them a few times a year."

The news that a young woman could still meet someone and fall in love even after graduation encouraged Esther. Perhaps she had been wrong to think her best opportunity for love had already passed.

Mrs. Peterson handed a pot full of potatoes to her husband. "I guess it was about twenty years ago that Stacy went off to travel on her own. We constantly thought about her, and we prayed for her all the time. I'm sure your parents are going through the same thing."

Esther scooped out a spoonful of potatoes and poured some gravy over them. "I'm sure my parents are concerned about me and praying every day. I wrote them a letter and sent it off before I came here."

"That was very thoughtful," said Mrs. Peterson. "They'll appreciate hearing from you as often as possible."

Mr. Peterson studied Esther, and he understood why his wife had taken to her so quickly—she resembled their daughter. Undoubtedly his wife would want to ask her to stay a few days.

He put his hand on his wife's shoulder and motioned toward Esther. "How would you like a job helping my wife for a little while. I've heard her talk about several tasks she keeps wanting to get done but doesn't have the time. You could stay here and use our daughter's old room."

Mrs. Peterson beamed. "That's a great idea."

Esther said, "That's very kind of you. I'll pray about it this evening, but I already feel so at home that I know I would enjoy staying here for a little while."

Mrs. Peterson reached for her hand. "There's a lot to do, and we'd insist on giving you some money."

"Oh no," said Esther, shaking her head. "I couldn't take anything from you. Providing room and board would be payment enough."

Mrs. Peterson patted her hand. "We'll work that out later. When you do go out on your own again, you're going to need a little money. Our daughter certainly did."

Esther agreed to stay the night and then check her path in the morning. She was very grateful for the offer. Her parents had given her some money for graduation, but it would soon run out. So taking a job to earn more, was an appealing idea.

They had some apple pie for dessert, then Mrs. Peterson showed her to her room. As Esther lay down on her bed to go to sleep, she thought about how God was revealing Himself as her Shepherd by providing exactly what she needed when she needed it.

2

NEW OPPORTUNITIES

Esther woke up, and after a time of reading and praying, she came downstairs. When she checked outside, she saw that her path had not moved. This was exactly what she had hoped for, and it was confirmation that God wanted her to spend more time with the Petersons. When she first started out on her own, the idea of being independent seemed adventurous and exciting, but now she was glad to be in a more predictable environment.

Mr. Peterson had left earlier to visit some members of his congregation, and Mrs. Peterson was busy putting some dishes away.

Esther entered the kitchen. "Good morning."

Mrs. Peterson glanced over her shoulder as she reached to place a saucer into the cupboard. "Good morning."

"Thank you so much for allowing me to stay."

"You're quite welcome." Mrs. Peterson dried off a cup and placed it on a shelf. "Will you be staying with us longer?"

Esther smiled and nodded. "I'd like that."

Mrs. Peterson gave her a hug and then pointed to a seat at the table. "Sit." She set out a bowl of hot oat cereal before her, then took a seat next to her. "I'm so glad you're going to be staying with us. I'll enjoy having the company as well as the help."

After Esther finished eating, Mrs. Peterson took her out behind the house and showed her the garden she had planted. While they discussed how often vegetables needed to be weeded and watered, a mom and her daughter strolled up.

"Good morning Mrs. Peterson."

"Good morning, Mrs. Walker, and good morning to you, Mary."

Mary looked to be about six years old, and she was carrying a doll made out of scrap pieces of fabric.

Esther knelt down in front of her. "That's a lovely doll you have. What's her name?"

Mary swayed side to side, smiling shyly at the ground, then glanced up at Esther. "Her name is Kelly."

"That's a great name. I used to have a special doll when I was your age too. Her name was Lisa."

Esther stood up, and Mrs. Peterson introduced her to Mrs. Walker.

"It's nice to meet you Esther. Are you going to be staying for a few days?"

"Yes, I will."

Mrs. Peterson put her hand on Esther's shoulder. "We're excited that she accepted our invitation to stay with us for a little while, and she's already proved to be quite helpful."

Mrs. Walker glanced around. "There's certainly a lot to do. Keeping up a home is enough, but with all you do for our House of Instruction, I'm not sure how you have the time to stay on top of everything."

"Which reminds me," said Mrs. Peterson, "be sure to spread the word about our women's meeting later tonight. Can you make it?"

"I'll be there," said Mrs. Walker, "and of course Mary will too."

With a wave, Mrs. Walker and Mary headed back toward their home.

Esther watched as they walked off, then turned to Mrs. Peterson. "A women's meeting sounds exciting. What do you do?"

"One of the ladies shares a teaching from the Book, and then we have tea and dessert. Of course, you're invited."

Esther clasped her hands together. "I can't wait."

Mrs. Peterson and Esther worked in the garden most of the day, and that evening they had a quick dinner with Mr. Peterson before getting ready to go to the women's meeting. When they arrived at the House of Instruction, they made their way downstairs. Esther helped Mrs. Peterson set out some chairs in a classroom. Soon others began trickling in, and those who had brought the tea and brownies set them on the table. Many of the women of the surrounding area came, and there were several that had daughters close to Mary's age. It was a great time of fellowship, and Esther enjoyed meeting and talking with all the women who attended.

When everyone else had left, Esther cleared off a small table that the younger girls had used when they ate their snacks. She brushed crumbs into her hands then dusted them into the trash can. "I don't want to speak out of place, Mrs. Peterson, but I was wondering if you've considered whether or not the young girls might benefit from a special time of their own?"

Mrs. Peterson finished straightening the chairs. "What do you have in mind?"

"Before I left to go to the House of Knowledge, I used to teach a class for young girls, and as I sat through the meeting tonight, I realized how much I missed that. What if I prepared a lesson just for them and they could learn stories from the Book? They could also have some time to play together and enjoy a snack."

Mrs. Peterson put her hand to her chin. "You know, that might be a really good idea. It would give the girls an opportunity to be together, and the moms would have some time to themselves. But if you did this, you wouldn't get to fellowship with the other women."

Esther picked up a broom and started sweeping the floor. "That's okay; I'm sure there will be other opportunities."

Mrs. Peterson said, "I tell you what. We'll let the other women know before next week, and if there's no objection, then we'll plan on it."

After the next service at the House of Instruction, Esther talked to all the mothers of the young girls about what she had planned. She also let the young girls know. "And be sure to bring your dolls," she said to each one.

When it was time for the next women's meeting, Esther was excited. She gathered up everything she needed and headed over to the House of Instruction early to set things up. Mrs. Peterson had told her about a smaller room down the hall from the one where the women met. Esther quickly put everything in place, and soon the ladies began to arrive. Seeing Esther in the doorway of the smaller room, they brought their daughters to her. As each young girl approached, Esther knelt to say hello and welcomed them in.

She had set up an extra seat for each girl so they would have a chair for their dolls. After all the girls had taken their places, four chairs remained empty because some had not brought dolls.

Esther moved to the front of the classroom and said, "I want to welcome all of you, and I also want to welcome your little friends." She reached down and retrieved a small basket, then set it on the table beside her. "I must tell you, though, that I have a problem, and I need your help. I have four dolls that do not have little girls to take care of them."

Earlier in the week, when Esther had asked each girl to bring a doll, she suspected from their reaction that some did not have one to bring. She had spent her spare time through the week collecting bits of fabric and other materials to make dolls.

Esther reached into the basket. "Who would like to take care of one of these dolls?"

The four girls who didn't bring one instantly raised their hands.

Esther waved for them to come forward. "Thank you so much for giving these a new home."

Each of the girls approached the basket and picked out a doll.

Esther placed her index finger to her cheek. "Now I have one more problem. They don't have names yet, so you'll have to decide what we should call them."

The girls were delighted to share with others the names of their new dolls.

Esther sat down in a chair in front of them. "Before we start our lesson I would like to ask if any of you need prayer for anything."

One girl asked for prayer for her little brother who had been coughing, and another said she would like prayer for her grandmother who had not been feeling well.

Esther noticed that another little girl looked like she was about to cry. "Emily, how are you doing?"

The little girl stared at the floor for a moment then said, "My doll is sad."

"Can you tell me why she is sad?" asked Esther.

Emily hugged her doll. "Sheila is sad because her daddy is sick, and her mommy has been crying."

Esther knelt next to Emily and grasped the doll's hand. "I'm sorry to hear that. Girls, let's pray for Sheila."

All the girls closed their eyes, and Esther prayed for Sheila's daddy to get better, and for her mommy not to be sad. After praying for the other girls' prayer requests, she told them the story of Jonah and the whale.

When Esther finished, she stood up. "Who would like some tea and cookies?"

All the girls raised their hands and said, "Me!"

Esther had prepared a cup of tea and a cookie for each of the girls, and she had a small plastic cup for each of them to pretend to give their dolls a drink. The girls enjoyed sipping tea and eating their cookies. They felt like big girls who were doing the same things their mommies did in the other room.

After everyone was done with their snack, Esther collected all the cups. She then led them in a time of singing songs such as "Jesus Loves Me." When they finished, she gave the girls some time to play with their dolls. Soon the women's meeting ended, and all the moms stopped by to pick up their daughters. After everyone left, Esther told Mrs. Peterson what Emily had said about her family.

"Oh yes, it's been very tough for them. The mother has not said much in our meetings because she doesn't want to burden others, but they are going through a difficult time. The father operates a small store, and he has not been able to work for over a week. The mom, Mrs. Jackson, has tried to carry on the business while also keeping up with everything at home. On top of that, she also has to take care of her husband."

Esther said, "Do you think it would be okay if I went over to help out tomorrow evening?"

Mrs. Peterson smiled and patted her on the hand. "I think that would be wonderful. I'll help you prepare a meal, and you can take it for their supper."

The next evening Esther took a freshly cooked roast and some steamed vegetables to the Jackson family, and when they were finished eating, she helped straighten things up around the house. Mrs. Jackson was very appreciative. For the first time in awhile, she was able to get everything done and have a few moments to herself. Esther spent some time playing with Emily, and they thoroughly enjoyed the evening together. When it was time for Esther to leave,

Mrs. Jackson thanked her. Esther hugged her, and Mrs. Jackson almost cried. Esther said goodbye to Emily, then made a special point to also say goodbye to her doll Sheila.

Over the next couple of weeks, Esther went back to the Jackson's a few more times. To their relief and joy, Mr. Jackson slowly recovered. The last time Esther went to help, she asked Emily how Sheila was feeling.

Emily held up her doll and smiled. "Sheila is happy now."

Esther hugged the little girl.

A few days later Mr. Jackson was back on his feet and returned to his store. The Jacksons never forgot how much Esther helped them during their time of struggle. After that, Esther began searching for more opportunities to help others, and God used her to be a blessing to many in the community.

Shortly after she'd arrived at the Petersons, Esther had found a lovely field to take walks in during the evening. It was close enough to the village so that she could see the houses and the people milling about, but far enough away so that she only heard the sounds from the small forest off to the left. It was the perfect place to be alone and just stroll around by herself after dinner. At times, she would look toward the woods and wonder what lay on the other side, but as the sun began to set, she always made her way back to the Petersons in plenty of time for their customary tradition—eating dessert and summarizing the events of their day.

As the weeks passed, Esther was grateful for all that God was doing in her life, but there was just one thing she felt was missing. When she would go on walks in her favorite field, she sometimes experienced a profound sense of loneliness. Ever since graduation, she had felt that her life really wouldn't begin until she met that very special man who would one day become her husband. When God had led her to stay in this village, she wondered if she would meet someone here, but weeks later she still hadn't met a young man who was single and close to her age.

She had heard wonderful stories about falling in love, and now, teaching young girls again, she realized how much she wanted to be a mom. One evening after dinner while on her walk, Esther found herself talking aloud. "There's nothing wrong with wanting to fall in love is there? If I were married couldn't my husband, and I do even more good together for the Kingdom of God?"

The next time everyone gathered at the House of Instruction for their weekly meeting, Mr. Peterson taught a lesson about putting God first in their lives. He read from the Book, "But seek first the kingdom of God and His righteousness, and all these things shall be added unto you." He also read, "Therefore since you were raised up together with Christ, seek those things which are above, where Christ is sitting at the right hand of God. Continuously set your mind on things above, not on things on the earth. For you died, and your life has been hidden with Christ in God."

Mr. Peterson taught that they should be seeking God and pursuing things that have eternal meaning. He said there was nothing wrong with desiring the good things God provided on this earth, but his followers should make Him and His Kingdom their priority and trust Him to add things to their lives as He saw fit. Esther heard the words, but her mind was in a different place. She was daydreaming about one day meeting the man God had prepared for her.

The next evening as she strolled through her field after dinner, she saw a young, attractive man at the edge of the woods. He started walking straight toward her with a slight grin on his face, and Esther felt her heart jump. As he drew closer, his handsome features came into focus. He was even more attractive than at first glance. He stood close to six feet tall, had a slender build and black curly hair. His black trousers fit perfectly, and his royal blue shirt was neatly pressed. Esther swallowed nervously as he confidently strode up to her and stopped.

He grinned at her with his piercing blue eyes. "I thought I was the only one who liked to take long walks during the evenings."

Esther blushed as she struggled to make eye contact. "I enjoy watching the sun disappear over the mountain."

"Well, it's nice meeting you—"

"Oh, my name is Esther."

The young man reached out his hand. "My name is Michael."

3

MICHAEL

Michael pointed beyond the field. "Do you live close by?"

"Yes," said Esther, glancing over her shoulder. "I'm staying with a family in that village."

"That's nice. I live on the other side of those woods. I usually don't come around this area, but I felt led to stop by here today."

Esther said to herself, *he was led here?* Could God have brought him here just for her? God knew she had been praying to meet someone, and this couldn't just be a coincidence could it?

"I take walks out here most every evening," said Esther.

Michael glanced at the ground while smiling. "I may have to start taking walks out here too."

Esther talked with him for a few more minutes, then noticed that it was starting to get dark. "I must be going. I don't want the Petersons to be worried."

"Yes, you should go. Maybe I'll see you again."

Esther started to walk off but then quickly turned around. "I'll be here tomorrow evening around the same time."

"That's good to know," said Michael as he turned to leave.

As Esther happily strolled back to the Petersons, a tantalizing question began to form in the back of her mind. Had she just met her husband? When she walked in the door, she was smiling from ear to ear and looked as if she was in a daydream.

Mrs. Peterson said, "Hmm, what has made you so happy this evening?"

"Oh nothing, it was just such a nice walk," said Esther as she glided across the room.

She didn't want to share anything about Michael since she'd just met him. For now, she would keep this to herself. After dessert, she went off to her room and got ready for bed. As she drifted off to sleep, she thought about Michael.

Upon waking up the next morning, Esther immediately looked forward to taking another walk that evening. The day seemed to go by quickly, and right after dinner, she rushed out to the field. She waited until sunset, but Michael didn't appear. She was disappointed, but she reassured herself that he would come back soon.

Two more evenings passed without him showing up, but on the following evening, he appeared again. Esther was overjoyed, and it seemed that not having seen him for those few days, served only to increase her interest in him.

While it would be another three days before she'd see him again, he began to appear more frequently after that, and their talks became longer. Esther chatted away about her entire life-story, and Michael would smile and listen. He'd share a few details about his life, but he seemed content to let Esther do most of the talking.

One evening Michael said, "I've enjoyed spending all this time with you, but what I'd really like to do is take you to see where I live."

Esther peered into the woods. "I can't. It wouldn't be right."

"Of course," said Michael. "I'm sorry for being so forward."

Esther shook her head. "Oh no, I didn't mean to imply that." She thought for a moment then said, "I'd like to introduce you to the family I'm staying with, but I think the best way to do that is if you would attend service with me at our House of Instruction."

Esther felt nervous as soon as the suggestion left her lips. As of yet, she hadn't asked him anything about his spirituality or what he believed.

Michael shrugged his shoulders. "Sure, I'll come with you sometime."

Esther glanced around and smiled nervously. "How about tomorrow evening?"

"I can do that. Will you meet me out here and walk with me to the service?"

Esther quickly nodded. "Yes, of course. I can't wait to introduce you to the Petersons."

Esther was so excited. After arriving back at the house, she stood in the doorway feeling as if she was about to burst.

"What is it Esther?" said Mrs. Peterson.

She closed the door and leaned back against it. "I've been waiting to tell you, but a few weeks ago I met a young man while I was out on a walk. His name is Michael. He's going to be coming to the service tomorrow evening, and I can't wait to introduce you to him."

Mr. Peterson leaned forward. "Where is he from? I don't know of anyone named Michael around here."

Esther made her way to the kitchen. "He said he lived somewhere beyond the woods where I've been taking my walks."

Mr. Peterson thought about the area she was referring to. "I don't know of any homes or communities in that direction."

"Oh, I'm sure you may have missed it, or possibly it's a little further away," said Esther.

Mrs. Peterson motioned for her to have a seat at the table while she set out a fresh strawberry pie. "Well come sit down and tell us about him."

Esther took her place at the table. "It was as if God was answering my prayers while I was praying them. Each day as I would go for a walk, I would think about meeting someone special and being married. Of course, I had no idea it could happen this soon, but one day he just came walking out from the woods and toward the field. I felt as if it were a dream."

Mr. Peterson sat back and tapped on the arm of his chair.

Mrs. Peterson glanced at her husband then patted Esther on the knee. "I believe God answers prayers, and if He intends for you to be married, then I'm sure he will bring the right person into your life at the right time. But aren't you moving a little too quickly? You hardly know this young man."

"Of course I'm going to pray about it, and I'm not saying I know for certain that he is the one, but so far there's something that just feels right about the whole thing." Esther grabbed Mrs. Peterson's hand. "And this is the part I haven't told you yet. When I first met him, he said that he had been led to come out to the field where I was taking my walks, and then he said he knew why once he was there. Isn't that romantic?"

Mrs. Peterson tried to be supportive, and she was trying not to show just how concerned she was. "Well, we'll look forward to meeting this young man tomorrow evening then."

Esther stood up. "Isn't this great? I've only been following my path alone for a few weeks, and already God has sent someone special."

Esther went to her room, humming as she left.

Mr. Peterson sighed. "I'm not sure about this."

"I know," said Mrs. Peterson, nodding. "I'm concerned too, but we have to be careful how we express our reservations. Esther is so excited, and she's convinced herself that God is the one behind this."

Mr. Peterson stood up to go to bed. "I will be ready to believe the best about this young man, but I'm anxious to meet him and see what he's like."

"That's a good attitude," said Mrs. Peterson, as she too stood up to get ready for bed.

The next day Esther could not wait for the evening to arrive. When it was close to time for the service, she came downstairs. "I'll be back soon. I'm going to meet Michael, and walk with him to the House of Instruction."

Mr. Peterson's eyebrows narrowed. "I wish he would have come here first to meet us and then walk you over."

Esther put her hand on the door and turned the knob. "I'm sure he's just shy. I think he would feel more comfortable if I walked with him into the village." She went out the door quickly and hurried to meet him.

When Esther arrived at the field, Michael was not there. She started pacing and constantly glanced toward the woods, hoping that at any moment he would appear. As time passed, she became worried. Was he not coming? Had she moved too quickly in inviting him to meet others? Did she scare him off by asking him to come to a House of Instruction so soon? Esther drew closer to the woods, hoping to catch the sound of Michael's approach. It was almost time for the service to begin, and if she didn't leave soon, she would be late. But what if he came after she left? What if he thought she had not shown up to meet him?

Esther decided to wait a few more minutes, and then a few more. Finally, she heard footsteps in the woods and then Michael emerged. Esther was so relieved. She knew they were going to be late, but that didn't concern her at the moment. What mattered was that he came.

Michael leisurely strolled up. "Sorry I'm late. Work went longer than I thought, and I had to stay to finish something up."

"That's okay, I understand. We better get going. The service has already started."

Michael edged up closer. "Well if that's the case then there's no need to be in a hurry. Let's not rush."

In fact, he made sure they walked a little more slowly than they normally did. When they were close to the House of Instruction, they could hear the singing. Esther was a little nervous because she had not been late before. She always sat up front with Mrs. Peterson, and she was always in her place before the service began.

As they walked in, Michael leaned over and whispered. "We don't want to draw attention so why don't we just sit here in the back."

Esther pointed to a pew near the entrance with two empty spots on the end. By the time they took their places, the singing came to a close. Mr. Peterson stepped forward and asked everyone to remain standing for prayer. When Esther bowed her head, she felt something brush against her arm. She opened her eyes. Michael smiled, and she smiled back before closing her eyes again.

After the service, Esther and Michael waited toward the back while Mr. Peterson greeted all the others who had come. When everyone else had left, Mr. and Mrs. Peterson joined them.

Esther nervously held out her hand. "This is Michael."

Michael nodded toward them, and then glanced over at Mrs. Peterson. "Esther, you didn't tell me you had a younger sister."

Mrs. Peterson tried to force a smile, but Mr. Peterson rolled his eyes. He clasped his hands. "Esther tells us that you live behind those woods just beyond the field she's been walking in. I don't know of any homes or communities back there."

Michael grabbed his shirt collar and quickly flashed a smile. "Well, hmm, we just moved here recently. We have a small home at the edge of the woods. If you didn't know where it was you'd probably never find it."

Mr. Peterson took a deep breath and pressed his fingers together.

Mrs. Peterson tried to lighten things up. "Michael, how did you enjoy the service?"

Michael shrugged his shoulders. "It was good."

"Have you ever been to a House of Instruction before?" asked Mrs. Peterson.

"Oh yes, I've been to many different kinds of services. I find God in all of them."

Mr. Peterson slightly shook his head, and his wife quickly grasped his hand and squeezed. She then turned to Michael again. "Would you like to join us for some dessert? I have a freshly baked apple pie that just came out of the oven before we left."

Michael glanced toward the exit. "Thank you for the invitation, but I must be getting home. It was nice to meet you."

It was dark so Esther knew it would not be proper to walk with Michael all the way back to the field. She turned to Mrs. Peterson. "I'll go with him for just a little ways, and then I'll be right in."

As they left, Mr. Peterson picked up his Book, then closed the door. "I don't feel good about that young man."

"I know," said Mrs. Peterson, "but Esther seems to be taken with him. We need to pray about how to talk to her about this. You remember that Stacy once went through a similar stage."

Mr. Peterson sighed. "I remember."

Esther walked with Michael to the edge of the village, and just briefly she felt his hand glance against hers. Had it been an accident as they were walking, or did he do it on purpose? Whichever it was, Esther felt a rush of excitement when it happened. She said goodbye, then hurried back home.

When she stepped into the house, Mrs. Peterson was coming out of the kitchen. "Come on over and have some pie."

Esther sat down at the table, putting her hands to her chin. "Isn't he great?"

Mr. Peterson took a bite of pie and looked over at Mrs. Peterson. "I would have loved to spend more time with him. I was hoping to get to meet him before service."

"Oh, yes," said Esther as she sat up in her chair. "I'm sorry we were late. Michael said he had to finish working on something before he came."

"I missed having you sit beside me," said Mrs. Peterson.

"I did too, but Michael said he didn't want to draw attention away from the service, so we sat in the back."

Mr. Peterson started to say something, but Mrs. Peterson quickly put her hand on top of his. "Esther, don't you think you're spending a lot of time alone with this young man."

Esther ate a bite of her pie. "We're not really alone. It's always light out when we're in the field together, and there are always people out and about who can see us. I know it's important not to give people a reason to think something is happening when it's not. My parents taught me that. Michael has been a perfect gentleman since I met him."

For the rest of the evening, Esther chattered away about all the great qualities that she had seen in Michael. Mr. and Mrs. Peterson listened, but they were quietly praying and asking God for wisdom. They didn't say anything that night, but they were concerned. Before they went to sleep, they prayed for Esther and asked God to protect her.

4

TOUGH DECISIONS

The next day Esther was trimming some bushes with Mrs. Peterson.

After an hour had passed, Mrs. Peterson straightened and rubbed the small of her back. "I think I'll use an outdoor stool for these low branches. I'll be right back." She then stepped inside the house.

All of a sudden, someone's hands covered Esther's eyes from behind.

"Guess who," said a familiar male voice.

Esther whirled toward him. "Michael! What are you doing here? I mean, it's nice to see you."

Michael pulled out a small bouquet of flowers and held them out. "I came to give these to you."

Esther accepted the flowers, then held them to her nose. "They're beautiful, and they smell so nice."

Mrs. Peterson came back outside carrying her stool and a pitcher of water for her flowerbed. "Hello, Michael."

"Hello, Mrs. Peterson. It's good to see you again."

Mrs. Peterson sprinkled some of the water on a row of daffodils. "I'm sorry you weren't able to stay and have some pie with us."

"I was too."

Mrs. Peterson saw the flowers Esther was holding. She thought they looked a lot like the ones Mrs. Walker kept in an arrangement on her front porch. "That's a nice bouquet of tulips and daisies."

Extending the flowers, Esther said, "Yes they are. Michael brought them."

He motioned toward the field. "Would it be okay if I took Esther for a short walk?"

As Esther dusted her hands on her apron, she glanced at Mrs. Peterson. Her eyes almost begged to go with him.

Mrs. Peterson knew there was only one answer she could give. "Sure. I'll finish up trimming the bushes, and I'll meet you over at the House of Instruction." She took a seat on her stool and picked up her trimmers.

Michael and Esther headed toward the field. As they neared the grassy open, Michael glanced over his shoulder to see if anyone was watching. When he didn't see anyone, he grasped Esther's hand. She peeked back as well, and when she didn't see anyone, she relaxed her hand in his. They strolled in silence for a few minutes, just smiling at each other.

When they came to the area where they normally stopped, Michael turned toward Esther and grasped her other hand. "I'm looking forward to our time together tonight. There's something I want to talk to you about."

Esther smiled and stared at her hands in his. "What is it?"

"You'll have to wait to find out. I better let you get back before Mrs. Peterson starts to worry. I'll see you later."

Michael let his hands slowly slide from hers, then he traipsed into the woods.

Esther made her way to the House of Instruction where Mrs. Peterson was inside sweeping the floors. Esther retrieved a broom from a closet and began helping.

Mrs. Peterson gave her a concerned look. "This is the first time he's come during the day. Was everything okay?"

Esther put both hands on her broom and leaned up against it. "Yes. He just wanted to bring me some flowers and let me know he was looking forward to our walk tonight."

After they finished sweeping, Mrs. Peterson motioned for Esther to have a seat on one of the benches. "It's a good time to take a break."

Esther looked like she was still in a daydream, but Mrs. Peterson felt it was time to probe a little deeper into what had been happening. "How much do you know about this young man? You've spent a lot of time with him, but do you really know anything about him?"

Esther had been gazing toward the field as in a daze, but she quickly faced Mrs. Peterson. "I know many things about him. He's thoughtful, kind, and he's so caring."

Mrs. Peterson placed her hand on Esther's shoulder. "But what do you really know about him? What is his relationship with God like?"

"Oh," said Esther as she shifted around, "we haven't talked much about that kind of thing. He knows how important my relationship with God is. He respects that, and he's never said anything negative about my beliefs."

"But has he said anything positive about them? You're an adult, and I don't want to pry into your affairs, but I'm sure you've been taught by many people how important it is to be in a relationship with someone who has gone through the Building of Reflection and up the Hill of Calvary."

Esther had briefly thought of these things at the beginning of her time with Michael, but she had also spent time thinking of answers to these kinds of questions. "I believe Michael is a good person. I think sometimes it's important not to go too fast on certain subjects. What if he hasn't yet begun his Quest? What if God has placed me in his life to be that person who helps him begin? Moving too quickly could scare him off."

Mrs. Peterson had a similar conversation with her own daughter many years ago, so she understood how Esther was thinking. "You've heard us talking about our daughter Stacy. When she was close to your age, she began spending time with a young man that her father and I had concerns about. Stacy convinced herself that their relationship was God's will, and she became upset if anyone suggested otherwise. One day she saw him kissing one of her friends, and she was devastated."

Esther quickly sat up and put her hands on the bench in front of her. "That would never happen with Michael. I'm sorry to hear about what happened to your daughter, but you shouldn't worry about me."

Mrs. Peterson took Esther's hand. "I feel God has brought you into our lives during this time for a reason. I've become very fond of you, and I don't want anything to happen that would hurt you."

Esther took a deep breath, then slowly breathed out. "I believe God has brought me here as well, and I'm thankful for how kind you've been to me. Please don't worry."

Esther hugged her, and then they finished cleaning up. That evening Esther couldn't wait to see Michael again. She helped Mrs. Peterson with dinner, but when they sat down, she hardly ate anything. She quickly asked to be dismissed and then darted toward the field.

When Esther was gone, Mr. Peterson stared at the door. "I don't know what's going to happen, but I don't have a good feeling about this."

Mrs. Peterson told him about Michael's visit earlier and her talk with Esther. "I feel like I've said all that I can."

Mr. Peterson nodded, then whispered a prayer.

When Esther reached the field, she didn't have to wait long before Michael arrived.

After a few minutes of listening to Esther talk about her day, he grasped her hands. "These walks have been great, but I feel like I want to spend more time with you. Remember when I asked about showing you where I live?"

"Yes."

"I want you to come with me tomorrow and meet my family, and then I'd like for us to go on a camping trip together."

Esther glanced back at the village. She knew the Peterson's would never approve. She knew no one would support such a thing, and even more, she knew that she shouldn't approve either. Esther stared at the ground and began shuffling her feet. "I don't know about that."

Michael put his right hand under her chin. "Don't you want to spend more time with me?"

"Of course I do," said Esther. "But it wouldn't be proper."

Michael cocked his head to the side. "Proper? Who decides what's proper? We'll have separate tents. You're an adult. At some point, you're going to be leaving the Petersons, and you'll be camping at times right?"

"Well yes, that's true."

"And at times there will be other people camping around you, right?"

Esther nodded. "I suppose so."

Michael shrugged his shoulders. "So what's the difference? If you're concerned about what the Petersons think, just tell them you're going on a short trip, and you'll be back soon. They'll understand."

Esther thought to herself, how could I lie to the Petersons after all they've done for me?

Michael could tell she was struggling. "Listen, I'll leave it up to you. I didn't want to say anything, but I may be going away soon. This might be our last chance to spend this kind of time together. In fact, it might be the last time I'll be able to see you at all for awhile."

Esther tightened her grip on his hand, but she didn't know what to say. If she didn't take this opportunity, maybe she wouldn't see him again. Maybe while he was gone, he would meet someone else. She felt conflicted and worried.

Michael began rubbing her hands with his thumbs as he gently held them. "I don't want to put any pressure on you. I'll be right here tomorrow morning just a few hours after the sun rises. If you don't show up, then I'll have your answer, but if you're ready to come with me, then we'll have a great time together."

Esther gazed into the forest. "It's so much to think about."

Michael released her hands and began backing away. "I understand. I hope to see you tomorrow."

Esther stood there and watched him disappear into the woods. As she turned to go back to the Petersons, she had many different thoughts going through her mind. She knew what was right, but she also knew what she wanted.

When she walked into the house, Mr. and Mrs. Peterson had just started dessert.

"Would you like a piece of cake?" asked Mrs. Peterson.

"No, thank you," said Esther.

Mrs. Peterson motioned for her to have a seat. "Is everything okay?"

Esther stared at the door. "Yes."

Mrs. Peterson scooted closer. "Is there anything you'd like to talk about?"

Esther shook her head. "No, I've just got a lot on my mind. I think I'm going to go on to bed." She stood up to leave. "Goodnight."

After Esther left the room, Mr. and Mrs. Peterson discussed what could be wrong, then prayed together and spent the rest of the evening quietly reading.

Lying in her bed, Esther's mind was racing. What was she going to do? Should she pray? Should she check her path? She knew deep down what she'd discover if she did those things. Instead, she began to think about what she could tell the Petersons. She'd have to make her story convincing. She was no longer thinking about whether or not she should go with Michael, but how she was going to do it. She continued to plan as she drifted off to sleep.

The next morning she had breakfast with Mrs. Peterson as usual, but Esther was uncharacteristically quiet.

She ate slowly. In fact, she barely touched her food. Finally, Esther set her plate to the side. "Do you remember when I talked about Melissa, my roommate at the House of Knowledge?"

Mrs. Peterson finished the last bit of her toast. "Yes, you mentioned she was married right after graduation."

"Yes, that's her. After the wedding, she gave me the address where Collins was going to build a house and told me to write to her when I settled in somewhere. I've been so busy, but I finally got around to writing her last week. I received a letter from her the other day, and she's not been feeling well. I've been concerned about her, and I believe I should go and spend a few days with her."

Mrs. Peterson put her hand on Esther's arm. "I hope everything will be okay."

Esther patted her hand. "I'm sure it will. It will be good to see her again."

"When will you be leaving?"

Esther hesitated then took a drink of orange juice. "I'll be leaving as soon as I get some things packed up."

"I wish you could stay for dinner. Mr. Peterson has gone to a nearby town for the day and won't be back until this evening. I'm sure he would want to say goodbye to you."

Esther did not want to sit through an entire dinner and have to lie to the Petersons. "Thank you, but I have just enough time to make it to an inn before sundown."

"How long will you be gone?"

"Just a few days, and then I'll be back."

Mrs. Peterson began to clear the table. "We'll pray for you to have a safe journey."

Esther picked up her plate and took it into the kitchen. "Thank you. I'm sure the time will fly by." She went to her room and packed enough for a few days journey. When she was ready to go, Esther joined Mrs. Peterson in the kitchen.

"Take this basket of food with you," said Mrs. Peterson. "It should be more than enough to last until you get to an inn."

Esther gave her a hug. "Thank you for everything. I'm sure I'll be back soon."

That evening when Mr. Peterson returned home, he greeted his wife with a kiss. Realizing they were alone, he said, "Where's Esther?"

Mrs. Peterson went into the kitchen to grab some plates and silverware. "She left for a few days to see Melissa—you remember, her roommate from the House of Knowledge. She's not been feeling well, and Esther wants to check on her."

Mr. Peterson sat down. "How did Esther find out that she was sick?"

Mrs. Peterson set the table. "She said she received a letter from her."

A concerned look came on his face.

Mrs. Peterson put her hand on his shoulder. "What's wrong?"

"I just spoke with Matt the letter carrier a few hours ago, and I asked him if any mail had arrived. He said there hadn't been any mail here for weeks."

Mr. and Mrs. Peterson stared at the door, both wondering the same thing. Where had Esther gone, and why had she lied?

5

THE DECEPTION OF SIN

As soon as Esther left, she hurried out the door and ran straight toward the field. She didn't look down to check her path because she already knew this was not where her path was leading. But couldn't God work with her on a different path if her heart was in the right place? No one always did everything perfectly did they? Esther made her way through the village and across the field. When she drew closer to the woods, she saw Michael standing at the edge waiting for her.

He smiled and reached toward her. "This is going to be great."

Esther grasped his hands. "I wasn't sure at first, but I'm ready."

Michael gently touched the side of her face. "I'm so proud of you for stepping out of your comfort zone."

Esther blushed at his praise. He had a way of making her feel so happy. Earlier in the day she may have had concerns, but his comfort and reassurance seemed to make all the doubts go away.

He turned toward the woods. "Let's go."

As they strode through the small forest, they talked about how fun it would be to finally be by themselves. There would be no time limits, so they could talk for as long as they liked. Michael reassured her that the spot where they'd be camping, would be in full view of his home, so it would almost be like they were being chaperoned.

After walking for what felt like an hour or more, Esther slowed. "How much further?"

He glanced around. "We should be there soon. I can't wait for you to meet my family."

"Who will I be meeting?" asked Esther.

"My parents and my little sister Amy. You're going to love her, and she's going to adore you."

"I can't wait to meet them."

Michael pointed toward a secluded trail. "We're almost there."

They stepped up their pace, and within twenty minutes they were out of the woods and into a large clearing. Rolling green grass stretched as far as Esther could see, and she felt as if they had just arrived at their own special part of the world. Michael pointed toward a small cabin about a hundred feet to their left, then grabbed her hand. "Here we are."

As they approached the small structure, Esther noticed that the logs looked freshly cut, possibly within the last few weeks. Michael had said that his family had been here for over a year, hadn't he? But maybe they'd put up a new place for some reason. Quickly dismissing any concerns, she decided to concentrate on making a good impression on his family.

Michael stepped up to the door and knocked. "Mom, Dad, Amy, we're here."

No one answered. He knocked again, but still, no one came.

Michael stepped back. "That's strange. I thought they would be back by now."

Esther said, "Where did they go?"

"My parents left yesterday to go shopping over in the next town. They were going to stay at an inn for the night, but they were supposed to be back by now. Let's go on in and wait for them."

Esther hesitated, but she reassured herself that Michael's family would be there soon. He led her in, and they sat down at a table and talked. As the hours passed, Esther suggested they eat what Mrs. Peterson had packed for her. They finished off the turkey and ham sandwiches, then spent more time talking. Esther was enjoying her time alone with Michael, but as the sun began to set she became nervous.

She stood up and looked out a window. "I don't think I can stay here tonight. It just wouldn't be right."

Michael slipped up beside her and slid his arm over her shoulder. "It's okay. You can stay in my sister's room. Besides, it's almost dark now, and I don't think we could find our way back through those woods with the little light that's left."

Of course, he was right. They could wander around in that forest all night and not find their way out. But still, staying with him alone in a cabin off by themselves–

Michael sensed her hesitation. "Isn't it great to be alone together and not have to say goodbye?"

Esther thought that it did seem freeing just to be able to relax and not worry about when it was time to leave. They spent the rest of the evening talking. Michael told her about his family and all the cute things his little sister did. When another hour passed, Esther started to feel tired, and she wanted to get a good night's rest to be fresh for the next morning.

She yawned and looked over at Michael. "I think it's time for me to get some sleep."

He put his hand on top of hers. "Thank you for trusting me."

Esther smiled. If a young man was going to try and take advantage of a girl, then this would have been the perfect opportunity, but Michael was being a perfect gentleman.

He stood up and gently tugged at her hand. "Come on. I'll show you to Amy's room."

Esther followed him to a small room off to the side. There was a bed, a small desk, and a chest of drawers, but besides that, there wasn't much that would make one think a little girl stayed there.

Michael said, "Amy likes to take a lot of things with her when she travels. We have a horse and small wagon, and Amy sits in the back and plays as they go." He turned to leave. "Goodnight and see you tomorrow."

"Goodnight."

Esther closed the door and set her backpack on the bed. As she unpacked, she saw her Book. It had been her custom to read in the Psalms and pray just before going to sleep, but she felt too tired to read, so she quickly got ready for bed and lay down. She looked around in the dark and thought of how her parents, the Petersons, and others would never have approved of this. But was it really that wrong? She had not committed any major sin. What if she was not only supposed to be a witness to Michael but to his entire family? Certainly, God could bring a lot of good out of this situation. Esther continued to reassure herself as she went to sleep.

The next morning as the sun pierced through the bedroom

window, Esther awoke and quickly got out of bed. After spending the next two hours straightening up and cleaning, she began to rummage through the cupboards, looking for items she could use to prepare a meal. But after opening all the cabinet doors, she discovered that the cupboards were empty. How peculiar that a family of four would not have any food in their home. Someone stirred in the room off to the right. Apparently, Michael was now awake.

A few minutes later he walked out of his room and raised his arms as he yawned. "Good morning."

Esther closed the cabinets and walked over to him. "How did you sleep?"

Michael smiled and gently stroked her hair. "I slept great. How about you?"

She leaned into his hand. "I was a little anxious, but I feel refreshed."

Michael noticed how clean and neat everything was. "The place looks great."

Esther stepped back and waved her hand around. "I've been trying to straighten up so your mother won't feel as stressed when she arrives."

"That was thoughtful of you."

Esther motioned toward the kitchen. "I was going to prepare a meal for when your parents arrived, but there was nothing in the cupboards."

Michael stared at the ground a second, then held up his hands. "Oh, we ran out of supplies completely which was why they had to go shopping."

How could a family run out of everything? But if she asked, she'd seem rude. She was a guest, and she had no reason to think Michael's mother didn't do a good job taking care of her home.

Michael said, "My parents should arrive soon. Let's just sit and relax as we wait for them."

They went out on the porch and talked for the next hour, but no one arrived. Another hour went by, and still, no one came. Esther was starting to become concerned, then out in the distance, a horse and wagon appeared. Finally, she was going to meet his family.

As the wagon drew closer, she saw that none of those riding in it were old enough to be Michael's parents. What's more, there was no young girl Amy's age either. In fact, all of those riding in the wagon appeared to be in their early twenties.

Michael went out to greet the new arrivals. A young man pulled back on the reins and brought the horses to a stop. Two other young men sat in the back along with two young women. Michael appeared to know the guys. He shook their hands, then helped the girls out of the wagon. Esther stood up as they approached the porch.

Michael held out his hand toward the young men. "These are my friends—Joe, Don, and Steve." He stepped onto the porch beside Esther. "And this is the young woman I've been telling you about— Esther."

Joe nodded. "Hello Esther. We've heard a lot of good things about you."

Michael held out his hand toward the young women. "Who are your new friends?"

Joe stepped beside them. "This is Polly and her sister Molly. We met them in Rock Creek just a few miles from here. They were looking for some adventure, and we told them we were on our way to a picnic. Polly asked if they could come along, and we said sure."

Polly seemed like the type that was up for some excitement, but Molly appeared more reluctant.

Joe put his arm around Polly. "Hey I know, Michael, why don't you and Esther join us?"

Michael shrugged. "Seems like a good idea to me. What do you think Esther?"

Esther stepped back toward the cabin door. "I don't know. We're waiting for Michael's parents to arrive."

Michael shot a look toward Joe.

He glanced at Michael and then back to Esther. "Oh, that's another reason we stopped by. We ran into Michael's parents in Rock Creek, and they wanted us to tell him that it would be later this evening before they would arrive, so you've got plenty of time. Besides, you have to have something to eat, don't you?"

Esther was a little hungry, and a picnic did sound fun.

Michael took her hand. "Come on, you'll love my friends, and we'll have a great time."

At least she wouldn't be the only female, and that made Esther feel more at ease. She smiled and nodded at Michael.

Joe clapped his hands. "That's great. Everyone jump in and let's go."

Michael helped Esther up into the wagon, and they were on their way. As they traveled, Esther talked to the two sisters and asked them about their village. She learned that their home was about two hours away. Polly was twenty-one, and Molly was nineteen. They were both pretty and well mannered.

Esther turned toward Polly. "How did you meet these guys?"

Polly replied, "Molly and I were walking around the town, and they pulled up to a supply store nearby. I started talking to them and found out they were going on a picnic. Molly didn't want to come, but I talked her into it. We never do anything exciting."

"Aren't your parents going to be concerned?" asked Esther.

Polly smiled at her sister. "No, we told them we were going to be with a couple of girlfriends for the day, and they agreed to cover for us. What about you? Where are you from, and how do your parents feel about you being out here?"

Esther realized she had been just as deceitful as Polly, but she didn't want to admit it. She was still trying to convince herself that everything was okay, and she wasn't doing anything wrong. "I just came to meet Michael's parents; they'll be here soon."

As they traveled, Esther and all those in the wagon were facing backwards, so she hadn't paid attention to where they were going. It felt as if they had been traveling for awhile, and by now she could barely make out Michael's cabin in the distance. The wagon stopped, and Esther turned around to see that they had traveled beyond the rolling green meadow to just outside a very dense forest.

Joe jumped down off the wagon. "This is a great spot."

Everyone hopped off and began to unload some of the supplies to set up for the picnic. Michael and Don started building a fire to cook the meats. Esther, Polly, and Molly rolled out a large blanket and started setting out the food and putting it in bowls. Within an hour, everything was ready, and everyone ate until they were full. They sat around and talked for a little while, and then Don went to the wagon and brought back a fiddle. Soon he was playing a lively tune.

Joe stood up and held out his hand to Polly. "Let's have some fun." He helped her to her feet, and they began to twirl around while holding hands.

Michael nudged Esther's arm. "Come on, let's join them."

"I think I'd just like to sit and watch."

Michael held her hand and smiled. "Okay by me."

Steve started to extend his hand toward Molly, but she quickly glanced away.

After dancing to a few songs, Joe and Polly sat down, and Polly tapped Esther on the elbow. "Come on, you've got to try it. It's a lot of fun."

"Maybe next time," said Esther.

Don played softly for several minutes while everyone talked, and then he changed to an upbeat tune. Soon Joe and Polly were on their feet again, dancing and having a good time. Esther watched for a minute and thought that it did look like a lot of fun.

Michael rubbed her shoulder. "How about it? Are you ready to loosen up a little bit?"

She hesitated at first then nodded toward him. "Okay."

"Great!" Michael stood up and reached for her hand.

After helping her up, he taught her a few simple moves where they would take a few quick steps to the left and the right, then turn in a circle. Esther was having a great time twirling about, and Polly seemed to be enjoying herself with Joe as well. Molly though sat quietly on the blanket. Don continued to play one tune after another until they were all tired. Steve added a few more logs to the fire, then Joe suggested roasting marshmallows. Time passed quickly, and soon the sun had set.

Esther peered off in the direction of the cabin and remembered that Michael's parents should have already arrived. She stood up and surveyed the area, but then quickly realized they had not seen anyone approaching the entire time they were out there. She grabbed Michael's hand. "Do you think anything could have happened to your parents?"

Michael elbowed Joe who was laughing and talking with Polly. "Are you sure my parents said they would be back this evening?"

Joe shifted his gaze toward Michael and then Esther. "You know, they did say they might stay an extra night with some friends. I wouldn't worry about them. They'll be back as soon as they can."

Esther shook her head. "It's getting late. What will we do for the night?"

Michael leaned forward. "It would take hours to get back to my cabin, and there's not enough room in there for everyone anyway."

Joe stood up. "I have an idea. We've got two big tents. We can set them up here for the night. One can be for the guys and one for the girls. We'll extend this adventure to an overnight camping trip."

Michael said, "Sounds great. Esther and I were planning on camping out anyway after she met my parents, and this is even better."

Molly turned toward her sister. "What will Mom and Dad think?"

Polly shrugged. "Don't worry. Our friends will just tell them that we stayed the night with them. We'll clear it all up tomorrow."

Esther was nervous about being gone another night, but she was also having a good time. There wasn't anything wrong with a little bit of adventure was there? Everyone gathered around the fire, and Don played his fiddle some more. Steve taught them some songs, and they spent the rest of the evening sitting around the fire and singing.

The next morning arrived, and everyone slept much later. The woods directly behind them blocked most of the sunlight until it was well into the morning. When everyone awoke, they came out of their tents and started working to prepare a meal. After they ate, Don took out his fiddle again, and the day seemed to pass quickly as they spent time singing, dancing, and talking for hours.

After a little while, Esther nudged Michael. "I still haven't seen any wagons approaching. I'm starting to get concerned for your parents."

"Don't be," said Michael. "They're probably just having a great time with their friends. They don't get to travel often, so I'm sure they're just making the most of their time. Since they ran into Joe, they know I'm being well taken care of. They probably figure I'm doing exactly what I'm doing which is relaxing and having a great time with my friends."

Esther was less concerned about another day going by without meeting Michael's family. She was having a great time, and another day wouldn't make that much difference.

When it was getting close to sunset, Michael whispered something to Joe and then motioned for everyone to give him their attention. "I have a great idea. Let's play some games. The first game Joe and I would like to play is Hide and Seek."

6

THE SEDUCTION OF SIN

Esther surveyed the field and the meadow beyond, wondering how they would play hide and seek in such a wide-open area. Surely, Michael and Joe weren't talking about going into those dense woods behind them.

Michael said, "We'll do this in teams of guys and girls. First, we'll hide, and you girls can try and find us. After that, we'll alternate. It'll be a lot of fun."

Esther stood up. "Where will you hide?"

Michael pointed toward the woods. "We'll be just inside there. We won't go too far." He patted her on the shoulders. "It'll be just fine."

Esther was concerned, but she thought as long as she and the other girls stayed together then it should be okay.

Polly was excited, but Molly was growing even more nervous. She realized though that she didn't have much of a choice other than staying close by her sister.

Michael and the other guys started toward the woods. "Alright girls, close your eyes and count to a hundred. And no peeking."

Polly closed her eyes and began counting, while Molly gave Esther a concerned look. Esther closed her eyes and started to count.

When they had reached a hundred, Polly turned around excitedly. "Come on let's find them!"

The girls started in the direction that the guys had entered the woods. They tramped through the underbrush for fifteen minutes but didn't see any trace of them. The girls were beginning to worry, and then they thought they heard whistling. They followed the sound, and soon they found the guys hiding behind a thick group of bushes.

Michael stood up and brushed off his pants. "We were concerned that you girls might be having a hard time, so we decided to give you a little help. Now it's your turn."

Esther was not excited about going deeper into these woods and hiding, but Polly took her and Molly's hands and said, "Come on, they've already started counting."

Polly led them deeper into the forest until they came to a big old oak tree with a hollowed out area at the bottom.

Polly walked around the tree. "This is a perfect hiding spot. Let's get inside."

The girls sat down within the hollowed out area and waited for the guys to come and find them. They sat and sat, but there was no sign of Michael or the others. Finally, the girls heard the sound of twigs breaking. Someone was approaching. Soon they heard voices and knew it was the guys. Polly put her finger to her lips to signal to Esther and Molly to stay quiet. Finally, the guys walked around the tree and found them.

Joe clapped his hands. "Great hiding place girls."

Polly jumped out, and Joe grabbed her hand. Michael stood beside Esther and put his arm around her. She was so relieved that Michael found her that she relaxed into his grasp. But just as Esther was feeling safe again, Steve motioned for the guys to come on.

Michael let go of Esther and backed away. "See you soon."

Steve, Don, Joe, and Michael took off running even deeper into the woods. Esther peered into the sky and realized that the sun had already set. She started to call out to Michael, but it was too late. What if they weren't able to find them before dark? What if they got stuck in these woods for the night? Esther hugged her arms to her body.

Polly was still counting, but Molly interrupted her. "Forget about counting. We've got to find them before it gets dark. They should have known better than to hide this late. We should have headed back to the campsite by now."

Esther knew that Molly was right, but she didn't want to say anything.

Polly shook her head at her sister. "When do we ever get a chance to have this much adventure? Think of all the stories we'll have to tell our friends." She started toward the direction the guys had headed, and Esther and Molly followed.

The deeper into the woods they went, the darker it became.

Esther grabbed Molly's hand. "It's okay. We'll find them soon."

Polly kept going, and as they pressed further and further, they started to hear loud screeching sounds. Was the wind making that awful racket, or was it something else? All three of the girls began to walk slower, and then they stopped. It was now dark, and with the scant amount of moonlight making it through the trees, they could barely see a few feet in front of them.

Molly glared at Polly and put her hands on her hips. "I told you we should never have come on this trip. This whole thing was a bad idea."

Polly took a step forward. "You worry too much. Everything will be all right. The guys can't be too far away."

At once they heard voices in the distance.

Esther called out, "Michael is that you? Steve? Joe?"

The voices came closer, and the girls yelled out even louder. The guys answered, and the girls guided them toward them. Finally, the girls could see their silhouettes. When Esther could recognize Michael, she raced to him and embraced him. It was their first hug, but Esther wasn't thinking about that. She was just thankful he'd found her. Joe held Polly, and Steve walked toward Molly.

Molly backed up. "What were you guys thinking, leaving us out in the woods like this so close to dark?"

Polly sighed. "Settle down Molly. It's not like they meant to leave us here. When they realized we couldn't find them, they started looking for us."

Joe said, "That's right. We realized you must have gotten lost, so we started back."

Esther glanced up at Michael. "What now? It's too dark to find our way back toward the campsite."

Michael pulled her a little closer. "It's okay. As we were looking for you all, we saw a place just on the other side of these woods where we can get something to eat and have a place to stay for the night."

Esther said, "Is it an inn?"

Michael replied, "It's something like that."

Michael led the way, and Esther stayed close by his side holding his hand tightly as they went. Joe and Polly followed behind them, and Molly stayed near her sister while Steve and Don trailed further behind.

Michael seemed to know where he was going, and he led them out of the woods and onto a road. "There's a place to spend the night not too far ahead."

They walked on, and soon they saw a tall building. As they came near, they could hear music coming from inside, then raucous laughter and loud shouts. At the entrance were two swinging doors. As the group approached, a man stumbled through the doors and almost fell down.

Michael held out his hand. "Here we are."

They went inside. A bartender stood behind a counter, while scantily clad women danced around the room serving drinks and sitting on men's laps. A well-dressed man sat behind a piano playing loudly, and many of the customers raised their glasses and sang.

Esther nervously glanced around, then she grabbed Michael's arm and whispered, "This isn't an inn. This is a tavern. Why did you bring us here?"

Michael patted her hand. "This might not be the best option, but it's the only place close by, and we have to stay somewhere."

Joe had already led Polly to the middle of the floor, and they began dancing around.

Michael turned to Esther and got close to her ear so she could hear him over the music. "I'll go see about some rooms. I'll get me and the guys a couple of rooms, and you girls can share a room."

Esther said, "I didn't bring any money."

"It's okay," said Michael. "I feel responsible for getting us into this, so I'll take care of it."

He found the person that appeared to be the manager and began talking to him.

Molly stepped closer to Esther. "What are we doing here? I don't even want to think about what my parents would say if they knew we were in a tavern."

Esther put her arm around her. "I'm uncomfortable too, but right now we don't have a choice. We have to stay somewhere. Let's just get through the night, and we'll come up with something tomorrow."

Michael strolled up, holding out a key. "It's all settled. I asked for a room that would be furthest away from all the excitement so you could get some sleep. Also, when I told the manager about what happened to us, he said one of his girls would bring up some pajamas for you all along with some other personal items."

Esther took the key. "Thank you. I know you're just trying to do your best."

Esther led Molly up the stairs and toward the direction Michael had pointed to. She found the room number matching the one on the key, and they went in. There were two beds, and in the center was a small dresser drawer with a mirror. Soon there was a knock on the door. When they answered, one of the girls they had seen working downstairs handed Esther some pajamas and personal hygiene items they would need for the night. She introduced herself as Linda and told them to let her know if they needed anything else.

After Linda left, Molly went over and sat on one of the beds. "Polly and I can both fit on this one."

Esther said, "I do hope she will be up soon. This is not a place for a young lady, especially this late at night."

Esther and Molly got ready for bed, but they could still hear the music and all the people yelling and singing. They lay down and did their best to get some rest, but it took them a couple of hours to relax and finally drift off.

The next day Esther woke up rather suddenly as a sharp banging noise emanated from downstairs. She peered out her window and concluded from the position of the sun that it was already late afternoon. How had she slept this long? She looked over to see that Molly was still asleep, but she didn't see Polly anywhere.

Esther reached out and gently shook her arm. "Molly. Molly."

She woke up and sat up quickly. "Where's Polly?"

"I don't know. I just woke up too."

Esther and Molly quickly got dressed and went downstairs. They didn't see Polly or any of the guys. There were a few men playing cards, and Linda and two other girls were clearing off the tables.

When Linda came near, Esther described Michael, Polly, and the other guys, asking if she had seen any of them.

Linda picked up some glasses off the table. "Yeah, I saw them. It was really late before they checked into their rooms. I'm sure they'll be down in a couple of hours."

Molly stepped forward. "Did you see my sister?"

Linda stared at her for a moment as if she was searching for how to answer. "There was a young woman with them, but I didn't see where she went. I'm sure she checked into a room and will be down in a little while too." She then offered to bring them some food while they were waiting.

Esther and Molly were grateful for the offer, and they talked together as they ate and waited for Michael, Polly, and the others to join them.

Molly glanced around as patrons began to file into the tavern. "Esther, how did we get here? I mean I know what happened, but I thought I was just going on a picnic for the afternoon, and now here I am getting further and further away from home."

Esther didn't have an answer. She could ask herself the very same question. Trying to reassure Molly and herself, she said, "We'll all be home soon. I'm going to talk to Michael the instant they come downstairs."

Esther and Molly finished their food, and while they waited, more patrons entered the tavern. The sun was starting to set, and they were both getting concerned. Some of the men sitting at a nearby table were leering at them. Esther couldn't fathom how she had ended up in a place like this. What must those men think of her? What were two young women doing alone in a tavern?

After thirty more minutes, Michael and the others finally came downstairs. Polly was walking arm in arm with Joe.

Molly stood up and pulled her sister to the side. "Where were you last night? We waited for you."

Polly smiled and patted her on the back. "You worry too much. I didn't want to come in and wake you two up, so one of the guys gave up their room for me."

Molly threw up her hands. "We have to get back home."

Polly smiled at Joe. "What's your hurry sis? You have the rest of your life to live in that little village and be close to Mom and Dad. What's wrong with a few days of fun and excitement?"

Molly joined Esther at the table, who had been making small talk with Michael. Molly gave her a look of desperation. Esther decided it was time to talk to Michael about getting back home.

Esther pulled on his arm. "Can we go outside and talk?"

"Sure."

When they were alone, Michael reached for Esther's hand. "What is it you want to talk about?"

"Don't you think we need to get back? What if your parents are worried about you?"

Michael motioned for her to sit down on a nearby bench. "Esther, there's something I need to tell you. Please don't be mad at me. I don't have any parents. I mean I don't know where they are."

Esther shifted to face him. "What do you mean?"

"My parents left me at some orphanage when I was a little boy, and I've been on my own ever since. Joe, Don, and Steve have been the closest thing to family that I've ever known. We look out for each other and take care of each other."

Esther shook her head. "Why did you lie to me?"

Michael shrugged. "As I got to know you, I started to have really strong feelings for you. When I heard you talk about your family and how close you were to them, I thought that you would look down on me if I told you the truth about my own family. So I made up a lie."

"But didn't you know I would find out eventually?"

"Of course I knew. But I thought that if you gave me a chance and spent some time with me, then you'd come to understand just how much I care about you, and you wouldn't hold my upbringing against me."

Esther was trying to process everything. She had suspected something wasn't right, but she kept telling herself everything would be okay. Now she was learning that the entire reason she left the Petersons and started on this journey was based on a lie.

Michael could tell she was having a lot of doubts. Putting his hand underneath her chin, he gently caressed her face. "Esther, I've been afraid to admit this, but I feel like I'm falling in love with you. I don't want anything to ruin what we have. Please forgive me."

So many things were running through her mind, but did Michael just say he was falling in love with her? Wasn't this what she had always wanted to hear from a man? Wasn't true love worth some sacrifices?

Esther put her hand on his. "I wish you had told me the truth from the beginning. I would not have thought any less of you. I have strong feelings for you too, but I need to get back to the Petersons. We can still see each other often."

Michael looked down. "I'm not sure we will be able to."

"Why not?"

"I don't really live in that cabin you saw. When I first met you, I wanted to be closer to you, so the rest of the guys helped me build it so I could spend some nights there and not be too far away from you. The truth is, I travel around with Joe, Steve, and Don, and we go wherever we can find work. Joe told me there was a great opportunity about two day's journey from here, and it might be a long time before we ever come back near your village again."

Esther felt sad and fearful. She had finally found someone to fall in love with, and now he was going to leave.

Michael quickly turned toward her and put his hand on her shoulder. "Come with me."

Esther looked away. "You know I can't."

He placed his hand on the side of her head. "Don't you have feelings for me?"

She shifted her gaze until their eyes met. "Yes, you know I do, but I can't."

Michael sat back and began to stroke her hair. "I understand. I'm going to miss you."

Esther put her hands in her lap, feeling as if she was going to cry.

Michael leaned over toward her. "I know what. The next place we're going is near a road that leads back to where Polly and Molly live. You can come along with us there, and then if you still don't want to come with me, you can walk them home and then go back to the Petersons."

This seemed reasonable, and she did want to make sure Polly and Molly got home safely. Esther smiled at him. "Okay."

Michael stood up. "That's great. At least we'll have another day together, and who knows, you may even change your mind."

"I wish there was somewhere else we could stay the night," said Esther as she stood to her feet.

Michael took her hand. "What's wrong with this place? Sure it's a little loud, but the people are nice, and everyone is having a great time."

Esther said, "But they spend their evenings drinking, and the women are selling themselves to these men."

Michael wrinkled his forehead, and his eyes narrowed. "Esther, aren't you being a little too judgmental? These men have had a hard day, and they're just loosening up a little bit. The women are only being friendly. They're waiting tables and bringing them their drinks. They have to make money too you know. There's nothing wrong with them dancing with these men and helping them to have a good time. I'm sure many of these girls are working to save up some money for their education."

Esther pointed toward the second floor of the building. "But I saw some of the girls go into a room upstairs with different men."

Michael sighed. "There you go again being judgmental. They probably just wanted a little bit of privacy. Didn't you call me out here so we could talk alone? Did anything happen with us? Those girls have their own rooms to sleep in. Not everyone can be like the Petersons or your family. Some people have it hard and have to make a living as best as they can. What if you weren't born with all the privileges you had in life? What if you had to do what was necessary to get by? Would you want people judging you?"

Esther thought about this. Maybe she had been too judgmental.

Michael pulled at her hand. "Come on, this will be our last night here so why don't we relax and try to enjoy it."

When Esther went back inside, she spotted Polly and Joe dancing around in the middle of the tavern. Molly sat nervously at a table with Steve gawking at her. As Esther approached, Molly grabbed her hand and motioned for her to have a seat next to her.

Molly leaned close. "What did you find out?"

Esther whispered, "Michael said we'll be leaving tomorrow, and heading toward a place that will lead back to your home. From there I'm going to travel with you and Polly until you reach your parent's house, and then I'm going to go back to the Petersons."

Molly looked around the tavern. "So we have to spend another night here?"

Esther patted her hand. "It'll be okay. We'll go back to our rooms soon, and then we'll start out tomorrow."

One of the tavern girls named Mindy came by asking if anyone would like anything to eat or drink. Esther and Molly asked if they could have some water. Mindy didn't appear happy about that, but she turned toward Michael to take his order.

Michael said, "Sure, bring me some of your best liquid and bring a little extra for my friends."

Esther stared at him in disbelief.

He leaned back and put his hands behind his head. "It's okay Esther, I'm just having one drink."

Joe and Polly finished their dance and arrived at the table just as Mindy was bringing the drinks.

Joe put his hand on Michael's shoulder. "You better have ordered me one."

Michael took a glass from Mindy and handed it to him. "You know I did."

Polly tapped Joe on the arm. "Let me have a drink."

Molly's eyes widened. "Polly!"

Joe grinned and handed Polly his glass.

She took a big drink and banged the glass down firmly onto the table. "Loosen up little sis. A drink of this would probably do you some good."

As Joe and Polly returned to the dance floor, Molly shook her head and stared toward the door. Esther kept telling herself that all of this would be over soon, and they'd all be back home.

Michael grabbed Esther's hand. "Let's dance."

Esther hesitated then glanced over at Molly who didn't seem thrilled at the prospect of being left alone at the table.

Michael stood up. "Come on. This could be our last dance."

Esther whispered to Molly. "I'll be back soon."

Michael took her to where Joe and Polly were dancing and began to spin her around. After each spin, he would pull her closer and closer. Since he'd had a few drinks, he seemed less concerned about where he put his hands. Esther tried to politely move them away, but he just smiled as if he were playing a game. She didn't want to make a scene in front of everyone, so as soon as the music paused, she started back toward the table.

Michael stood still and held his hand out. "Come on back. We're just getting started."

Esther glanced over her shoulder and politely smiled, but kept walking toward the table. Michael followed and sat down beside her. He downed his glass of ale, then grabbed another glass from the tray and took another drink. Esther wasn't sure what Steve had said to Molly, but she looked even more uncomfortable.

Esther took out their room key and motioned toward Molly. "I think it's time we went to our room. We'll need to get up earlier tomorrow."

Steve didn't look happy that his time with Molly was ending, and while Michael appeared slightly irritated that Esther was heading upstairs already, he did his best to seem cheerful.

When Esther stood to leave, Michael rubbed her arm. "The manager said to leave your clothes outside your room after you changed into your pajamas, and he'd have a few of the girls wash them before we head out tomorrow. I've also asked if he could get each of you a few changes of clothing since I know you left your bag at the cabin, and Polly and Molly didn't pack anything for an overnight trip."

Esther patted his hand. "Thank you."

Michael hugged her then stepped back. "Well you ladies have a good night's rest, and we'll see you tomorrow."

Joe and Polly returned to the table just as Esther and Molly were about to leave.

Polly twirled around and put her arm around her sister. "Where you going? The night has just started."

Molly removed Polly's arm from her shoulder. "We're going to our room, which is where you should be going too."

Polly picked up Joe's glass and took another drink. "You're not my mom. Go on and get some sleep. You're just dragging the party down anyway."

Esther and Molly went upstairs and into their room. When Esther closed the door, Molly collapsed on the bed and started to cry.

Esther sat next to her. "I know this is hard, but you'll be home soon. I understand why you're worried about your sister, but once you get back, I'm sure she'll see how wrong she's been."

Molly turned over and wiped her eyes. "I wish we had never left to begin with. Polly has always been a little rebellious but nothing like this. And the way Steve keeps looking at me makes me really uneasy."

Esther handed her a tissue. "It's going to be okay. We'll be leaving tomorrow."

Molly felt reassured and soon went to sleep. Lying down on her bed, Esther wished she could do as good a job reassuring herself as she had done for Molly. She was starting to see things in Michael that she hadn't noticed before, but that wasn't what was really bothering her. What was even more disconcerting was what she was seeing in herself. Things that would never have been okay a week ago were now becoming acceptable. As much as she was put off by everything going on in the tavern, there was a part of her that wished she could be just as free as Polly and take it all in.

As she lay there on her bed, Esther realized she had left her Book in Michael's cabin, but her hunger to read it was not nearly as strong as it once was. She tapped on her chest twice just to make sure her armor was still there. It was, but she could tell it was much weaker. She said a quick prayer asking God to help her to get back home safely, and to help Molly and Polly get home as well.

7

THE ROAD TO NOWHERE

The next morning Esther and Molly woke up earlier than the day before, but as they peered out their window, they could tell from the position of the sun that it was at least 10:00 AM, possibly later. Once again Polly had not come to their room, but Molly consoled herself that soon all this would be over. They packed everything up and hurried downstairs, but when they arrived, no one else was in the tavern as of yet.

They sat at a table to wait, and Linda came by. "Did you get the extra changes of clothing I set outside your door?"

"Yes we did," said Esther. "Thank you."

"You're welcome. Can I get you two something to eat?"

Esther and Molly decided they might as well have some breakfast while they waited, so they ordered some scrambled eggs and toast.

They finished their food then talked for another hour. When Linda came back to check on them, Molly said, "Did you see where my sister went last night?"

Linda didn't make eye contact. "I don't know. I may have seen her go upstairs, but I'm not sure."

"Could you please tell us which rooms our friends are in?" asked Esther.

Linda glanced around as if she was concerned about getting in trouble.

Esther reached out and touched her arm. "Please?"

Linda surveyed the bar to make sure no one was looking, then wrote three room numbers on a napkin.

Esther stood up quickly. "Thanks." She turned to Molly. "Why don't you go on up and gather our things. I'll round up the others and meet you back down here."

Molly headed toward their room, and Esther went up the stairs toward the opposite end of the tavern. When she found the first room matching a number Linda had written on the napkin, she knocked on the door. No one answered. She knocked again. She waited then knocked louder and longer. After a few more attempts, she heard a low groan. Finally a voice she recognized as Michael's mumbled something. He didn't sound happy about being woke up, but he said he would get Steve and Don who were in the room next door.

Esther then went to the last room number Linda had given her and knocked on the door. To Esther's surprise, she heard a man's voice. More precisely, it sounded like Joe. She had assumed that Joe was in the room with Michael and just hadn't woke up yet.

Esther called out, "I'm looking for Polly."

Esther heard someone stumbling around, and then the door opened slightly.

Polly's face appeared, then she whispered, "So are you going to tell Molly?"

Esther didn't know what to say. "Right now I just want to get out of here so we can all get home. You can tell Molly later."

Polly stepped away and closed the door.

When Esther came downstairs, Molly asked, "Is everyone ready? Did you see Polly?"

Esther struggled with how much she should say. "They'll all be down soon."

An hour passed, then all the guys and Polly joined them downstairs. Michael insisted on having a quick breakfast, so another hour passed before they were finally ready to leave. Joe had arranged to borrow another horse and wagon since they had abandoned the other one. They loaded everything up and were soon on their way. Don was driving, while Joe and Polly were curled up next to each other in the back. Michael was holding Esther, and Molly was trying to keep her distance from Steve.

After three hours of traveling, they came to a stop.

Joe jumped off the wagon. "This is a good place to rest and make some lunch."

Everyone hopped off, and they unloaded some of the supplies they had purchased from the tavern.

After they were finished eating, Michael stood up and held out his hand to Esther. "Let's go for a walk. You know, like we used to when we first met." He led Esther to a spot where they were out of eyesight of the others then stopped. "Do you remember that first day we met?"

Esther smiled. "Yes I do."

Michael gently squeezed her arm. "I really do feel we were supposed to meet. It's hard for me to think about not seeing you again."

Esther stared at the ground. "I feel the same way, but everything has changed. I can't just run off with someone. What would my parents think about something like that?"

Michael put his hands on Esther's shoulders and looked directly into her eyes. "If we're supposed to be together, then why are you letting something stop you? Don't your parents want you to be happy?"

"Of course they do, but they wouldn't believe this could make me happy."

Michael shrugged his shoulders. "If God put us together then who should be able to keep us apart?"

This was the first time she had heard him use the word *God* as if he thought He actually existed. Was she starting to have an impact on him? Was this more evidence that God was blessing her time with him even though it might not have been the best way to go about it? Yes, Michael had a lot of rough edges, but he also had a lot of potential.

Esther shook her head. "I don't know. You just don't realize what you're asking."

"I'm asking the woman I love to come with me. There, I said it. I love you Esther."

She had wanted to hear those words from a man for as long as she could remember. She had dreamt of this day since she was a young girl. Now that it was happening, what was she to do?

She stared into his eyes. "I've felt such strong feelings for you since the day I met you. A part of me wants to come with you, but you're asking me to give up everything I've known."

Michael touched the side of her cheek. "I'm asking you to give up all the things that are keeping you from living your life. All these rules that everyone has put on you are holding you back. Let go and just live."

All of this sounded so appealing to her. "I'll think about it. I really will."

Michael bent over and kissed her on the forehead. "That's all I ask."

As Michael and Esther returned to the others, they could hear the sound of a fiddle playing lively music. Joe and Polly were up dancing around. Michael motioned for Esther to dance with him as well, and they began to twirl around. Then after a few minutes, Michael made a gesture toward Don, and he began playing a much slower tune. Joe and Polly immediately embraced one another and began swaying to the music. Michael held out his hands, but Esther seemed unsure. He cocked his head to the side and smiled at her. Slowly she reached out until her fingers met his, then he pulled her close.

As they were dancing, Michael whispered in her ear. "I love you."

Don continued to play, and Esther began to relax. She closed her eyes and imagined it was just the two of them, all alone in the middle of nowhere. The music went on for almost twenty minutes. When at last, it stopped, Esther slowly took a step back. She gazed into his eyes, and he caressed her face.

Joe stepped up to them. "Time to pack up and get going."

They all loaded up and headed off. After a couple more hours of travel, Joe signaled for Don to halt the horses.

Molly sat up. "Why are we stopping?"

Don jumped off the wagon. "It's going to get dark soon, and this looks like a good place to camp."

Molly started shaking her head. "I thought we were going to arrive at a road today that would lead back to our village?"

Polly stepped off the wagon. "Pipe down Molly. I'm sure we'll be there soon."

Joe motioned for Steve and Michael to help him unload the tents. "Looks like I may have misjudged just how far we were from that road. I'm sure we'll run into it sometime tomorrow."

"See Molly," said Polly. "You're always getting worked up about nothing."

Molly walked off by herself while the guys unloaded everything.

Esther strode up next to her. "It's just one more night."

"That's what we thought last night too."

Esther didn't know what to say, but a part of her was glad she would have another day with Michael before having to make the decision to leave him. She rejoined the others and helped with the unpacking.

When they were finished setting up the tents, Steve and Joe built a fire. They all sat around and snacked on some of the leftovers from lunch, then as it grew dark Don took out his fiddle. He played a quiet and relaxing tune, and Joe and Polly snuggled next to each other. Michael put his arm around Esther, and both couples were whispering to one another. Molly pulled a blanket tightly around her as if she was trying to isolate herself.

After a few minutes, Joe and Polly picked up a couple of blankets.

As they were heading off, Joe turned and said, "As much as we love being around all of you, we're going to take a little bit of time to ourselves. We'll be back soon."

Esther stood up. "I think it's time for me to get some sleep."

Michael hugged her, and then Esther and Molly climbed into their tent.

When they were lying down, Molly whispered, "I'm worried about Polly. Why is she spending so much time alone with a guy that she barely knows?"

Esther turned over. How was she supposed to answer? "I'm sure she'll be okay."

The next morning Esther and Molly awoke, and once again Polly was not with them. Molly quickly got ready and went outside. No one else was awake yet, but she noticed that a third tent had been set up. After an hour, Polly stumbled out of it.

"Why did you sleep there?" asked Molly, pointing toward the tent.

Polly put her index finger to her lips. "Shh, people are sleeping."

Molly heard someone snoring. "Who's in there?"

"Listen," said Polly, placing her hands on her hips. "I don't have to answer to you. I don't owe you an explanation for what I do."

Molly shook her head. "It's Joe, isn't it? And I bet this isn't the first time either?"

"No it isn't, but what business is that of yours."

"What would Mom and Dad think if they saw you right now?"

Polly turned as if she was going to walk away but then spun around toward her sister. "You want to know what they would say? I'll tell you. They'd say, 'Polly what a disappointment you are. Polly, you've managed to mess up once again. Polly why aren't you more like your sister.' I'm tired of hearing all that."

Molly threw up her hands. "You've changed so much. What's happened to you?"

Polly angrily pointed at her sister. "No, I haven't changed at all. I'm just tired of hiding who I am."

Molly looked as if she was about to cry. "Are you even planning to go back home?"

Shrugging her shoulders, Polly said, "I'm not sure. Joe has invited me to stay with him, and I'm thinking about it."

Molly shook her head again and walked away. Esther climbed out of the tent just as Molly was going back inside.

Polly said, "What about you. I hear Michael has invited you to go with us as well."

Glancing over her shoulder, Esther replied, "I don't know. How would Molly get home?"

Polly edged toward her tent. "Joe said that once we get to the next place, he'll look for a family heading in that direction and pay them a little bit to take her back with them."

Esther sighed and turned away. "I don't know what I'm going to do."

Soon everyone climbed out of their tents, and after a quick meal, they were on their way again. Joe and Polly were curled up together, and Michael was pulling Esther closer than they had been before. Molly just stared off into the distance and tried to keep from crying. They traveled for hours, and after a quick stop for a meal, the guys announced that they would be at their next destination by sundown if they hurried.

After a while, they noticed that the trails started to go further and further downhill. It also seemed as if they were forking off onto different trails and constantly winding around. As the sun was setting, the road they were now on led them into another forest. The further they traveled the denser the forest became. Esther realized that they had taken so many different paths that she had no idea how they had gotten to where they were. Within a few minutes, they started to hear the faint sound of music in the distance.

After they had gone a little further the wagon suddenly stopped. Joe leaned up and whispered something to Don, who then jumped off and started down the trail.

Esther looked back. "Where did he go?"

Joe sat up. "He's just going to make sure the place where we're going has plenty of room for us to stay the night."

Molly hurriedly glanced around as if she was about to panic. "Where are we, and how do we get home from here?"

Joe said, "This is where we're meeting the people that have a job for us. Don't worry Molly. We'll find you a way home."

Esther put her hand on Molly's shoulder trying to reassure her.

Don returned and climbed up in the driver's seat of the wagon. They continued along the path, and the further they went, the louder the music became. They could also hear the voices of a crowd of people. Esther wondered if they were headed to another tavern.

They cleared the forest, and the wagon came to a stop at the edge of a large campground. People roamed about while laughing and shouting. Fireworks shot into the sky, and a sense of excitement filled the air.

The guys jumped off the wagon and helped the girls down. Esther grabbed Michael's arm. "What is this place?"

Two men were up on a ladder, hanging a banner that looked freshly painted. Michael glanced up at the banner. Pointing toward it, he said, "This is the Camp of Fun."

8

THE CAMP OF SIN

Don slapped Michael on the back and snickered.

Esther said, "What do you do here?"

Michael shrugged. "We have fun of course. As Joe said, this is where we're meeting the people hiring us. They should arrive in a day or two."

Michael stepped up and talked to the two men at the entrance.

Molly tugged on Esther's arm. "I'm not sure who is going to come by here that can take me home. Are you still coming back with me?"

Esther gave the only honest answer she could. "I don't know."

Michael joined them again. "I have good news. The first night here, everything is free. Let's go have a good time."

Joe and Polly headed straight to the center of the campground, but Molly stayed close to Esther.

A lot of yelling and cheering broke out on the left side of the camp, but Michael steered them to the right. "Let's go over here. It's a little quieter."

They hadn't had anything to eat for a while, so Michael led them to a make-shift stand serving hamburgers and hot dogs. When they finished eating, they wandered to a tent where a group of actors performed a comedy routine on an improvised stage. Esther thought some of the jokes were a little questionable, but most of it was just funny. She laughed and had a good time. Molly was starting to relax and not be as nervous.

When the actors finished their performance, a rough looking man with tattoos on his arms came on stage and began telling jokes containing sexual innuendo. Esther felt uncomfortable, but Michael was laughing hysterically. Then a slender, nice-looking man and an attractive woman wearing a low cut blouse and short skirt came on stage. They took the parts of a boyfriend and girlfriend who had gotten into a fight. The male actor went by the name of Jack, and he addressed the woman as Melinda. There were a few minutes of dialogue, then Jack told her how sorry he was, and slowly Melinda began to forgive him. Jack began to kiss her passionately and caress her. Esther thought they should not be doing such things in public. She looked away, but in a moment she glanced back at the stage to see what they were doing.

When the show ended, everyone left the tent.

Don approached Molly. "I know I haven't talked to you very much, but you seemed like you were having a hard time earlier. I understand you want to get back home, and I'll do whatever I can to make sure that happens."

She stared at the ground and didn't answer.

Don said, "I also noticed that Steve was making you uncomfortable. I told him to back off."

Molly looked up. "Thank you."

Don pointed toward Michael and Esther. "Why don't we give those two a little time to themselves. I know of a nice place where we can sit and watch the fireworks. We'll stop and get some cotton candy along the way. I'll let Michael know where we'll be, and I'm sure they'll join us in a few minutes."

Molly tapped Esther on the elbow. "See you soon."

As Don and Molly were walking away, Michael gestured toward a group of people laughing. "Come on. Admit it. You're having some fun."

Esther smiled. "I guess I am. I've never been to anything like this before."

Michael gave her a short tour. As they neared the entrance again, Esther turned toward the other side of the camp at the sound of raucous shouting.

Michael stepped in front of her, blocking her from that direction. "It's a little too loud over there for my taste. Let's stay on this side."

Soon they caught up with Don and Molly and sat down with them to watch the fireworks. Molly appeared to be a lot more relaxed now. After a little while, Esther became tired and asked Michael where they could sleep.

He pointed to his left. "I know a great place where you and Molly can get some rest. It's quiet and for females only."

Molly realized she hadn't seen her sister since they first arrived. "Have any of you seen Polly?"

Don said, "I saw them earlier. They were having a good time. Polly said not to worry about her, and she would see you tomorrow."

Michael led Esther and Molly over to a tent. An older woman with bleached hair and thick make-up was at the entrance taking each girl's payment, but Michael motioned to her, and she let the girls go in for free. Esther didn't realize it, but it was almost time for the sun to rise, and they were just starting to get some sleep. By the time she awoke, it was late in the afternoon. She woke Molly up, then they dressed and came outside.

Michael and Don joined them within a few minutes. Michael took Esther's hand. "How did you sleep?"

Esther rubbed her eyes and yawned. "Very good, but I'm not used to sleeping so late though."

"You get used to it," said Michael.

Joe and Polly soon came around the corner. Putting his arm around Polly, Joe said, "Since we're all together, let's go get something to eat."

He led them to a place where a cook grilled steaks over an open fire. The food was great, and everyone seemed to be having a good time.

Polly asked Molly if she could talk with her for a minute.

The two sisters walked off a little ways, and then Polly took her by the hand. "I'm sorry for snapping at you the other day. I just didn't want to be judged. I've felt judged all my life by Mom, Dad, and everyone else at the House of Instruction, and I just didn't want to be judged by you too."

Molly hugged her. "I don't want to judge you." They then returned and joined the rest.

Michael stood up. "Okay everyone. This was the last free thing we can get. From this point, we have to pay."

Holding out her hands, Esther said, "But we didn't bring any money."

"That's okay," said Michael with a grin on his face. "They take a different kind of payment here. You just put your hand on a small table, and it takes a little bit of your energy."

Esther stared at her hand. "Is that safe?"

"Of course it's safe," said Michael. "We do it all the time. You've got enough energy to last for decades."

That evening Michael and Don took the girls back to the same tent where they had seen the show the night before. Esther and Molly put their hands on the small table at the entrance to make the payment. When Esther's fingers first made contact, a shock zapped through her.

They went into the tent and sat down to get ready for the show. Different comedians appeared on stage one after the other, and as the night wore on the jokes seemed more crude and sexual. The same male and female actors from the night before came out on stage again, but this time they acted the parts of lovers who had just been reunited after a long absence. There was less dialogue in this routine and much more kissing and caressing. Esther realized she wasn't as put off as she was the day before. In fact, she actually enjoyed the show. Molly seemed to be having a good time too.

When the performance was over, Michael led Esther in one direction, and Don took Molly in another. Later they all ran into Joe and Polly. Joe told them that someone had contacted him, and it would be another week before the people they were meeting would arrive. Esther didn't mind, and Molly seemed to be okay with it as well. Don had even started talking to her about coming with them when they left.

When the night was over, Esther and Molly went back to the tent where they were staying, and the next day they got up and started the whole routine over again. Five days passed, and Esther was becoming more comfortable with everything going on around her.

They continued to attend different shows each night. The comedy routines became even raunchier, and the couples on stage were starting to take off some of their clothes. In fact, in one scene the couple was in a bed, underneath the sheets and apparently had no clothes on. Esther would have been appalled at all of this weeks ago, but now the activity seemed like a necessary part of the show.

That evening Michael took her to another tent that served

beverages of all kinds. He put his hand on the small table to pay and then ordered a drink. "Esther, you should at least try this. It will help you to relax and enjoy things even more."

She had already crossed so many lines, and it didn't seem like a big deal to take a sip. She reached out to take the glass from him.

Michael pulled it back and smiled. "You'll have to get your own, but first you have to pay."

Esther put her hand on the table and felt a short tingling. She grabbed the glass the server extended and took a small drink. She had never tasted anything like this before.

Michael pointed to the glass. "Take another sip. You need a few before it starts to have an effect."

Michael and Esther carried their drinks with them as they watched a few shows, admiring all the fancy costumes and how free everyone seemed to be. No one seemed to care about what anyone else thought of what they were doing, and no one seemed to be living according to any set of rules. When the night was winding down, she said goodnight to Michael, then went to look for Molly. After finding her, the two headed for their tent. On the way, Esther tripped and started giggling as if she'd done something really funny.

Molly wasn't sure what was wrong with her, but she thought she must have just enjoyed herself a lot that night. They went to bed again, and the next morning, which was really the afternoon, Esther woke up feeling as if she was in a fog.

Michael and Don quickly found them, and Michael suggested they get something to eat to help Esther feel better. That night was much like the others except Michael took Esther to get something to drink earlier in the evening. Esther gladly took the drink, and they walked around just like they had before. When the night came to an end, Esther was stumbling a little bit. Michael grabbed hold of her to keep her from falling. He then pulled her in close as if to kiss her.

Just as his lips almost touched hers, Esther turned to the side so that he kissed her cheek. "I don't know if I should."

"Of course you should. Don't you want to?" Michael placed his hand on her cheek and slid it downward toward her shoulder.

As his hand reached the base of her neck without stopping, Esther grabbed it and stepped back. "What are you doing?"

Michael tried to pull her closer again. "I'm not doing anything you don't want me to do."

Esther gently pushed him away. "I've got to go. Molly will be going to bed soon, and I promised I would meet her at the usual time."

Michael grabbed her arm. "Molly can wait."

She removed his fingers, then turned to leave. "I'll see you tomorrow."

Esther wasn't sure what just happened. She felt like she was in a daze. She made her way over to the tent where they were staying, and Molly was outside waiting for her.

"Are you okay?" asked Molly.

Esther put her hand on her stomach. "I don't feel too good."

Molly helped her into the tent, and they lay down to go to sleep. Esther tried to drift off, but she kept feeling sick at her stomach. She stumbled out of her tent, thinking she better find a place where she wouldn't disturb anybody if she threw up. She stumbled between tents. She couldn't see straight, and her head felt woozy. Maybe if she did throw up, she'd feel better. She stopped and plopped onto the ground.

Suddenly, she heard familiar voices coming from a nearby tent. Michael, Steve, and Don were talking and laughing.

Steve snickered. "You owe me for this one, Don. You must admit I set Molly up really well for you."

Don chuckled. "You did, and I'm going to enjoy every bit of my time with her, too."

Steve said, "Yeah I really creeped her out, but just remember, the next time we bring a girl here you get to be the set-up guy, and I get to be the closer."

Don slapped Steve on the back. "No problem."

"So how long before you get Molly into the Tent of Fornication."

Don smiled a sly smile. "I'll get her to take her first drink tomorrow. I should have her a few days after that."

Steve turned to Michael. "How about you? How long will it take you for Esther?"

Michael placed his hand on his chin. "I've had to go slow with her, but a few more days should do it. I thought I had her tonight, but it appears I've got to get her to drink more than two glasses."

"Do you think we'll get a bonus from the Master for those two?" asked Don.

Michael nodded. "I'm thinking a large bonus. I figure we can get at least a year from both before they're used up and ready for the garbage dump. I must admit though, Esther will be hard to replace. It will be difficult to find another girl of her quality."

Esther couldn't believe what she was hearing. Was she dreaming? Michael had never intended to marry her. This whole time he had played her for a fool. How could he? She had loved him, hoped for a life with him, and now she realized he only wanted to use her. She felt so dirty, so ashamed. Tears streamed down her face.

Hearing someone crying, Michael stepped out of the tent and saw her. "What's wrong? Where did you come from?"

Esther was sobbing. "Get away from me. I heard everything."

Michael knelt beside her. "What do you mean? What do you think you heard? You know how guys joke around. You can't take that kind of thing too seriously."

Esther shook her head. "No, don't do it. Don't do it anymore. I'm tired of all the lies. You brought me here to use me, and then you were just going to toss me away like garbage. How could you? You said you loved me." She placed her hand on her stomach as a pained look came on her face.

Michael stood up and glared down at her. "Look at you. You're about to throw up. You're not the perfect little girl you think you are. You are exactly where you want to be. Nobody forced you to come here. You've known the truth since that first day you saw my little cabin. How did you like that by the way? Joe and I put that shack together in a couple of days."

He knelt down beside her again. "Ah come on Esther. You could last for years here before you're used up. I promise to take good care of you between now and then."

Esther pushed him away.

Michael stood up and spit on the ground next to her. "Fine, suit yourself, but you're going to be staying here whether you like it or not. And this isn't the kind of place you want to be without having someone like me as your friend."

Esther covered her face with her hands. "I just want to go back to the Petersons."

Michael laughed. "Oh yeah, I almost forgot about them. That old couple almost ruined things for me. I knew they didn't like me, but obviously, I'm much more persuasive than them because here you are. Forget about going anywhere. There's no way out of this place."

Esther wiped her eyes and looked at her surroundings in the dim light of the moon. The campground was in a deep canyon. Steep cliffs surrounded them, and there was no way to climb out.

Michael pointed to the entrance of the camp. "And don't even think about trying to find your way out through the woods on those trails. You'd be lost for weeks."

Michael kicked some dirt toward her. "And from now on you need to call me by my real name, Rebellion. Yeah, that's right, you've been following Rebellion this whole time, and it's led you to the Camp of Sin."

Esther stared at him in confusion.

"Don't look at me like that. You've known all along where you were. Sure, when we first arrived, we sent Don on ahead to ask them to change the banner, but you knew this was no Camp of Fun. This whole time, you've been deceiving yourself."

Between sobs, Esther said, "Why, Michael, why?"

Rebellion laughed. "You know why. Joe, Don, Steve and me—we all work for your enemy. Our job is to pull people like you off your path and fix it so you can't go back. I'll get a nice bonus for you."

Esther doubled over and placed her palms on the ground. "I wish I had never met you."

Rebellion shook his finger at her. "Don't you think it's time to start telling yourself the truth? If it hadn't been me, it would have been someone else. By the time I showed up, you were ready to leave your path. Each step along the way, you convinced yourself that what you were doing was okay. You're no different than me. I'm just honest about it. Go on and get some sleep. You'll change your mind about things once you realize you don't have much of a choice."

Esther continued to sob as Michael walked back into his tent. The happy married life she had hoped for with him was now gone. After a minute, she heard them all laughing. She stood up and tried to walk, thinking about how far she had strayed from her path. How could she have turned her back on God like this? What would her parents think if they could see her now? What would the Petersons think?

Would anyone even want her back?

Esther had grown up in a Christian home, and as a little girl, she asked her parents to walk with her to the Building of Reflection and then up the Hill of Calvary. She knelt before the cross on that day and accepted Jesus as her Lord and Savior. From that point on, she did her best to live according to the principles of God's word. Now all of that had changed. She had followed Rebellion to the Camp of Sin. Michael was right about one thing—she had known all along that what she was doing was wrong.

Esther stumbled a little ways and then fell to the ground. She called out to God. "Dear Lord, I'm so sorry. This is all my fault. I knew what I was doing was sinful, but I didn't care. I've sinned against you. Please help me!"

As she tried to get to her feet, Esther saw a bright light toward the edge of the mountain. She crawled toward it, and when she drew closer, she saw that it was a heavenly being.

"Esther, the Lord Jesus has heard your prayer. He wishes to restore you to your path."

She began to sob again. "I'm so sorry, and I feel so dirty. I can't return to my path until I've gotten cleaned up."

"If you could clean yourself up, then you wouldn't need Jesus, and you wouldn't need His grace. You must receive His forgiveness right now, where you are, without trying to do anything to earn it."

Esther felt so vulnerable. In the past, she always felt comforted by the fact that she was a good, moral person, but now she had to totally rely on grace. She gazed at the heavenly being. "Why does my Lord even want me anymore? Look at me. Look at where I'm at. I've brought disgrace upon myself and upon His name."

The heavenly being motioned toward her. "Esther, our Lord has wanted to be in relationship with you before you were even born— even before you had done anything good or bad. His love for you is not based on what you can do for Him. It's all about what He's already done for you."

Esther could barely hold her head up. "Why does He still love me? I don't deserve it."

"No you don't, but you didn't deserve His love before you came here either. Our Lord loves you because He loves you."

Esther glanced around and realized that for the first time she was truly seeing her surroundings as they really were. The sun was starting to rise, and this was the first time she was able to see the Camp of Sin in the morning light. "I want out of here. I want to serve my Lord again. I'll do anything."

The heavenly being said, "You just have to take my hand, and I'll carry you out."

Esther stood up and took a step toward the heavenly being. "Wait, I can't go yet. I've got to go tell Molly the truth about this place and ask her to go with us."

The heavenly being pointed toward the tent where Molly was sleeping. "Hurry, and go talk to her."

Esther was still a little unsteady on her feet, but she felt better than before. She hurried back and woke Molly up, then led her outside. Esther explained everything she had overheard from Michael and the guys, then she told her about the heavenly being waiting to take them away from here.

Molly began to cry because she too had also known all along that what she was doing was wrong. "I want out of here too, but I have to go see Polly. Maybe she'll listen to me. I don't want to leave without her."

Esther knew they didn't have much time, but she also knew how important Molly's sister was to her. They dashed through the camp to Polly and Joe's tent.

Molly pushed opened a corner of the tent flap and whispered, "Polly, Polly. Come outside. I need to talk to you."

She heard a low groan, and Polly stumbled out, rubbing her eyes and yawning. "What do you want? Couldn't this wait until later this afternoon?"

Molly began to tell her everything that Esther had told her.

Polly frowned at Esther. "Molly, are you going to believe everything you hear? Esther is not as innocent as you think she is either."

Molly grabbed her sister's hand. "But don't you understand? They are just using you. And when you're used up, they're going to take you to a garbage dump."

Joe climbed out of the tent and put his arm around Polly. "Joe has already told me about that. They only take the weak ones to that garbage dump, and I'm not weak." She pulled her hand away from

Molly.

Joe kissed Polly. "That's right honey. You're going to be just fine. These two though need to learn to keep their mouths shut."

Joe swatted Polly on her backside and laughed. "You go on back inside, and I'll be there in just a minute. Don't worry about these two. They'll learn how things work around here."

Polly staggered back inside.

Joe glared at them. "I told Michael you two might be trouble. You're going to have to learn a lesson."

Two other guys came around the corner, and Joe pointed toward Esther and Molly.

Esther pulled on Molly's arm. "Let's go, we've got to get out of here now."

Molly didn't want to leave Polly behind, but Esther jerked her forward, as the two guys moved closer. With the two thugs giving chase, Esther and Molly ran toward the place where the heavenly being would be waiting. Just as they were almost there, Michael, Steve, and Don stepped out in front of them.

Michael grabbed Esther and smiled. "Where are you going all in a hurry? Did you decide to spend some more time with me after all? And I see you brought a friend. I'm sure Don and Steve will appreciate that."

All the guys laughed.

Esther pushed Michael away. "We're getting out of here."

Michael grinned at the other guys. "Oh really, and how do you plan to accomplish that?"

The two thugs who were chasing them barred the way the girls had come, and Michael motioned for Don and Steve to block their escape. Just then a bright light radiated all around them, blinding the guys. They put up their arms to block the light, but it didn't help.

The heavenly being held out its hands. Esther grabbed one and Molly the other, then they ascended up the side of the mountain.

9

RESTORATION

The heavenly being carried them out of the canyon and far away from the Camp of Sin. Soon they crossed over a small forest and touched down in the middle of a field. Esther immediately recognized where she was—the field where she had been taking her walks. In the distance, she could see the steeple on top of the House of Instruction.

The sun was rising higher in the sky, and Esther knew the Petersons were probably just finishing breakfast.

Esther stared at the ground. "What am I going to say?"

The heavenly being lifted her chin. "The truth."

Esther knew this was the only right answer. "What will happen to Molly?"

"I'll be taking her to a place just outside of her parent's home."

Esther embraced Molly. "I'm so sorry I didn't do more to help you get home sooner. Throughout this whole time, I was only thinking about myself." She started to cry.

Molly squeezed her tight then stepped back. "Please don't cry. I could have insisted on going home, but I didn't. I knew what I was doing. What matters is that you came back for me. You could have left by yourself, but you cared about me. Thank you for that."

Esther gave her another hug. They cried some more then said goodbye. Esther watched as the heavenly figure departed with Molly.

After Molly arrived home, she ran up to her house just as her mom was coming outside to begin the daily chores. When her mother saw her, she called out to her husband, and they both sprinted toward her. They embraced her and cried tears of joy, but then they realized Polly wasn't with her. Molly sat down and told them everything. Her parents were relieved that she made it back, but at the same time, they were devastated upon hearing about Polly.

Molly dedicated herself to walking her path again, and God restored her to a place of strength. It would be over a year before they would see Polly again, and when she finally came back, she was six months pregnant. Polly continued to have a difficult time after giving birth to her daughter. Different men came in and out of her life, and she struggled to be a single parent. When her daughter turned thirteen, they constantly fought and argued. At sixteen Polly's daughter ran away from home, and Polly knew where she was heading.

It was that night that Polly knocked on Molly's door, who by that time was married and had two children. Molly sat out on the porch with her where they talked, prayed, and cried throughout the night. That morning Molly walked with Polly to the Building of Reflection and waited until she came out. They then climbed the Hill of Calvary together, and Polly dedicated her life to serving her Lord and Savior that day. After that, they began to pray for Polly's daughter, but it would be another year before they would see her, and when they did, Polly's daughter was pregnant.

That day Polly embraced her daughter and apologized for not being the mother she should have been. Her daughter cried, and a few months later, both Polly and her Aunt Molly accompanied her to the Building of Reflection and the Hill of Calvary. Life wasn't easy after that, but they were at least going in the right direction. Esther would one day see both Polly and Molly again, and they cried and prayed together as they talked about the goodness of God's grace.

After the heavenly being flew off with Molly, Esther stared down at her path, knowing where it was leading. She wasn't sure how she was going to do this. The Petersons had been so gracious to her since the day she had arrived. They tried to tell her she was going in the wrong direction, but she wouldn't listen. Esther knew she had to face them and tell them the truth.

As she walked back into the village, she saw Mrs. Peterson outside watering her flowers. Esther remembered that first day when she arrived and saw her doing the very same chore. She felt such remorse and sorrow. If only she could go back and undo everything that had been done.

As she came closer, Mrs. Peterson turned around. Esther stopped.

Barely able to hold up her head, she began to cry. Mrs. Peterson put down her watering pot and hurried toward her, then she threw her arms around her and held her tight. Esther couldn't move. Her hands dangled at her sides while she sobbed.

Mrs. Peterson held her for what seemed to be hours, and then she whispered in her ear. "We've been praying for you. We knew you would return."

Esther sobbed even harder.

Mr. Peterson had come back to the house to get something, and he saw Esther crying in his wife's arms. He knew this was a time for Esther and his wife to be alone, so he quietly retrieved some notes, and then went back to the House of Instruction to pray.

Mrs. Peterson led her inside their house. They sat on the couch while Esther shared everything that had happened. She alternated between crying and talking while Mrs. Peterson sat and listened.

When Esther finished sharing everything that had happened, Mrs. Peterson embraced her again.

Esther leaned back. "I'm so sorry. You've done so much for me, and I just ran off like that and lied to you."

Mrs. Peterson patted her hands. "What matters is that you're safe. A lot worse could have happened to both you and Molly if you had stayed there even a few more days."

Esther thought of Molly. "I can't believe how irresponsible I was. If something would have happened to her, I don't think I could have forgiven myself."

Mrs. Peterson sighed. "Sin has terrible consequences, and it affects more than just the one committing the sin. You learned a very valuable lesson, and it sounds like God intervened and protected you both by His grace."

Esther sat up. "I know. I think about what would have happened if I hadn't overheard Michael and the guys talking. I was okay with sin as long as I could maintain the deception."

"Sin is very deceptive. It allows us to believe what we want to believe until it has us fully in its grasp. I'm so thankful both of you got out of there when you did."

Esther wiped her eyes. "I will gather up my things and be going."

"Where will you go?"

Esther peered through the front window. "I don't know. I don't feel like I can stay here though."

Mrs. Peterson took her hand. "Running away is not an answer."

Shaking her head, Esther said, "But, I've lied to you. Why would you want me to be here? What will people think about me?"

Mrs. Peterson looked at Esther with caring but stern eyes. "It doesn't matter what people think about you. What matters is facing things and not running away from them."

Esther thought of the people in the community and those who attended the House of Instruction. Then she thought of the young girls she had taught during the women's meetings. What had those little girls thought when they realized she wasn't going to be there to teach them anymore. "What happened to my class?"

"Mrs. Kramer's daughter, Sally, stepped in and has been teaching them. She's only fourteen, but we felt the young girls needed to have their time together."

Esther realized this was another consequence of her sin. She had abandoned her responsibilities, and this affected others as well.

Mrs. Peterson said, "Tonight is our meeting. You need to come."

Esther turned away. "I don't know. What will they think about me?"

Mrs. Peterson firmly grasped her hand. "They will love you, and they will care about you."

Mrs. Peterson saw that Esther looked exhausted and suggested she lie down for a little while before the meeting. After a good sleep, she got ready and came out of her room. Mrs. Peterson was waiting for her in the kitchen, and as soon as she saw her, she held out Esther's Book.

"How did you get this?" asked Esther.

"On the day you left, Mr. Peterson had talked to the letter carrier, and we knew you hadn't gone to visit your friend. We were both worried, so Mr. Peterson asked around to see if anyone had seen you leave. The next day he finally found someone who saw you and Michael heading toward those woods. It was almost dark by then, so he had to wait until the next day to try and find you."

Esther sighed and looked toward the door. "I'm sorry I put the both of you through all of this."

Mrs. Peterson put her arm around her. "We were concerned about your safety. Later the next day, Mr. Peterson hiked through those woods for hours before he finally found the little cabin. He knocked and knocked, and after no one came to the door, he realized it was unlocked. He went in and discovered some of your things on the table, and then he found your Book. He walked around for the rest of the day, but there was no sign of you, so he gathered up all of your things and brought them back."

Esther reached out to take her Book. "I'm so grateful to have this back again. I must thank Mr. Peterson for everything he did, and of course, I owe him an apology as well."

Mrs. Peterson picked up her Book and started toward the door. "You will have a chance to talk to him later, but for now we need to get over and get ready for the women's fellowship time."

Esther and Mrs. Peterson arrived early and set up all the chairs. Not long afterward, Mrs. Kramer arrived with her daughter, and Sally began setting up the classroom next door for the young girls. Esther greeted her and thanked her for taking over the class.

When all the ladies had arrived, Esther asked Mrs. Peterson if she could step into the young girl's classroom and say hello to them. Esther stopped at the door, as all the young girls were getting ready to sit down. When they saw her, they ran toward her and hugged her.

Emily held up her doll. "Ms. Esther, Sheila missed you."

Tears began to stream down Esther's face.

"Ms. Esther, why are you crying?"

Esther reached out and grasped the doll's hand. "I missed Sheila, and I missed you too." She gave Emily a hug.

One of the girls asked Esther if she would be teaching them, and she told her that she was going to be with their mommies in the other room, but she would see them at the end of the class. She waved goodbye to the young girls and then joined the other women. They all greeted her and let her know how much they missed her. Esther then took a seat beside Mrs. Peterson.

Mrs. Johnson had prepared this week's lesson. She led the women in a short prayer, then read from her Book that it was the goodness of God that leads people to repentance. Then she turned to Isaiah and read, "I, Yes I, am the One who wipes out and cancels your transgressions for My own sake, and I will not remember your sins."

She then read from the Psalms. "He has not dealt with us according to our sins, Nor punished us according to our iniquities."

Mrs. Johnson held out her hand. "If you are in Christ, God is not mad at you. Jesus was our propitiation, which means He was our wrath-bearing sacrifice. All of us deserve God's wrath because we are sinful, and we continue to commit sins even after receiving Christ as our Savior. But Jesus took all of our sin and the wrath that we were due and bore it on the cross."

Esther thought about this. She could believe that God would forgive her, but wasn't He still mad at her for all the things she had done? Wasn't He mad at her while she was in the Camp of Sin?

Mrs. Johnson folded her hands. "This does not mean that sin doesn't have consequences. The wages of sin is death, and when a person willfully follows after sin, it brings death into their life. When we sow to our flesh, then we reap the harvest from those seeds. God disciplines us by allowing us to experience the consequences of our sins so we will learn from them."

Esther realized that she certainly learned a lot of things since she had run off. She had let so many people down, and she had violated the trust of those who had given so much to her. But most of all she had sinned against her God. He had always been gracious and loving toward her, and yet she openly rebelled against His goodness.

Mrs. Johnson then read from another Psalm. "If You, Lord, kept account of and treated us according to our sins, who could stand? But with You, there is forgiveness that You may be reverently feared and worshiped."

Esther could feel the truths of God's word reaching into her soul, but at the same time, these truths made her feel uncomfortable. There was a part of her that wanted to be treated according to her sins. Shouldn't she have to do something to make up for her failure?

Mrs. Johnson glanced at each of the women. "If God gave us what we truly deserved for even the smallest of our sins, no one could stand before Him. As sinful human beings, we have nothing to offer God in exchange for His forgiveness. We must completely rely upon His grace."

Esther remembered back to the words of the heavenly being. Why had the offer of grace made her feel so vulnerable, and why was she still feeling vulnerable hearing about grace now?

Esther felt as if the Holy Spirit was moving through Mrs. Johnson to speak directly to her because next she said, "Relying upon grace is hard because our old nature tries to convince us that we must do something to earn back God's favor. But in reality, our sinful flesh is trying to avoid the cross. For only through repentance and surrender at the foot of the cross can sin be dealt with at its roots."

Mrs. Johnson instructed everyone to turn to Hebrews chapter four. She then read, "And there is no creature hidden from His sight, but all things are naked and open to the eyes of Him to whom we must give account." She pointed up and said, "All things are revealed and open before God. We stand before Him completely naked and exposed. We cannot bring our works, our own goodness, or anything else into His presence to cover ourselves with. Our only covering is Christ's righteousness, which we cannot take any credit for."

Mrs. Johnson then asked everyone to turn to Second Corinthians. She read, "For godly sorrow produces repentance leading to salvation, and leaves no regret, but worldly sorrow produces death." She set her Book in her lap. "Our first reaction to sin is worldly sorrow because it gives us a way to pay for our sin without having to give it up. Worldly sorrow prompts us to make up for our sins through our own efforts. In contrast, godly sorrow recognizes that our real problem is not what we do but who we are. Godly sorrow goes to the very core of our sinfulness and teaches us to turn toward God and His grace as our only solution."

Esther realized she had been planning to follow a path of worldly sorrow. She had been thinking about what she could do to make up for her rebellion. She planned to work even harder for the Petersons, while also doing more for others in the community so she could earn back the favor and approval she had before. But what then? The Holy Spirit showed her that none of these activities would have brought change to her heart. All the roots of sin that had caused her to follow rebellion in the first place would still be there untouched.

Mrs. Johnson bowed her head and said a short prayer. When she finished, she asked if anyone would like to share something that God had laid on their heart. Some of the women talked about their own struggles with receiving forgiveness. They too could relate to wanting to make up for their sin in order to feel good enough to approach God.

Mrs. Peterson spoke up. "Often when we sin, we want to do

something to get rid of the guilt, but we aren't willing to go before God and do whatever it takes to get rid of the sin. Worldly sorrow may produce a lot of tears, but it will not produce a lot of change."

Mrs. Kramer said, "I know there have been times when I've beaten myself up over something, and then once the guilt passes I move on as if it never happened."

Others nodded in agreement.

Mrs. Johnson asked if anyone else would like to share. Esther felt the Holy Spirit prompting her to talk about her recent experiences, but she was hesitant. All of these women had given her so many compliments in the past. She had been seen as an upstanding young lady in the community. Some had even remarked that they hoped their daughters grew up to be just like her someday. Now, what would they think? Esther stared at the floor.

Mrs. Johnson closed her Book. "If that's all, then Mrs. Kramer will you dismiss us in prayer?"

Esther put her hand on Mrs. Peterson's shoulder. "I would like to share something."

Everyone had been wondering if Esther was going to talk about where she had been. She started from the beginning and told them about all that had happened over the last few weeks. When she described feeling trapped in the Camp of Sin and calling out for grace, some of the women teared up. When Esther finished, she was crying as well. Mrs. Peterson asked the women to gather around and pray for her. Esther felt comforted and loved. Mrs. Johnson closed the meeting in prayer, and all the women hugged Esther and told her how glad they were that she was back.

Before she left, Mrs. Kramer approached Esther. "I want you to come over for lunch with Sally and me sometime. Sally is a good Christian girl who loves God, but I can tell by her questions that at times she wonders about the enticements of the world. She's heard stories that sound very appealing. It would be good for her to hear what you've experienced, and what sin is really like."

"I'd be glad to come over anytime." Esther wished she had never taken the first steps off her path, but she hoped that her experience could be a warning to others.

As the women left, Esther stood out in the hall and waved goodbye to many of the young girls. At last, she joined Mrs. Peterson in the classroom to straighten up.

When they finished, Mrs. Peterson gave her a hug. "I'm proud of you for sharing and being honest tonight."

Esther said, "I didn't want to, but I felt I had to. I do feel better, but at the same time I feel vulnerable."

Mrs. Peterson said, "And you will feel like that for some time. The path of worldly sorrow can give you immediate relief because you feel you've made up for your sin, but when you turn to God in true repentance, His work of grace is a process. That's because God is doing a complete work that is causing you to be different from the inside out. God does not just want to change what you do, but He wants to change who you are."

They left the House of Instruction and headed home. Halfway there Esther stopped. "I've not seen Mr. Peterson yet? How will he feel about me staying?"

"We'll talk with him when we get home. I know how much he cares about you."

When they arrived, Mr. Peterson was waiting and greeted his wife with a kiss. "How was the meeting tonight, Anna?"

Mrs. Peterson took off her shawl and set it on a chair. "It was wonderful. Mrs. Johnson led a marvelous teaching on the goodness of God."

Mr. Peterson turned to Esther. "It's so good to see you again. While you were resting earlier, Anna came over to my office and shared with me everything that's happened. I'm very sorry you've had to go through all that."

Esther nervously rubbed her hands. "I'm sorry for what I put you two through. Before we left to go to the meeting, Mrs. Peterson told me how you came to look for me. Thank you for getting my Book. I just wish I had listened to both of you in the first place."

Mr. Peterson motioned for Esther to sit down, and Mrs. Peterson sat beside her on the couch.

He could see that she was nervous. "Esther, I want you to know that we both feel about you as if you were our own daughter. It grieved us to see what was happening to you before you left, and when we figured out that you followed Michael, we knew it was going to lead to a lot of heartaches. We're glad you came back, and I want you to know that you're welcome to continue staying here."

Esther breathed a sigh of relief. "Thank you so much. I promise that I will not do anything like that again, and I will listen to what you have to say."

Mr. Peterson leaned forward. "I know you will, but I don't want you to go back to being the person you were when you first arrived."

Esther didn't understand what he meant. What was wrong with her before? Yes, she had drifted off her path after being here a few weeks, but wasn't she just fine before that?

Seeing her reaction, Mr. Peterson said, "Let me explain. I believe that you have always relied on being the good girl that everyone approved of. I'm sure you always knew your memory verse in Sunday school, and as you grew up, you received lots of compliments on how good a Christian you were. I'm also sure your professors at the House of Knowledge were always holding you up as a good example for others to follow."

Esther listened carefully, identifying with what he was saying.

Mr. Peterson sat back and clasped his hands together. "I think what happened is that you began to put your trust in your own goodness. So when you started to become deceived by rebellion, you weren't able to see it because you didn't believe you were capable of being deceived."

Esther knew he was right. "I understand how deceitful sin is now. All along, I was convincing myself that everything was okay, but with each step I took, sin was slowly leading me further and further away."

Mr. Peterson continued, "Sin is always looking for an opening. Your main enemy is never the devil or the temptations of the world around you. Your biggest enemy is always your sinful flesh. The moment you think you are standing, you should watch out lest you fall."

Esther leaned forward. "I see what you're saying. I always thought of myself as a good person, but I forgot that I am what I am by the grace of God."

"Yes," said Mr. Peterson, "that's something we all have to be constantly reminded of. Focusing on our own efforts either leads to pride or a sense of failure."

"I can see that now," said Esther. "It seems like over the years I've drifted from one to the other. When I followed all the rules, I felt a sense of accomplishment, and without realizing it, I felt better than others. But if I had one of those days where I didn't feel I measured up, then I felt like a complete failure."

Mr. Peterson held up his finger. "And I bet you worked even harder the next day to make sure you made up for it."

"Yes I did."

Mr. Peterson nodded. "When we realize just how sinful we are, then we also realize that fulfilling our Christian To Do List won't even scratch the surface of dealing with our problem. But when we realize we are completely covered in Christ's righteousness despite our sinfulness, then we also realize there's nothing we can do to earn any more of God's favor. Being constantly aware of our sinfulness drives us to the Throne of Grace. Being constantly aware of our acceptance in Christ assures us that we'll be welcomed once we get there."

"Thank you," said Esther. "I need to remind myself of those truths daily."

Mr. Peterson stood up. "We discussed earlier that we believe you need to write your parents and let them know everything that's happened."

Esther knew this needed to be done, but she wasn't looking forward to it. Her parents had worried so much about her going out on her own, and now they were going to be even more concerned.

One more consequence of her sin—but she wouldn't hide what she'd done from them. She replied, "I'll do that."

Mr. Peterson leaned over to give Esther a hug. He then kissed his wife on the cheek and let her know that he was going on to bed. Esther and Mrs. Peterson spent another hour talking, and then they went to bed as well.

10

REBUILDING

The next day Esther settled back into her role as Mrs. Peterson's helper. She worked with her around the house and at the House of Instruction. However, Esther didn't continue one part of her old routine. No longer did she walk toward the field where she had met Michael. When dinner was over, she would take walks through the community, greeting many of those who were sitting outside and enjoying a relaxing evening. If she noticed someone who appeared to have had a hard day, she would offer to talk and pray with them. After this, Esther always reserved plenty of time to go back to her room and read in her Book. Reading and praying was how she started her day, and it's what she wanted to do just before going to bed as well.

That first week after being back, Esther began to work on the letter she needed to write to her parents. It was one of the most difficult things she had ever done. It took her eight days to complete it, and then she sent it off. Ten days later she received a reply with some encouraging words, but also an announcement that her parents planned to visit because they wanted to see her.

Esther always enjoyed spending time with her mom and dad, but she was concerned about how they were going to react on this visit. They had not said much in their letter, and she knew they were waiting to talk to her in person before sharing most of their feelings.

A few days later her parents arrived, and the first thing they did was embrace her. Her mom cried as she held her, and Esther cried as well. Her father was very loving toward her, but he was also angry at Michael and the other guys. Esther learned later on that her father asked Mr. Peterson how he could find Michael, but Mr. Peterson assured him that Michael and his friends were long gone.

Mr. and Mrs. Prescott stayed three days in a guest room that the Petersons had prepared for them. On that first evening, Esther's father brought up the subject of wanting her to return home with them. Esther knew this was coming, and she had already prayed about it. She reassured her parents that she was in a safe place where God could help her rebuild her spiritual walk. The Petersons also reassured them that they felt Esther was in a good place and was again using good judgment.

On their last day there, Mr. Prescott saw that Esther's path stayed at the Petersons while he and his wife's were pointing toward home. Reluctantly, her parents accepted that she would not be returning with them. This realization was especially tough on Esther's father who wanted to take her back so he could make sure nothing bad happened to her again.

Before they left, Mr. and Mrs. Prescott gathered around with the Petersons and Esther for prayer. After giving their daughter one more hug, they said goodbye. Esther stood on the porch as they traveled out of sight. The last time she had said goodbye to them was right after graduation. At that time, she felt she knew everything and was ready for anything. This time she knew there was still much she needed to learn.

The following weeks and months seemed to go by quickly. Esther was growing stronger in her walk with God each day, and within five months she was back to teaching the young girls class. This time though, Mrs. Peterson suggested that Esther and Sally alternate teaching so they both could also be in the women's meeting every other week.

Following up on Mrs. Kramer's invitation, Esther also made time to come by and have lunch with her and Sally. While she was there, Mrs. Kramer asked her to share some of the things she had said during the women's meeting that first night back. Sally listened intently and expressed surprise that a godly woman like Esther was able to fall into sin. It helped Sally realize that sin was capable of deceiving anyone. Esther helped her understand that the world with all its allurements could seem attractive and desirable, but once a person got there, she'd see it wasn't as fun and exciting as she thought it would be. Esther assured her that God had his own special adventures for her, and if she'd be patient, she'd get to experience all of them.

As time went by, Esther told her story to other young women. Each time, she felt some of the pain from the experience, but the more she shared, the less painful it became. God was using these times of sharing with others as a process of healing for her as well.

After nine months, Mrs. Peterson asked her if she would teach at the next women's meeting. Esther was excited and afraid all at the same time. She would only have six days to prepare. What would she teach on? These were all mature women of God who knew their Books. What could she add to them?

Esther asked Mrs. Peterson if she could pray about it and let her know the next day. That evening when Esther was alone, she prayed and asked God what she could possibly share that would bring value to the ones hearing it. God began to impress upon her to think about what He had been doing in her life over these past nine months. She meditated on all the Scriptures the Holy Spirit had been working in her heart, and the truths these verses taught.

Esther started to understand that the most valuable thing she could offer these women was what God was doing in her own life. Sharing principles from God's word was valuable, but what really made them powerful was the ability to show how these truths applied to a person's daily life.

Esther studied and read for the next hour and then went to sleep. The next morning she told Mrs. Peterson that she would be honored to share a teaching with the women's group. It was Sally's turn to lead the young girls class, so the timing was perfect.

When the day for the meeting arrived, Esther was a little nervous, but Mrs. Peterson helped to reassure her. Together they set up the classroom, and the other women soon began to arrive. Everyone was delighted to hear that Esther would be teaching that week.

Esther opened in prayer, took a deep breath, and then began. "I feel like I've gained more insight and wisdom over these past nine months than I have in my entire Christian life. I've learned more about the depths of my sinfulness, while at the same time experiencing a greater depth of God's love and acceptance. I know that sounds odd because it would seem like the more we discover what's wrong with us, the more depressed we would become."

A few of the women nodded.

Continuing, Esther said, "We think the more of our faults we admit, the more reason God has to reject us, but that's not how it works with Him. He already knows all about our sinfulness, and He sent Jesus to die for every single bit of it. Nothing we admit to God is a surprise or causes Him to love us any less. In fact, He is waiting for us to bring Him our sins so He can forgive us, as well as cleanse us from the guilt and shame that comes with our sins. Transgressing against God's commands is like being stung by a bee. The initial act of transgression brings pain into our lives, but the remaining stinger continues to inject unrighteousness into our systems through the venom of guilt and shame. The only way to have this stinger removed is through repentance and receiving grace in the presence of God."

Motioning toward Mrs. Johnson, Esther said, "I want to thank you for the teaching you did on that first night when I came back. I needed to hear about the goodness of God, and I needed to hear that there was no way I could earn this goodness through my own efforts. It was humbling to realize I couldn't earn my way back into God's favor, but it caused me to go deeper rather than looking for a quick fix to my problems."

Mrs. Johnson smiled and nodded.

Esther turned a few pages in her Book. "I want to read from Luke chapter seven, beginning in verse thirty-six to the end of the chapter." When she finished reading, she set her Book on her lap. "I'm sure that when Simon the Pharisee invited Jesus to his home, he believed Jesus to be a good and honorable man. And I'm also sure that Simon felt he was worthy to have such a man eat with him. But when a woman who was known to be sinful came in and began to anoint the feet of Jesus, Simon's true heart was revealed. He saw himself as superior to this woman, and he even judged Jesus for allowing this type of person to wash His feet."

Esther held up her finger. "But this woman had a very different attitude. Some would think she was humiliating herself with this public display of crying and washing a man's feet with her tears, but she didn't care how she looked. She recognized Jesus as much more than just a good man. She saw Him as someone who could bring relief to her spiritual condition. That was worth risking public humiliation."

Esther pointed at her Book. "Knowing what Simon was thinking,

Jesus told him a story. There were two men who owed a debt. One owed fifty days worth of wages, and the other five hundred days worth of wages. When neither could pay back their debt, the creditor forgave both of them. Jesus asked Simon which of the two would love their creditor more. Simon said he supposed the one to whom more was forgiven. Jesus wanted Simon to understand that unlike himself, this woman truly understood just how in debt she was. Because she grasped the level of her sinfulness, she was able to experience a greater depth of love for Jesus and a greater appreciation for the forgiveness He could offer."

All of the women sat quietly without moving.

Esther glanced at Mrs. Peterson. "It's hard for me to admit this, but before I followed rebellion to the Camp of Sin, I had a lot of Simon in me. If you would have asked me about my relationship with God, I would have told you how much I loved Him and how grateful I was for what Christ did for me on the cross. But deep down there was a part of me that thought I deserved God's love more than others because I wasn't as sinful as they were."

A few of the women sighed and slightly nodded.

"It's been a process, but I've come to understand that the only thing that separates me from the most sinful person on earth is God's grace. Without it I'm nothing. Each day I can be like that woman at the feet of Jesus, or I can be like Simon."

Esther picked up her Book. "I'd next like to read from Psalms 51. In this passage, David is crying out before God after the prophet Nathan had confronted him about his adultery with Bathsheba and the murder of her husband, Uriah. David wrote, 'For I acknowledge my transgressions, and my sin remains continually before me. Against You, You only, have I sinned, and done this evil in Your sight, so that You may be justified when You give your sentence, and be blameless when You judge.' "

Pointing toward her Book, she said, "Before these last nine months, I would have told you that this was the perfect prayer for the really sinful people. I'm sure Simon would have thought it was a perfectly fitting prayer for the woman at Jesus' feet. But what Jesus wanted Simon to understand—what He wants all of us to understand, is that this prayer is fitting for all of us all the time. We shouldn't wait until we end up in the Camp of Sin to pray these words, and in fact, if we would daily acknowledge the truths in

David's proclamation, then we could avoid the Camp of Sin altogether."

Turning in her Book, Esther said, "Let me read this to you from Isaiah, 'For thus says the High and Exalted One, Who inhabits eternity and Whose name is Holy, I dwell in the high and holy place, with those who are thoroughly sorrowful for their sins and who are of a humble spirit, to revive the spirit of the humble, and to revive the hearts of the ones who are truly repentant for their sins.' "

Esther smiled as she glanced around the room. "Many would not understand, but since I've become more aware of my sinfulness, I've actually experienced a greater depth of joy. The woman at Jesus' feet understood something that Simon didn't. She wasn't humiliating herself—she was humbling herself, and God gives grace to the humble. When we approach the Throne Room of Grace, we are entering God's presence, and in His presence is fullness of joy!"

Esther closed her Book.

After a moment of silence, Mrs. Walker raised her hand. "Thank you so much, Esther, for sharing that. As I've been sitting here, the Holy Spirit has shown me how much energy I've expended, trying to prove I'm not that sinful. Sometimes it feels exhausting. I say all the right words and quote all the right Scriptures, but at best this only provides temporary relief."

Mrs. Johnson spoke up. "That was very good Esther." She turned to Mrs. Walker. "I've felt the same way as you at times, and it's so freeing not to have to prove ourselves anymore. We often hear of those who quote Romans 8:1, 'There is no condemnation to those who are in Christ...' in an attempt to deal with their guilt and shame, but what is overlooked is that it was the Apostle Paul's revelation about his sinfulness throughout Romans 7 that gave birth to that proclamation in Romans 8. He didn't have to repeat 'There is no condemnation...' in an attempt to convince himself of this truth— the truth of these words rose up in his spirit as a result of his honesty before God. Only when we fully acknowledge who we are outside of Christ, do we more fully comprehend who we are in Christ."

"Amen," said Mrs. Peterson.

Esther closed in prayer, and as they were enjoying a time of fellowship afterward, several women thanked her for sharing what they needed to hear.

When all the women had left, Mrs. Peterson hugged her. "That was so good tonight. You did a great job."

Esther smiled. "Thank you."

The next few months were filled with lots of activities at the House of Instruction. There was a weeklong series of meetings that were conducted by a special guest speaker, and there was always a lot to do before and after each meeting. Esther enjoyed being a part of all of it, and she felt like God was using her in so many different ways. Yet Esther knew her time with the Petersons was coming to a close, and they sensed it as well. Just as they had to release their own daughter to go out on her own, they knew God was preparing them to do the same for Esther.

11

MOVING FORWARD

A few weeks later Esther woke up one morning and saw that her path was moving away.

Mrs. Peterson joined her on the porch. "I thought this day was coming soon. We'll be having our women's meeting tomorrow evening. Why don't you stay for that? It will be a great opportunity for all of the women to say goodbye to you."

"I'd like that."

Esther felt excited, but there was also a slight bit of sadness. The Petersons were like family to her, and this had been her home for over a year. She had made so many friends in the community, and she had grown close to the young girls in her class.

Mrs. Peterson began to spread the word that the next women's meeting would be Esther's last, and she would be leaving the next day. The women were saddened by the news, but they were glad to have an opportunity to say goodbye. When it came time for the meeting, Esther and Mrs. Peterson went over early to prepare as usual. When they arrived though, they found that some of the women were already there. They had set everything up and had hung a banner that read, "God Bless You Esther, and May You Always Remember Us As You Travel." There was a big cake, and some punch set out on a table.

That night there was no lesson, but all the ladies went around and shared the different ways that Esther had impacted their lives and their children. Esther wiped away a few tears as she listened. Then Mrs. Peterson shared how much Esther meant to her. Mrs. Peterson said that she knew from the very first moments of Esther's arrival that God was placing her in her care for a season. There was a time of prayer, then they cut the cake and began fellowshipping with one another. Esther let the ladies know that she was going down the hall for a few minutes to say goodbye to the young girls.

She made her way to the classroom, thinking of all the time she had spent with these girls. When Esther entered, Sally had just finished passing out the juice and cookies.

Emily skipped up to her and held up her doll. "Look Ms. Esther, Sheila is having a birthday!"

Esther kissed the doll. "Happy birthday Sheila!"

She then gave Emily a hug, and a tear rolled down her cheek.

Emily tugged at her arm. "What's wrong Ms. Esther?"

She wiped the tear away. "I have some news, but let's get everyone in their seats so I can talk to all of you."

Sally directed all the young girls to get their dolls and return to their seats.

Esther smiled at them. "I want all of you to know just how much I love you. I have enjoyed every moment that I've spent with each of you. You have been such good girls, and you have learned so much about Jesus. One day when you get older, God may send you on a journey, and when that happens, you have to say goodbye to some people that you care about. God is sending me on a journey, and I don't know when I'll be back. Sally is going to continue to be your teacher, and I know you'll continue to do great. I'm going to miss you."

One by one, the girls came up to Esther and hugged her.

Emily grabbed her hand. "Where will you go Ms. Esther?"

"Wherever God leads me."

"Will you be back?"

Esther knelt beside her. "I believe that someday I'll see you all. I know you'll grow up to be women who serve God, and I can't wait to hear about all your adventures."

Emily gave her one more hug, then Esther returned to the women's meeting. They all assured her that they would be praying for her. As the women began to leave, they gave Esther a hug and let her know how much they would miss her. Mrs. Johnson told Mrs. Peterson they would clean up, so she and Esther returned home where Mr. Peterson was waiting. He had always been a man of few words, but he felt just as close to Esther as his wife did. He had watched her progress over this past year, and he was so proud of her. He shared this with Esther and started to tear up a little bit. She gave him a hug and thanked him for all he had done for her.

Mr. Peterson went on to bed, and Esther and Mrs. Peterson were left alone to share the final moments of their last evening together.

Mrs. Peterson placed her hand on Esther's shoulder. "I'll be praying for you."

"Thank you."

"Letting go isn't easy," said Mrs. Peterson. "But I know you're ready. God has great things in store for you, and I'm thankful He used me to play a small part in your preparation."

Esther wiped away a tear. "I wouldn't be where I am without you."

Mrs. Peterson handed her a tissue. "I believe that one day you're going to meet a special young man, and it's going to be very different than your last experience."

Esther shook her head. "I want to believe that, but I'm afraid I'll make a mistake again. How will I know when it's right?"

"You'll know," said Mrs. Peterson smiling. "God will place him along your path. You just keep seeking God and His plans for your life, and He'll add this young man to those plans."

Esther smiled and gave her a hug goodnight, then she went to her room to pack up the rest of her things. She looked around and thought of all the wonderful memories she would take with her from this place. She then lay down and went to sleep. The next morning she had a nice breakfast with the Petersons, and then it was time to leave. Esther reassured them that she would stay in touch. As she walked through the community, some of the women came out to wave goodbye to her.

Esther checked her path, and to her surprise, it was going by the field where she had spent so much time with Michael. This field represented her failure, but God was taking her by it one last time to show her just how far she had come since then. Her path then turned toward the edge of the community. She looked back one more time, then continued on.

She traveled the rest of the day, and just as the sun was setting, she came upon an inn. The Petersons had been very generous and given her a nice sum of money for all her help, and the women had taken up an offering for her as well. She paid the lady at the front desk, then settled into her room for a good night's rest. The next day she rose up early and continued on her path. Toward the end of the day, she came upon a forest. There was only about an hour of daylight left, but there didn't appear to be a suitable place to camp, so she decided to try and make it through to the other side.

As she approached the entrance, Esther felt an eeriness as if the trees were watching her. She checked her path to make sure she was going in the right direction and confirmed that she was. She left the sunny grassland and entered the forest, keeping her hand on her satchel, ready to draw out her Book in case she needed her Sword. The air seemed to get heavier, and a cold breeze whipped through the trees, sending chills down her arms. After plodding along the darkened path for what felt like an hour or longer, a loud shriek resonated off to her right. Esther drew out her Book. She held still for a moment to see if she could detect any movement or sounds. When she heard and saw nothing, she crept forward.

The sun had already set, and the deeper into the forest that she went, the darker it became. Further ahead Esther heard a hissing sound. The closer she got, the louder the hissing grew. The faint light of the moon trickling through the trees ahead exposed a long, dark object looming up from the path.

Cautious and concerned, Esther raised her Book until it became a Sword. After several more steps, she recognized what the object was—a giant snake swaying back and forth. The large reptile swung forward, as the moonlight glistened on its head. Its mouth opened, revealing fangs as long as a four-penny nail and a forked tongue darting in and out. The snake's rounded, hooded head rose seven feet off the ground.

"Hello, Esssssther. I've been expecting you. My name issss Leviathan. Welcome to the Foressst of Fear."

12

THE FOREST OF FEAR

Leviathan continued to sway back and forth. "Are you afraid Essssther? You should be. I know all about you, and I know what you fear the most."

Esther took a step back. She had never encountered such an enemy as this. She tried to think of words from her Book, but seeing the giant snake and hearing the constant hissing almost put her in a trance. She began to imagine the worst things that could possibly happen to her, and a sense of dread and terror flooded her thoughts. Behind her, off to the left, she heard rustling among the leaves on the ground.

She backed away slowly while holding up her Sword.

Leviathan said, "That's right, Essssther. Go back where you came from, and don't ever return."

Still retreating, Esther glanced over her shoulder. A twig snapped, then something that looked to be a small shadow darted from behind a tree.

Holding out her Sword, she said, "Who's there?"

A faint, soft voice said, "Please don't hurt me."

Esther stepped closer. "Come out so I can see you."

A figure emerged from behind the tree. "I'm Naomi. Who are you?"

Esther lowered her Sword and introduced herself. Naomi looked to be a few years younger than Esther. She had long brown hair and gentle facial features. Her gaze flicked from place to place, and even after Esther put away her sword, Naomi still clung to the tree, staying partially behind it. Her face and hands were smudged with dirt, and her hair was unkempt, as if she'd been in the forest for days with no chance to comb it.

Esther took a step toward her. "How long have you been here?"

Naomi glanced around to make sure nothing else was nearby. "I arrived three days ago, but as soon as I saw that giant snake, I ran and hid behind this tree. I think that creature still knows I'm here though, because each night I hear it hissing and calling my name. I've barely been able to get any sleep, and I ate the last little bit of my food yesterday."

Esther set down her backpack and took a seat a few feet from where Naomi was standing. Esther pulled out some bread and honey, then held it out.

Hesitant at first, Naomi sat down beside her and eagerly accepted the food. She gobbled it down, then said, "I've made so much progress following my path, and I didn't want to retreat, but I don't see how I can get past this enemy."

Esther took out her canteen and a cup, then poured Naomi some water. "It looks like we're in this together now. This enemy has become our enemy."

Naomi gulped down the water. "How are two young women a match for this giant snake?"

Esther fixed another piece of bread for Naomi and poured her another cup of water. "It's not going to be easy, but our paths have led us here, and I know God does not intend for us to stay trapped in this forest."

After Naomi finished eating, Esther took out her Book. "I think anyone would be afraid of such a fearsome creature, but I can't help but notice that you seem to be almost paralyzed by your fear. Has it always been like this?"

Naomi nodded. "I think I've been afraid all my life."

"What are you afraid of?"

Naomi shook her head. "That's just it. I don't know. I'm always taking short quick breaths, and I'm never able to fully relax. I'm constantly thinking about all the terrible things that could happen to me."

Esther opened her Book. "John says that when we abide in God, His love is perfected in us and this gives us confidence."

Naomi said, "I don't feel very confident. I know I've accepted

Christ as my Savior, but I always wonder if God is pleased with me."

Esther glanced down at her Book and continued to read. "There is no fear in love, but perfect love casts out fear because fear has to do with the dread of punishment. The one who fears has not been made perfect in love."

Pointing to the passage, Esther said, "John is teaching that the root of fear is the feeling that we are going to be punished for something. Jesus already took the punishment that we deserved when He died on the cross. As we learn to trust in what Christ has done for us, we see that we are worthy to receive God's love. And as this love is perfected within us, it casts out our fears."

Naomi thought about this, then glanced up at Esther. "I think I understand now. Because I have doubted God's love for me, I have lived with the constant fear and dread of what will happen to me."

Esther nodded. "That's right. Our enemies want us to focus on our performance, then accuse us when we fall short. But when we instead focus on God's unconditional love for us because of Christ, we can face our enemies without fear."

Esther smiled and put her hand on Naomi's shoulder. "Now let's go face this enemy together."

After praying for strength and wisdom, Esther and Naomi stood up. They held out their Books until they became Swords and marched toward the giant snake. Leviathan hung over the path up ahead, swaying back and forth in the moonlight.

The creature saw them approaching and began swaying more rapidly. "Essssther, do you dare to challenge me? And Naomi, why are you being so foolish? You know you can't defeat me."

The two women took a few more steps, then Esther signaled Naomi to split off to the left.

"Yesssss, do come closer. I shall make a meal of both of you." Leviathan reared back its head, preparing to strike. "Do not think God will protect you, Esssssther. Did you not sin against Him in your thoughts this morning?" The snake lunged toward her.

For a brief moment, Leviathan's words had taken Esther off guard, but she quickly recovered and threw up her Shield. "God does not deal with me according to my sins but according to His mercy."

Leviathan's sharp fangs bounced off her Shield. The creature hissed at Esther, then reared back its head and glared at Naomi. "You have no strength to fight me. Give up now while you still can."

Naomi remembered a verse she had been taught in Sunday school. "I have no strength of my own, but I am becoming strong in the Lord and in the power of His might."

Naomi's bold words enraged Leviathan. How dare she speak to him like that! He lunged at her, but she held up her Shield and blocked the attack.

The giant snake hissed loudly and bared its fangs. "You are only making this worse. I shall punish the both of you before I eat you."

Esther and Naomi inched forward. Leviathan thrust his head toward Esther, then toward Naomi. Determined not to give into their fears, they braced themselves and dug in with their Shoes while keeping their Shields in front of them.

Leviathan began to laugh a low hissing laugh. "You cannot keep up your guard forever. Soon you will lower your Shields, and then you will have no defense."

Esther knew their enemy was right. Simply blocking their fears wouldn't be enough. They needed to go forward and confront them. She glanced over at Naomi, then took another step forward. Naomi nodded and did the same.

Leviathan swung its head toward Naomi and tried to bite her from the side. She thrust out her Shield, then swung her Sword toward Leviathan's neck. The creature saw the weapon slicing toward its head and quickly recoiled. Again the giant snake reared back, this time taking aim at Esther's feet. She dropped to her knees and lowered her Shield just in time to block the strike.

Leviathan coiled up, as venom dripped from its fangs. "You two will not be able to hold out much longer. I can smell your fear."

Esther held out her Sword. "I fear God, and not you Leviathan. Our God has given us authority to trample on serpents, scorpions, and over all the power of the enemy, and nothing shall by any means hurt us. Today you will not taste our flesh, but you will taste our blades!"

Leviathan furiously lunged at Esther, but she sidestepped and struck at the creature's neck. Leviathan swung its head away, hissing angrily and appearing to be in pain. In the glimmer of moonlight shining through the trees, blood dripped from a cut on the creature's head where her sword had connected.

Naomi closed in from the other side. Leviathan saw her and snapped out at her. She dodged, then slammed her Shield into the snake's head. She followed up with a blow from her Sword, but Leviathan jerked back and evaded the attack.

Naomi stood tall and gripped her Shield tightly. "Through my God, I shall do valiantly, for it is He who will tread down my enemies."

Leviathan slithered toward her but stopped just out of reach of her Sword. His tongue flicked in and out of his mouth as he swayed in front of her in a hypnotic motion. "Do you really believe that? Why would God fight for someone like you?"

As Naomi stared into Leviathan's eyes, a sense of terror invaded her thoughts. Her body tensed, and her arms started to go limp. Her Shield slid lower.

Esther yelled, "Don't let down your guard!"

Startled, Naomi shook her head and raised her Shield. "My Heavenly Father gives me so great a love that I can be called His very own child. That is why He fights for me!"

While the creature maintained its focus on Naomi, Esther crept closer and raised her Sword. Leviathan caught a glimpse of light reflecting off the blade and raised his head to its full height. In a sudden strike, he plunged toward her neck. Esther thrust her Shield upward, blocking the blow, but the force of the assault knocked her backward and onto the ground. Seeing that she was vulnerable, Leviathan struck at her again, but she rolled over and jumped to her feet just as his long fangs were about to dig into her shoulder. Before the giant reptile could recoil back out of range, Esther swung upward with her Sword and pierced the creature's neck all the way through.

Leviathan violently wriggled its head, trying to free itself from her Sword, but Esther dug in with her Shoes and held on. Naomi dashed in from the side and brought her Sword down on the giant snake's neck, slicing all the way through and severing its head from its lifeless body.

Still impaled on her Sword, Leviathan's head stopped moving. Esther swung around in a circle and cast it off into the woods.

Naomi ran over and hugged her. "We did it!"

Esther stepped back and smiled. "Yes we did. We stood up to our fears, and God gave us the victory."

Naomi took a deep breath. "I can breathe! I mean I can really breathe now."

Esther noticed she could breathe in deeper as well.

They rolled the rest of Leviathan's body to the edge of the woods, then continued their journey through the Forest of Fear. Even though it was night, the moon gave them enough light to see their path. Once they were clear of the woods, Esther and Naomi traveled for another hour then stopped to set up camp. Both were tired and fell asleep almost instantly.

The next morning they saw that they had stopped near a House of Instruction. They packed up and made their way toward it. When they drew close, they could hear someone singing around back. Soon a cheerful older woman appeared, carrying a pair of hedge trimmers.

"Hello, young ladies. Where did you come from?"

Esther stepped forward. "We both traveled through the Forest of Fear last night."

The woman put down her trimmers and took off her work gloves. "Oh my, that must have been a dreadful experience. We do get many travelers who've gone through that forest. My name is Mrs. Green. My husband is the leader of this House of Instruction. Why don't you come inside and get cleaned up while I make you some breakfast. You can tell me all about what happened while you're eating."

Esther and Naomi were grateful for her invitation and followed her into the house. Mrs. Green showed them where they could get cleaned up, and when they came back out, they joined her at the table where she had set out fresh toast, oatmeal, and a large pitcher of orange juice.

When they finished their breakfast, Mrs. Green cleared the table and brought out some fresh blueberries and cream. "I'm anxious to know what you encountered in that forest. It seems each person that goes through it faces a different enemy."

Esther and Naomi took turns telling her about what they had learned in their Books and their battle with Leviathan.

Mrs. Green was fascinated. "I've heard of all kinds of different enemies, but the one you faced seems to be the scariest yet."

Naomi said, "I'm so thankful God caused Esther to come by when she did. I don't know how long I would have been stuck in that forest if she hadn't arrived."

Esther said, "God gave us both wisdom and courage. When I was reading through John's letter, I saw truths I hadn't seen before. To Naomi, it must have seemed as if I had always known the things we were discussing, but God was pointing them out to me as we were reading."

Mrs. Green poured them some more juice. "Sometimes that's how God works. He gives us what we need when we need it."

She took her Book from a desk shelf and then returned to the table. "Often when travelers come out of that forest, God leads me to read these verses to them. 'Fear not, for I have redeemed you; I have called you by name, you are mine. When you pass through the waters, I will be with you; and through the rivers, they shall not overwhelm you; when you walk through fire you shall not be burned, and the flame shall not consume you. For I am the Lord your God, the Holy One of Israel, your Savior.' "

Naomi said, "That's exactly what we needed to hear after what we've been through."

Mrs. Green smiled. "As you learned while in the forest, when God's love is perfected within us, it drives away fears. That's why it's important to recognize that nothing can separate us from the love of Christ."

Naomi nodded. "I've always heard that God's love is unconditional, but I acted like it was based on my performance. No wonder I had so many fears."

Mrs. Green said, "If God's love was based on any of our performances, then we would not be able to stand before Him for a single second. But since Jesus is our High Priest and Advocate before the Father, we can come boldly into His presence, knowing that He will always accept us."

"That helps me to understand what it means to abide in God," said Esther. "Daily I am to come before Him without trying to earn my way first. As I abide in His presence, I am filled with His love, and fear is driven away."

Mrs. Green clapped her hands. "Yes, that's right. Instead of trying to work for His approval, we receive His grace apart from works, and then His grace produces His works through us." She read from her Book, "But I am what I am by the grace of God, and His grace toward me was not wasted, for I worked harder than they all, yet it wasn't really me that was doing the work, but the grace of God in me."

They continued to talk for another hour. At last Esther pointed outside. "I saw that you were trimming those bushes when we arrived. Please let us help you in return for your kindness."

"You don't have to help me with that. I'm always glad to serve those who are on their Quest."

Naomi said, "Please do let us help you."

Mrs. Green smiled and thanked them for their offer. She found each of them a pair of gloves and a set of trimmers. They had a wonderful time working and talking together. Esther and Naomi spent the rest of the day working outside, and when evening came, she invited them to stay the night.

The next day Esther saw that her path was continuing on, but Naomi's remained.

Naomi stepped outside and stood beside her. "I wish you could stay too."

Esther hugged her. "God is giving you the same opportunity that I had earlier in my Quest. You're going to grow stronger as you stay here, and one day you will be sent out as well. When that day comes, you'll be ready to face whatever is out there."

Mrs. Green came out and joined them. "Well let's all have one more breakfast together before you have to go."

They enjoyed the meal and their time together, then Esther packed up and prepared to leave.

Mrs. Green handed her a sack of food to put in her backpack. "Take this with you."

"Thank you so much," said Esther as she gave her a hug.

Naomi and Mrs. Green waved goodbye, and Esther set out on her path once again. She was emboldened by the victory God had given her over Leviathan, and she was excited to see what else lay ahead.

She traveled throughout the day until she came upon an inn. After settling into her room, Esther spent the evening reading in her Book and praying for those she had met on her journey. The next morning she woke up refreshed and traveled on. Toward the end of the day, she came upon two young women who were talking.

One looked distraught, and the other appeared as if she were trying to encourage her. "Elizabeth, I know you can do this. Don't leave now."

Elizabeth shook her head and stared at the ground. "I don't think I can."

Esther drew closer to the young women and stopped. "Hello. I've been traveling all day. Is there a good place nearby to stop and rest for the night?"

The young woman who had been giving Elizabeth encouragement stepped forward. "It looks like your path is heading in the direction where we're staying. There are many camping there."

"Thank you. My name is Esther."

"It's nice to meet you. My name is Overcomer."

13

THE STORY OF OVERCOMER

Seeing that Elizabeth was discouraged, Esther asked, "Is there anything up ahead that I should be concerned about?"

Elizabeth was silent.

Overcomer glanced over her shoulder. "You will see soon. It's an important part of your journey, but it's also challenging. You'll come to a sign that will explain everything. We'll be there soon to talk with you about it some more."

Esther left them and headed toward the camp. Soon she saw the sign. "All those on this Quest must defeat the Giant of Shame and enter the River of Healing. Once you bring the giant to his knees, he must let you come back and forth as you wish."

Esther wondered what the warning and the promise could mean. She had not faced a giant before. Was this why Elizabeth looked so discouraged? Esther continued until she reached the base of a massive rock wall which appeared to rise up out of the ground a thousand feet into the air and stretched for miles on either side. A small opening had been carved out in the middle, and the Giant of Shame stood in front of the opening, blocking the entrance. On the other side, a beautiful river flowed with crystal clear water.

The Giant of Shame stood about nine and a half feet tall with massive shoulders, muscular arms, and legs the size of a tree trunk. He had a thick, scruffy beard that looked as if it hadn't been cleaned in months. He wore armor made out of thick black leather, and he carried a large club, which he could swing so fast that it created a gust of wind as it passed.

The ground in front of the giant looked like a battlefield—the soil had been trampled by any number of assailants and packed down until it was as hard as concrete. Those waiting to confront this enemy had set up camp on either side of the narrow path leading to the space in front of the giant.

Esther heard footsteps and turned. Overcomer and Elizabeth had just arrived.

Overcomer had her arm around Elizabeth. "You won't regret this. You can win this battle."

Elizabeth smoothed out a wrinkle in her blouse and straightened her shoulders. "Thank you for believing in me." She made her way over to a group of tents and began setting up hers as well.

Suddenly the giant roared.

He hit the palm of his hand with his club. "So no one wants to fight me today? You all are very wise. It's better to sit on the sidelines and think you can succeed rather than to try and fail."

A part of Esther wanted to challenge him, but after seeing how discouraged Elizabeth was, she thought it best to first learn more about this enemy.

Overcomer edged closer to Esther. "Don't be intimidated by him. He can be beaten."

Esther turned toward her. "Have you seen anyone defeat him?"

"Yes, I've defeated him myself, and now I help others to as well. Set up your tent near mine and Elizabeth's. We'll have a meeting in a few hours to discuss how to win the battle against shame."

Overcomer had been helping people defeat the Giant of Shame for many months. Ever since that day she met Disciple, God had been using her mightily. When she told her life-story, everyone was amazed at the abundance of grace that God had bestowed on her. She had been abandoned at birth and ended up in an orphanage. There she learned to be tough in order to survive, but she also became manipulative and deceitful.

When she turned fifteen, she ran away from the orphanage and began living on her own. She would steal or do whatever it took to get by, but as smart as she believed herself to be, she soon found that there were others who were even more experienced in the ways of deceit. She met men who promised to take care of her but in fact, only wanted to use her. These relationships turned abusive, and eventually, Overcomer would run away, only to meet some other man promising the same thing.

By the time she was seventeen, Overcomer was living in outright rebellion and did not appear to care what happened to her. Through a series of events, she found herself a prisoner in a house with several other young women, who were being used to make money for their captors. While enslaved there, she realized just how out of control her life had become. Due to what she thought at the time was a bit of good luck, she escaped from the house and ran as far away as she could.

Soon afterward, while traveling one evening, she came upon the sound of singing coming from a white building with a slanted roof. The music was joyful and peaceful, and she wondered what kind of people would sing in such a manner. She crept into the building and stood in the back. A group of fifty people or more were lifting up their hands and their voices in praise to God.

As Overcomer watched and listened, she felt anger rising up within. If this God they were praising was so good, where had He been during all the times of suffering in her life? Despite her anger, she sensed an immense peace around her. When the singing was over, an elderly man went to the front and asked everyone to sit down. Overcomer started to slip out the back and leave, but her curiosity caused her to stay.

The man at the front had stooped shoulders and was practically bald, but he appeared to be full of joy. He set a large Book on the podium in front of him, then introduced himself as Pastor Jensen and welcomed everyone to the service. Overcomer felt as if he was looking straight at her, so she shifted in her seat to try and hide behind the person in front of her. Pastor Jensen prayed then opened up his Book. He read about a woman who was caught in adultery. According to the story, some men had brought her to a person named Jesus and plopped her down in a public place where He stood. They then proceeded to tell Jesus and all those around what this woman had done.

Overcomer thought how humiliating that must have been, then she realized that after the life she had lived, she could easily have been that woman. Pastor Jensen said that when these men questioned Jesus about what to do with the woman, He did not respond. This woman's very life hung in the balance because those religious leaders were ready to stone her, and all they were waiting on was Jesus' consent. Overcomer wondered what she would have done in that situation. Was there anything she could have said to save her life? The woman in the story sat before Jesus in silence, and Overcomer realized that was all she could have done as well.

The story continued with Jesus addressing her accusers. He told them that the one who was without sin could cast the first stone. He then knelt to write on the ground, and when He did, slowly her accusers faded away. At last, He addressed the woman and asked where her accusers were—the ones who had condemned her. She informed Him that they were gone. Then He told her, "Neither do I condemn you. Go and sin no more."

Pastor Jensen then shared that the Person who bestowed mercy on this woman was the same Jesus who was still willing to show mercy today. Overcomer listened intently as the speaker taught that Jesus had existed as God the Son through all of eternity. Then one day God the Father sent Him to be born on the earth through the virgin Mary.

Overcomer had never heard such a thing, but at the same time, it didn't seem strange. If this God truly existed, then He could do anything. Pastor Jensen went on to say that Jesus lived a perfect, sinless life and then offered Himself as a sacrifice on a cross for her sins.

Pastor Jensen stepped to the side of the podium. "If anyone will acknowledge their sinfulness and put their faith in what Christ did for them, then they can be forgiven and placed in perfect right standing with God."

Overcomer thought this was an incredible statement. Did God really care about her that much? Could she be forgiven of all the things she had done in her life? Was it possible for God to see her as righteous?

Pastor Jensen closed his Book. "I'm about to dismiss in prayer, but if there are any who wish to go to the Building of Reflection, there will be some members at the back who will lead the way."

Pastor Jensen dismissed them, and Overcomer noticed that some of the people were crying. She sat thinking about what she had just heard. For the first time in her life, she was encountering someone who wanted to give something to her instead of wanting to take something from her. God was freely offering salvation to her. She could feel all of her walls coming down, and in that moment, she felt it was safe to trust.

Overcomer left her seat and followed those who were going to the Building of Reflection. She noticed that some of those who had cried at the end of the service didn't come to the building. They cried and cried, but then they just left. Some stood in line for a few minutes and then turned around and left. Some walked into the building and then came right back out, but some were going all the way through and out the other side.

When it was Overcomer's turn to go in, she was fearful of what awaited her on the inside, but she was ready for a change in her life. After standing at the entrance for a moment, she opened the door and went in. As she passed through the different rooms, she saw all of her sinfulness, and she saw all the deceitful and manipulative behavior that she had practiced throughout her life. After heading into the last room and witnessing the sacrifice of Christ, she collapsed on the floor and sobbed in repentance.

The voice of the Holy Spirit reassured her that God loved her and was ready to forgive her of all she had seen in the different mirrors. She exited the building with tears in her eyes, and Pastor Jensen and others waited to walk with her up the Hill of Calvary. Climbing to the top, she saw the cross where Jesus had given His life for her. She knew this was the only payment that could erase her sin. She fell down before the cross, asking Jesus to forgive her and to come into her life and save her.

She felt so unworthy to even call upon His name, but within an instant, she felt overwhelming peace and joy.

A strong voice thundered, "From this point, you shall be known as Overcomer! Your old life has passed away, and behold all things have become new."

She had been called by so many different names and nicknames that none of them seemed to be important, but now she had a new name and a new beginning! She was a new creation. Overcomer shed many tears of joy that evening, and after a time of fellowship with those who had accompanied her, an elderly couple invited her to stay with them. The next morning she attended another service at the House of Instruction, and afterward Pastor Jensen baptized her.

Overcomer spent the next year with the elderly couple, helping them with their pottery business and learning about the Quest. She grew in her knowledge of God's word and learned much from Pastor Jensen's preaching and teaching. After a year, she discovered that her path was moving away. She thanked Mr. and Mrs. Hampton, the couple she had lived with, and she thanked Pastor Jensen for all he had taught her.

The next morning Overcomer set out on her journey. Nearly a year passed before she arrived to fight the Giant of Shame, and throughout her travels, she learned from various groups different ideas about her Book. Not everything she learned was helpful, a fact she discovered when she first fought the giant. She failed, but rather than becoming discouraged, she spent time praying and reading her Book. After a time of meditation and study, she received the strength and wisdom she needed.

Overcomer defeated the Giant of Shame that day, and she had been helping people to win their own battles ever since.

14

THE GIANT OF SHAME

A number of those waiting to fight the Giant of Shame gathered around when Overcomer called for a meeting. Elizabeth was there, and so was Esther.

Overcomer said to Esther. "I know you've just arrived, but I believe God has laid some things on your heart that we need to hear."

Esther glanced around for a moment, then slowly stood to her feet. "God has been so gracious to me, but I still have much to learn about dealing with guilt and shame. A little over a year ago, I followed rebellion to the Camp of Sin. God delivered me when I called out for grace, but I still felt a lot of shame afterward."

Several sat up and listened more intently.

Esther continued. "The same day I returned to my path, I heard a teaching about the goodness of God. You would think we would welcome such a message, but I felt myself resisting. I didn't understand why at first, but then I realized that after having fallen into sin, I was much more comfortable with God being angry at me than with receiving His love and forgiveness."

Overcomer could tell that many were identifying with what Esther was saying.

Esther swallowed and took a deep breath. "I figured if God was mad at me, then I could work toward winning back His approval. What I came to realize though was that God didn't want my works—He wanted my honesty."

Overcomer said, "What did He want you to be honest about?"

Esther held up her hands. "Everything, God wanted me to confess all the things that led me to follow rebellion, without making any excuses or trying to blame anything or anyone else."

"And how hard was that?"

"It was very difficult," said Esther. "I desperately wanted to feel right with God again, but all I could do was surrender and admit I wasn't capable of doing anything to earn His approval. I had to rest in the truth that the only reason He has favor toward me is because of Christ."

Overcomer looked out over the others sensing a breakthrough was near. "And what was the result of this process?"

"I felt like I was dying inside. There was nothing I could reach out to for comfort except God's grace. It took time, but as I stayed vulnerable before Him, He healed my pain and gave me His strength."

Overcomer noticed that Elizabeth had tears in her eyes. She had been trying to minister to her, but it seemed Elizabeth had put up thick walls and wasn't letting anyone in.

Overcomer said, "Would anyone else like to share something?"

Elizabeth waited to see if someone else would start speaking, then raised her hand. Overcomer nodded, and Elizabeth stood up. "I was always told I was no good, and that I would never amount to anything. I tried so hard to prove them wrong, and I strived to be the best person I possibly could. I was always friendly to everyone I met, even when they weren't friendly toward me. I volunteered to help wherever I saw a need, and I tried to serve God in every way I could. But no matter how much I did, it never felt like enough."

Overcomer held out her hands. "You'll never feel good enough because you'll never be good enough. There is no one who is good. Only God is good."

Several of those listening would later say that this was the turning point for them. They had believed that if they could just reach that point where they felt good enough for God, then they could be free of their guilt and shame. Now they realized that point was never going to come. God did not want their goodness, but He wanted to give them His goodness.

Elizabeth said, "I've always felt that if I admitted anything bad about myself, then I would be agreeing with those who told me I was no good. Now I'm realizing that if I'm not able to go before God and freely admit my faults, then I cannot receive His grace. I've been trapped this whole time. My own efforts have kept me in a cycle where I'm chasing the impossible while running away from the very thing that would set me free."

Overcomer nodded. "All of the guilt and shame of our sin has been placed on Jesus at the cross. God is just waiting for us to come to Him and confess our sin so He can forgive us and cleanse us from its effects."

A few more shared about their own struggles with guilt and shame, and then they prayed for one another and their upcoming battle with the giant.

Overcomer hugged Elizabeth. "I know you're going to defeat that giant."

Elizabeth thanked her, then returned to her tent where she planned to read in her Book for the rest of the evening.

Overcomer turned toward Esther. "Thank you for sharing tonight. I've been trying to minister to some of these for weeks, and I could see that your testimony was having an impact."

"I'm glad God was able to use my experiences, but I still know that my battle with the Giant of Shame is not going to be easy. I'll spend the rest of the evening getting ready."

They said goodnight, and Overcomer went back to her tent to pray for those who would do battle the next day. In the morning, there was a sense of anticipation, and it appeared the Giant of Shame seemed to sense this as well. He looked on edge and shouted even louder, trying to intimidate those who wished to fight him.

The first person to step up to the narrow path leading to the battleground was Elizabeth.

The Giant of Shame stared at her with curiosity. He would not have predicted that she would be the first to challenge him that day. "Well if it isn't my good friend Elizabeth. I hope you're doing well today."

Elizabeth was taken off guard, and for a second she forgot who was speaking to her. "I'm doing well, thank you."

The giant leaned forward and roared, "No you're not! You're doing terrible just like you always are. You're not fooling anyone with this whole nicey-nice routine. You're a horrible person, and everyone knows it."

The words of her enemy blasted Elizabeth back into reality. She realized that her need to please even manifested itself when approaching the giant. Elizabeth thought, why do I have such a need to please everyone? Why do I feel like I only have value if everyone approves of me? Standing there, she began to realize how working to please others served to cover over her insecurities. However, this strategy only provided temporary relief, so she had to constantly work to get more approval.

The Giant of Shame could see that Elizabeth was searching for answers. "You really think others like you? They think you're weak. They think you're clingy and needy. They just wish you'd go away."

Was her constant desire for approval annoying and exhausting? Elizabeth thought the giant was actually right about this, but what could she do? What was the alternative? If she quit trying to win the approval of others, what would be left? She had placed all of her identity into being the nice girl that everyone liked. If she gave that up, then who would she be?

The Giant of Shame struck the ground with his club, startling her. "You're a nobody, and if you died tomorrow, no one would even care."

"Don't listen to him Elizabeth, we care about you," said one of the onlookers.

She was grateful for the support of those standing by, but she knew she needed something more, something deeper. Elizabeth thought she heard within, 'I cared enough to die for you.'

She heard herself saying back, "But why Lord? I have nothing to offer you."

Elizabeth thought she again heard a voice within saying, 'I don't want what you can offer Me. I only want you.'

Tears began to flow down her face. How could someone love her so much when she couldn't do anything for them in return? The Holy Spirit reminded her of the verse which said, "He has saved us, and called us with a holy calling, not according to our works, but according to His own purpose and grace, which He gave to us in Christ Jesus before the world began." The truth was starting to sink in that God had saved her because of His own goodness and grace, and not because of anything she could do for Him.

The Giant of Shame became nervous as he saw Elizabeth standing up straighter. "If you fight me I will expose all of your faults to everyone here. They will know just how sinful you really are. Do you think they'll ever look on you with approval after that?"

Elizabeth held out her Sword and took a step forward. "Even when I was nothing but sinful, God showed His unconditional love by sending His only Son to die for me."

The giant cocked back his club, preparing to knock her out as soon as she was within reach.

Elizabeth darted toward him, and when he swung his club toward her, she rolled under it. She then thrust her Sword into his knees. The giant winced in pain and tried to bring his club down on top of her head.

She jumped to her feet and scuttled back so that the blow landed harmlessly in front of her. "I will no longer try to earn the love and approval of others. For I have been persuaded that nothing can separate me from the love of God which is in Christ Jesus my Lord."

The giant swung his club at her again, but Elizabeth easily blocked it with her Shield. She then spun around and slashed his right arm with her Sword.

The Giant of Shame was desperate, and although he had been holding back on his best weapon, he felt now was the time. "Nobody wants you Elizabeth. Not even your dad wanted you enough to stick around. Don't you ever wonder what was so wrong with you that your own father didn't want you?"

Elizabeth retreated several steps, and her hands dropped to her side. Seeing the effect of his words, the giant let out a roaring laugh. Elizabeth had tried so hard to bury the feelings of rejection from her father. He had left before she could even remember him. What was so wrong with her? Was she a burden? Why didn't he love her? Was this feeling of rejection the root of her need for approval?

As she stood with her hands at her side, she heard a still small voice within. 'I am your Father. I have loved you with so great a love that I have adopted you and called you as one of My own.' She realized that she might never know why her earthly father left, but she could be confident in knowing that her Heavenly Father had chosen her as one of His very own.

Elizabeth raised her head. "God is my Father, and because I'm His daughter, He has sent forth His Spirit into my heart giving me the right and the privilege to call him ABBA FATHER!"

Elizabeth dashed toward the giant and struck him in the side. Using her Shield, she then blocked another blow from the giant's club. "It is my Heavenly Father that has qualified me and made me fit to share in the inheritance of all His children."

The giant stumbled, and Elizabeth plunged her Sword straight into his chest. Now weakened, the Giant of Shame was desperate to do something to turn the battle in his favor. He reared back his club with the little strength that remained and swung toward her head. Elizabeth saw the weapon coming toward her and easily moved out of the way. The momentum of the giant's attack caused him to lose his balance, and he staggered forward and bent over.

Elizabeth forcefully brought her Sword down on top of his head. "I give praise to God's glorious grace, by which He has made me accepted among the beloved."

The Giant of Shame desperately tried to stay on his feet.

Elizabeth reared back with her Sword. "I do not have to work for His acceptance. I've been *made acceptable* by His grace." She connected with a perfect blow to the giant's temple, bringing him to his knees.

Overcomer bolted toward her and congratulated her. Elizabeth collapsed on her shoulder and began to cry tears of joy. They then waded into the River of Healing together. They both stood there, praising God for the victory. As the waters rushed over her, Elizabeth felt cleansed from years of rejection. After enjoying the cleansing effects of the river for several minutes, they went back to encourage Esther who was next up to challenge the giant. They joined hands with her and prayed, then Esther stepped out onto the path leading to the battle area.

The Giant of Shame, who was back on his feet, leered at her. "Hello Esther. Why don't you lift up your skirt? Michael tells me you'll lift it for anyone."

The remark took her off guard. Had Michael been lying about her? How many others had heard these lies?

The Giant of Shame smirked as he motioned toward all those watching. "I know what Esther, why don't you bring Molly along, and we'll call it a party."

Esther paused. The feeling that she had failed Molly still haunted her. She so wished she could go back and change what had happened.

The giant could tell he had hit her where she was the most vulnerable. "Come on Esther, don't feel so bad. I'm sure Molly found a friend who really cared about her."

Each word the Giant of Shame spoke, felt as if it was a punch in the stomach. Even though she had repented of her indiscretions and rebellion, the remembrance of them still hurt. Esther understood that while the forgiveness of God was instant, the healing of her soul took time. The Holy Spirit reassured her that while she still felt the pain of her sins, they were not separating her from the love of God.

Esther glanced over at Overcomer and Elizabeth, and they both gave her a look of support, letting her know that nothing the giant said changed their view of her. She knew she couldn't change her past, but she could surrender to God and let Him change her future.

The Giant of Shame smirked at her. "No matter what happens here today, you will never be able to forget your failures. I'll haunt you in your thoughts, and I'll always be there to remind you of your sins."

The Holy Spirit reminded Esther of the Psalm, which assured her that God did not treat her according to her sins or reward her according to her iniquities. She realized that God wanted her to learn from her past, but He didn't want her to constantly relive her past.

Esther defiantly stared at the giant and raised her Sword. "If God kept a record of sins, no one could stand in His presence, but with Him, there is forgiveness that we might fear His name."

Running toward the giant, Esther prepared for battle. The Giant of Shame aimed his club at her legs, but she jumped over it. She then delivered a hard whack with her Sword to his exposed arm. "God does not want my guilt offerings or else I would bring them. He only wishes that I bring him a truly repentant heart."

The giant pivoted toward her, preparing to swat her away, but she darted to one side and slammed her Shield into his knee. He swung his club toward her head, but she ducked out of the way and backed up a step.

Esther raised her Shield. "It was by grace through faith that I was saved, and not because of anything I could do."

The Giant of Shame angrily swung his club at Esther's Shield in an effort to knock it out of her hand.

Holding firm, Esther shouted, "The same grace by which I was saved, is the same grace in which I stand."

The giant's club crashed against her Shield, but she held steady. Again she spun away and struck the giant on the side of his leg. He staggered and reached down to catch his balance.

Seeing an opening, Esther struck the giant's hand with her Sword and followed the blow with a strike to the side of his face. "As far as the east is from the west, this is how far He has removed my sins from me."

The giant righted himself and cocked his club back, but before he could even begin his swing, Esther dashed toward him and sliced his thigh with her Sword. Screaming in pain, the giant went down to one knee. She then delivered a blow to the side of his head. He dropped his club and placed his hands on the ground, barely keeping his other knee from making contact with the earth.

The Giant of Shame gave her an evil frown. "It's only a matter of time before you sin again, and when you do, I'll be waiting to remind you of how much you've failed once again."

Esther readied her Sword for the final blow. "I know I'll fall short each and every day, but that's why I'll continuously come before the Throne of Grace for the mercy and forgiveness that I need."

Esther slammed her Shield into his face, then gashed him in the neck with her Sword. The giant collapsed and fell face first with a thud.

A loud cheer erupted as Overcomer and Elizabeth ran over to congratulate her. Esther was exhausted from her battle, and they each helped her wade into the River of Healing. Once they reached the deepest part, Esther knelt down, letting the water flow all over her. The grace of God washed over her memories just as the water washed over her body.

After several minutes, they all returned to the other side where the others were waiting to battle the Giant of Shame. Several more defeated the giant that day, and Overcomer, Elizabeth, and Esther encouraged many more over the next three days, as they also got ready for their battle.

On the morning of the fourth day, the three of them gathered for prayer in front of Elizabeth's tent. When they glanced down, they saw that Overcomer's path and Esther's path were leading away in the same direction.

15

ESTHER AND OVERCOMER

Overcomer studied her path. Was it time to leave? What about all those she had been teaching? What about the ones who would soon arrive and need help?

Elizabeth said, "I see that your paths are leading away, but mine hasn't moved."

Overcomer placed her hand on Elizabeth's shoulder. "Should we stay a few more days to see if your path moves too?"

Esther said, "Yes, I don't mind staying. I feel the three of us have been brought together for a reason."

Elizabeth looked back at many who had just arrived to fight the Giant of Shame. "No, I believe God is calling me to stay and share with others the things I've learned. I sense that He's going to use this time to further heal and strengthen me as I minister to them and their needs."

Elizabeth hugged them. "I know you two are going to make a great team. Maybe I'll join you someday."

"We'll be praying for you," said Esther.

"Yes," said Overcomer. "I'm sure we'll see you again, and I can't wait to hear about all your victories."

They prayed together, then Overcomer and Esther packed up and departed. They waded through the River of Healing, then looked back one more time and waved goodbye to Elizabeth.

As Esther and Overcomer traveled together over the next week, they spent lots of time getting to know one another. They talked about their different backgrounds and experiences, and they learned about each other's strengths and weaknesses. One day after hiking for many hours, they came upon what looked like an abandoned shack. There were no other buildings around, and the whole area appeared desolate.

Overcomer stepped up on the porch and tried to look through a dirty window. "It doesn't seem like anyone is living here."

Esther joined her. "It doesn't appear anyone has lived here in a long time."

Taking hold of the doorknob, Overcomer said, "Let's go in. I saw an old table and chairs. We can sit down and rest for a little bit."

They went inside, and after cleaning off some dirt and cobwebs, Esther and Overcomer sat down. They took out their canteens to enjoy the water they collected from the River of Healing and then talked for an hour.

Feeling refreshed, Overcomer stood up to explore the cabin some more. As she was looking around the kitchen, they both heard voices in the distance.

Overcomer hurried to a window and peered out. "Oh no, they're coming straight toward this shack."

Esther quickly stood up. "What is it?"

"It looks like two trolls."

"Should we run, should we fight, what should we do?" said Esther, looking around in a panic.

As Overcomer backed away, her foot got caught on a loose board. She bent down to examine it. "This looks like the entrance to some kind of cellar. Let's duck down there and get out of sight."

They lifted the trap door and climbed down a narrow set of steps into a small opening. They pulled the door after them, making sure it was tightly shut, then huddled together quietly in the dark. The door opened with a slam, then heavy footsteps plodded across the floor above them, followed by two loud thuds as if something had been thrown on the table.

By the sound of the footsteps, one of the trolls was much bigger than the other.

The smaller troll backed away from the table. "So now what? We've collected these two bags of seed just like we were told. What does the Master want us to do with them?"

The second larger troll who sounded like he was in charge said, "One of our scouts spotted a group of warriors heading toward our house. We're going to plant this seed just across a stream that they'll have to pass through if they continue in our direction. This seed will sprout up quickly into tall weeds and produce seedpods. By the time they get to us, they will be in no shape to fight."

"How do you know this will work?"

The other troll shouted angrily, "Do you dare to question me or the Master?"

The smaller troll stumbled backwards as if trying to stay out of reach of his superior. "Oh no, never, I just want to know what effect our work is going to have. I'm sure you and the Master have a great plan."

The larger troll grunted, then spoke in a harsh tone. "We're planting seeds of discord, envy, rivalry, and anything that will kill their unity. I instructed Gorbor to plant a smaller crop earlier in their journey, and some effects have already begun. If they're able to continue on, then this much larger crop we're going to plant now should finish them off. Grab that bag and let's go."

Esther and Overcomer waited until the footsteps faded into the distance, and then they waited a little longer just to make sure. When they came up out of the cellar, they peered through the windows but couldn't see the trolls in any direction.

Esther sat down at the table again. "That was close."

Overcomer gave one more look out the window, then sat down as well. "It appears those trolls are trying to cause problems for some group that is nearby."

"Perhaps God wanted us to overhear their plan?"

Overcomer shifted around in her seat. "Our paths did lead us here."

After a moment of silence, Esther made her way to the door. "Our paths are now heading toward that hill over there."

Overcomer stepped outside. "I've got a feeling we're about to start an adventure. Let's go."

As soon as they reached the top of the hill, Esther and Overcomer saw a group of twelve young men and women who were folding up their tents and preparing to leave. Seeing that their path was going straight toward the group, they picked up their pace, reaching them just as they were preparing to move out.

A young man with a deep tan named Joseph, who appeared to be the leader of the group greeted them. "Hello, it's good to see others walking their path. We haven't seen anyone else in days."

An older female teen named Haley, who had long, braided hair stepped up beside him. "We started to wonder if we were ever going to see anyone anytime soon."

"Where did you all come from?" asked Esther as she set down her backpack.

Haley pointed off to the south. "We come from a small village about five day's journey from here. We represent all the youth in our town. For several months we've been meeting together, and we felt like God was calling us to go on a mission."

Esther took notice of the other young men and women who were now gathered around. "Is this the first adventure you all have been on?"

Joseph nodded. "Yes, I've sort of been leading our time of study and prayer together, and one evening as we were praying, we all sensed we were supposed to do something as a team. The next day we saw that all of our paths were leading away from the village. We then talked to our parents, and the leader of our House of Instruction, and they all agreed God was directing us to go on a journey."

Haley put her arm around one of the younger girls named Susan. "So after everyone prayed for us, we set off. We didn't know what type of adventure we might be heading for, but we all thought we'd be back to our village by now."

Overcomer saw that many in the group looked tired and worn out, and most stared at the ground. "How have things been so far?"

Joseph tried to force a smile. "We're doing our best to keep our spirits up. It's been a tough journey. It's been five long days, and our paths seem to take us further and further away from home."

Haley glanced over at Joseph. "I think we need to be honest. It's been more than just tough. For all the months that we were meeting together as a youth group, everything was going great. We were learning more about God's word, and we were able to support one another in whatever each one was going through. But a few days into our journey problems started to arise."

A young man named Sean stepped forward. He appeared to be

the smallest of the guys and probably the youngest as well. "This wasn't what I was expecting. I thought we were going on a camping trip, but instead, it's been one problem after another. It hasn't been any fun at all."

"If you don't mind me asking, what kind of problems?" said Overcomer.

Joseph shook his head. "I feel responsible. I was so sure, I was following the right path, but the further we've gone the more uncertain I've become. I don't know if any of us really know where our path is going right now."

Susan started to cry. "I just want to go home. All we do is fight and argue. I don't understand why we've turned on each other."

Haley hugged Susan and tried to comfort her. "I want to go home too, but I do think we've been going in the right direction. I don't understand what's going on, but we've come this far so we have to keep trusting God."

Esther raised an eyebrow. "Do you remember when all this trouble started?"

Joseph glanced around. "I think it was the second day of our journey. I remember it because right after we finished lunch, we started through this large field that was covered with briars and thorn bushes."

Haley nodded. "That does seem to be the point when all this trouble began. As we were making our way through that field, I started to sneeze. All those tall plants were giving off that weird smell. Pretty soon, a bunch of us started to complain about different things, and then that night it was like everyone was snapping at each other over silly stuff. Whose turn was it to set out the food, why was one tent bigger than another, how come one person had to gather wood, and someone else didn't? Insignificant things that didn't really matter."

Joseph held up his finger. "That's right, and each day it seems to have gotten worse. It hasn't made it any easier that we've almost run out of food, and we haven't come across a stream or any source of water since we started out. There's been no shade of any kind during the day, and the sun seems to beat on us as we travel. Today we didn't even want to move out again, and it's taken us most of the morning just to pack everything up."

Esther glanced at Overcomer then back toward Joseph. "I think we may know what has caused part of your problems."

Esther and Overcomer then told the group what they had overheard in the shack.

Haley sighed. "Do you think that field we came through was where those trolls had planted their seed?"

"Yes I do," said Esther. "And if what we overheard was true, they've got something even worse planned for you ahead."

Susan wiped away a tear. "I don't know if I can take anything else. This has been hard enough."

Overcomer took one of Susan's hands. "Whatever it is that you are supposed to face, I believe God has sent us to help. You don't have to do this alone."

Shrugging his shoulders, Joseph said, "So what do we do next?"

Staring toward the sun, Overcomer said, "I agree that this heat is making things more miserable. Since everyone is ready to leave, let's all go together and see if there's some relief up ahead."

They joined hands to pray. Afterward, Joseph studied the ground, trying to see where his path was going. Overcomer and Esther were able to clearly see their path, as well as the paths of the others, but they remained silent. They wanted Joseph and the rest of the youth group to gain some confidence.

Joseph took out his Book and quietly read in the Psalms. When he looked up again, he pointed toward the north. "There, that is where our path is leading."

Overcomer smiled. "I agree. You all lead the way, and we'll follow."

After traveling for an hour, they came to a small stream with several large shade trees. Immediately everyone in the youth group threw down their backpacks and waded into the stream. The water was refreshing both to drink and to cool them off. After they splashed around for a little while, they made their way a little further upstream and filled up their canteens. At last, they gathered underneath a large tree and sat on some blankets.

Joseph took out his Book. "How many days has it been since we spent time discussing God's word?"

Sean shook his head. "Too many. That's probably why we've had a hard time seeing where our paths have been leading."

"I don't understand," said Susan. "We got along so great back in our village. What happened?"

Haley came over and took a seat next to her. "I think we're experiencing some of the realities of life that we've been sheltered from so far in our lives. Our parents have always been there to take care of us and solve all of our problems, but now we don't have them to rely on."

Joseph nodded. "So far we've had it easy. When we came together during the evenings back home, we were only together for a couple of hours, but since leaving the village we've been around each other all the time, and that's made it a lot harder."

Another young girl about Susan's age, named Michelle scooted up next to Esther. "I just wish we could all get along once again."

A young man named Mike, who appeared to be the tallest and most athletic spoke up. "I know I've been tough to live with these last few days, and Joseph, I need to be honest and tell you that many times I've thought I should be leading this group and not you. I realize now this was due to my own pride and envy. That's probably why I've been finding fault with just about every decision you've made."

"In some ways, I don't blame you for feeling like that," said Joseph. "I don't know if I've been a very good leader. I'm not even sure I'm supposed to be a leader."

Haley said, "I think you've done your best, and to be honest I don't know if the rest of us have been much help. I've struggled with my own pride and feelings of superiority."

Joseph turned a few pages in his Book and read, "Confess your faults to one another, and be praying for one another so that you may be healed."

Overcomer spoke up. "That's exactly what you've been doing since we sat down here. What I like about all of you is that you didn't blame those trolls or the seeds they planted as the cause of your problems. You recognize that while those seeds may have made things worse, they could only have an effect to the degree you let them."

Esther nodded. "I agree. Don't be too hard on yourselves. Being able to recognize your faults and taking responsibility for them is a very mature thing to do. There are many others on this Quest who are much older who are still learning this lesson. I know it's something I still have to be reminded of myself."

Mike said, "I guess when things get hard it's easier to blame someone else rather than looking at yourself."

Susan straightened up and took a deep breath. "So what's next? Why have we been led out here so far away from home? Was it just to learn this lesson?"

Overcomer stood up and peered out over the horizon. "I think you've been brought here for more than that. Those trolls mentioned some kind of house that is up ahead. They have something planned, and it's not good."

16

TRAPPED

Susan scooted closer to Haley. "I don't know about this. I agree with Sean. I thought this was going to be a camping trip where we'd sit around at night and discuss our Books together. I just turned sixteen, and I'm not ready to fight any trolls."

Haley looked concerned as well. "I'm not sure I'm ready either, but God didn't bring us all this way to fail."

Esther rose to her feet and shouldered her backpack. "You don't know what you're capable of until you're in the midst of the battle. No matter how big your enemy may be, God is always bigger."

Joseph took out his telescope and surveyed the countryside. "I can't see anything in the direction our paths are heading, but I have a feeling we're going to come up on something soon."

Haley picked up her backpack and joined Overcomer and Esther. "I'm ready to find out why God has brought us all this way."

After drinking some more water and refilling their canteens, everyone started off. The terrain was much more friendly on this stage of their journey. Soft grass cushioned their steps, and rather than barrenness all around them, they passed through meadows filled with trees and small wildlife. Thin clouds hovered above them in the sky, serving to lessen the heat from the sun.

When they crested over a small hill, a valley appeared below that was teeming with all kinds of different plants and flowers of various shapes, colors, and sizes.

Joseph motioned for everyone to stop and then pointed straight ahead. "Those tall brown weeds just across the stream look familiar."

Haley stood beside him and peered out over the valley. "Yes, those are the same plants we encountered on our second day."

"That must be the crop from the seeds those trolls planted," said Esther, as she joined them.

Overcomer nodded. "The trolls must have thought they could plant their seed among all the other vegetation, and those weeds would go unnoticed."

Mike took out his canteen and took a long drink of water. "What do we do? That crop appears to spread out for miles. I don't see how we can go around it."

"We don't," said Joseph. "We go through it."

Mike blurted out, "Go through it? Are you crazy?" He quickly glanced around at the others, realizing what he'd just said. "What I mean to say is, are you sure? Won't we have the same problems as before if we try crossing through all those poisonous plants?"

Joseph shook his head. "It doesn't have to be the same this time. We know what we're up against. We can take out our Swords and cut our way through those plants. Instead of becoming weaker, we can become stronger."

Joseph gave the signal, and they all started out together. Overcomer and Esther followed in the back, feeling their role was to support and not to lead. They sensed God was doing something with this youth group and preparing them to be a team. After crossing the stream, they reached the edge of the field where the tall brown weeds were scattered throughout. Everyone stopped.

Joseph took out his Book and read, "Make my joy complete by being like-minded, having the same love, being united in spirit, and being focused on one purpose."

Haley nodded and read from her Book. "I appeal to all of you, by the name of our Lord Jesus Christ, that you walk in harmony with one another, and that there be no divisions or rivalry among you. Be perfectly united together sharing the same understanding and judgment."

Mike scratched his head. "That sounds good, but how do we determine what we're all supposed to be in unity about?"

Joseph said, "The simple answer is we're supposed to be focused on God and His word, but what I think you're specifically asking is how do we know what we're supposed to be doing right now."

Mike said, "I guess you're right. We all probably have our own ideas about what God wants us to do and how He wants us to do it, but without some kind of leadership we could be pulled in twelve different directions."

Joseph held out his hand toward the group. "So far I've taken on the role of a leader, but if God wants to use someone else, then I'm okay with that."

Haley said, "I think this is something we need to settle now. If those trolls do have something planned for us, then we need to be in unity before we try to go into a battle."

Sean stepped forward. "I agree." Turning toward Joseph, he said, "I do think God has called you to lead us, but I also think you need to be more open to listening. It's going to be a lot easier for us to follow if we feel we're part of the team and have some input."

Joseph looked around and nodded. "You're right. When things got tough, I didn't want to hear anything that sounded like criticism, so it was easier just to shut everyone out. I think I felt the need to prove that I was a good leader, but the most important part of leadership is listening to others. So let's start fresh right now. We're about to enter this field, and we still don't know what awaits us on the other side. What do you all think we should do?"

Mike spoke up. "Joseph, I think you need to trust that the rest of us can pull our weight. I think you've tried to make sure all the jobs get done instead of trusting us with some responsibility. It's the only way for us to grow, and it will keep you from being over-burdened."

Haley said, "I agree that we each need to be ready to carry our part of this mission. But we also need to recognize that it's been easy to sit back and blame Joseph when things weren't going well rather than stepping forward and offering solutions of our own. Being part of a team means that once we agree on a plan, it's our plan and not just the leader's."

Everyone joined hands in a circle and one at a time each prayed and confessed their shortcomings as well as pledging their unity to the mission that was ahead. When they finished, Joseph led them into the field. They each took out their Sword and sliced through the poisonous plants while quoting the verses that Joseph and Haley read earlier.

When they came to the end of the field, they climbed to the top of a hill. A few hundred feet away, they saw what looked to be a large house with several trolls roaming around outside.

Joseph motioned for everyone to get down and out of sight, then took out his telescope.

"What do you see?" asked Haley.

After a few minutes, Joseph placed the telescope back in his satchel, and a disturbing grimace formed on his face. "I see several young women who look like they're being kept as slaves in that house. The trolls appear to be carefully guarding the outside, and they only allow the girls to come out to get water from a well."

Susan stood close to Haley. "Why would they be keeping those girls trapped in that house?"

Overcomer crawled forward. "May I see your telescope?"

After peering through the lens for a few minutes, Overcomer handed it back to Joseph. For a moment she sat quietly, then took a deep breath, and motioned for everyone to gather around. "I think I know the purpose of that place. It doesn't seem that long ago when I was trapped in just such a house." She paused, then stared into the distance.

Esther reached over and put her hand on her shoulder. "What happened?"

Overcomer shook herself just a little, then started speaking again. "When you don't have a home and are out on your own, you're always looking for a place to stay. Word gets around where you can go to find food, shelter, or whatever you're looking for. Sometimes you can't be real choosy about where you end up, and you don't ask a lot of questions when you finally find a place to stay."

Haley pointed over the hill. "Are you saying that you traveled to a house like this and were trapped?"

Shaking her head, Overcomer said, "No, that's not how it works. In my case, the trolls paid some local men to set up a large shack and throw a party in it with everything you could want to eat or drink. There was lots of music, and after a few cups of their ale, I didn't care to ask any questions about where everything came from. They let us stay there for a week, and then one morning the trolls showed up."

Susan said, "Doesn't everyone run as soon as they see the trolls?"

Overcomer sighed. "Maybe we would have at the beginning, but as time passes you feel like you're in a daze. The trolls took all the girls to the side and told us that the party was being moved to another house, and if we would come with them we could keep enjoying ourselves like we had been. They said all we had to do at this new place was dance with some men during the evenings and see that they had a good time. We were even promised some extra money if we did well."

Haley said, "That sounds like a trap."

"It does," said Overcomer, "but by this time all we cared about was keeping the party going. We all followed them to a large house where there was, even more, to drink and eat then there was at the small shack. Everything was going great. There was lots of music, and all of us girls were having a great time. When night came, several older men arrived. Each one of them gave a gold coin to one of the trolls, then entered the house. At first, the men were really friendly. They danced with us and acted as if they wanted to get to know us, but after an hour passed, two of the men grabbed a couple of girls by the arm and marched them upstairs."

Esther said, "I think I know where this is going. That must have been terrible."

Overcomer stared blankly ahead and clasped her hands tightly. "It was. One of the first girls tried to resist, but a large troll hit her on the back with a belt. The trolls then angrily pointed at the rest of us and said we could either cooperate or be beaten, but no matter what, we were going to go upstairs with those men. The head troll said that if we were cooperative, he could make life easier for us."

Susan hugged her. "I'm so sorry you had to go through that."

"That's heartbreaking," said Mike. "How did you get out of there?"

"Those next few days seemed like a really bad dream. We realized that we were trapped, and the trolls weren't going to let us leave. We were drinking and inhaling whatever we could get our hands on just so we could feel numb and forget about what happened the night before. On the third day there, I decided not to touch anything the trolls offered. I tried to stay alert, and I waited until just before the men were to arrive. This was the only time most of the trolls stayed on the inside. As soon as they opened up the door to start collecting the money, I jumped up and ran out the entrance."

"That sounds dangerous," said Susan.

"It was, and if I had been caught—" Overcomer looked as if she was thinking back to that time and feeling the danger of the moment. "I can look back now and see how God was with me even when I didn't believe in Him." She glanced around at the group. "I heard the trolls yelling and their loud thumping footsteps behind me, but I ran as fast as I could and never turned around. I just kept going until I ran through a stream. When I reached the far bank, I didn't hear anything sloshing in the water behind me. I glanced over my shoulder and saw that I was alone."

Esther hugged Overcomer. Haley and Susan dabbed at the tears in their eyes.

Joseph crawled up to the edge and peered through his telescope again. "So this is why we've been brought on this journey. God wants to use us to set those girls free. No wonder those trolls wanted us weakened or defeated before we could get here."

Mike shook his head. "I can't believe I let all those petty little things get to me along the way. There was something so much more important that God wanted to do through us, and we almost blew it because of our pride, envy, and rivalry."

Overcomer raised up on her elbows. "There will be more time for reflection later, but by the looks of the sun, we've got about three hours before men from local towns start arriving. We need to do something soon if we're going to help set the girls free."

Joseph leaned forward. "She's right. We need to come up with a plan and the sooner, the better."

Mike looked around at the others. "Joseph, what do you think we should do?"

"I count eleven trolls. Right now eight seem to be guarding the outside, and three are coming in and out. We need to figure out a way to catch them off guard."

Overcomer raised her hand. "I think I have an idea." Glancing over at Esther, she said, "Are you ready to act like a lost girl?"

17

THE LOST GIRLS

Esther gave Overcomer a curious look. "What is a lost girl?"

"A lost girl is someone who was lured in like I was," said Overcomer. "Many of them are runaways, and some just ended up at the wrong place at the wrong time. When they first arrive at a place like this, they don't know what they're getting into. Some are excited because they think it's just going to be a never-ending party."

"What are you thinking?" asked Haley.

Overcomer motioned toward the house. "If we try to rush them, those trolls are going to have an advantage. Let's remember they've been alerted that your youth group was heading in this direction, so they're prepared for a large group of young men and women. In order to catch them off guard, we need them to think that Esther and I are some new girls that have been sent there. They'll let down their guard because new girls don't know what they're getting into, and the trolls have no reason to feel threatened."

Joseph sat up and folded his hands. "I don't know. You two would be at great risk walking up there by yourselves like that."

Esther tapped her chest twice to reveal her armor and then twice again to make it disappear. "I know we've been sent to help you, and Overcomer and I will be ready. Besides, the rest of you will not be far behind."

Overcomer nodded. "That's right. We're the only two that can do this. At some point, these trolls spotted your group. If they happened to recognize one of you, they would immediately be on guard."

Joseph surveyed the whole area with his telescope. "There's a small grouping of trees to the left and just behind that house. But it's going to take us an hour to make it there because we're going to need to go a long way around to make sure we can't be spotted. Once we're in position, we'll wait for your signal, then we'll all run out and join the fight." He handed Overcomer his telescope. "Take this. When you see us approaching that group of trees, you'll know it's time for you to move forward."

Joseph led the others on the long trek, descending into several large gullies that kept them out of sight. Overcomer and Esther stayed on the hilltop, keeping watch through the telescope to make sure the trolls didn't spot the others as they moved into position. After an hour, they could see that Joseph and the rest of the group were nearing the trees.

Overcomer pointed toward the house. "Are you ready?"

"I'm not sure. How does a lost girl act?" asked Esther.

"When first arriving at a house like this, they would act like they were about to experience something new and exciting. So we'll skip and laugh as if we're expecting to have a good time." Overcomer stood to her feet. "Do you think you can act like that?"

Esther stood up. "I guess so. I saw a few tavern girls once, so maybe I can pull this off."

Overcomer gave her a quizzical look, trying to figure out how a girl like Esther had ever seen the inside of a tavern.

Checking her satchel and her Book, Esther said, "It's a long story. I'll tell you later."

They started toward the house, and as they drew closer, Overcomer said, "Once we're there, I need to find a way to check the inside before the battle begins."

"How will you do that?" asked Esther.

"I'm not sure yet, but just follow my lead."

Soon they spotted the trolls looking in their direction, and they began to skip and twirl around. At first, the trolls stared at one another, and a few reached behind their backs for their spears, but as the girls came closer, they started to laugh and smirk.

One of the large trolls who was called Jamik, said, "I didn't know we were expecting anyone new today."

A smaller troll whom they called Bomar said, "I didn't either. But we can always use more girls, and these two look like they could bring in a lot of gold."

Jamik barked at the smaller troll, "Go inside and tell Bekar that we have some new guests."

As Esther and Overcomer drew closer, Overcomer whispered under her breath, "Those are the two trolls I saw coming toward the shack."

Esther kept smiling and skipping around while whispering back. "I recognize the voices."

Bomar hurried inside, and soon, the biggest troll who looked to be in charge came out.

Bekar stepped forward. "Well, who do we have here? You girls look like you're ready for a good time."

Overcomer stopped and giggled. "We've already been having a good time, and we were told to come here to have even more fun."

Bekar grinned at the other trolls. "If it's fun that you want then you've certainly come to the right place. In fact, just as soon as the sun goes down, the fun really begins."

All the other trolls let out a roaring laugh.

Overcomer pointed toward the house. "May I go inside and have a look around? I was told that one of my old friends would be here."

"Sure," said Bekar. "Go on in. Balek is in there somewhere, and he will be glad to give you a tour."

Overcomer stepped inside. All the girls were sitting on sofas or overstuffed chairs, staring at the floors and doing their best not to make eye contact. She quickly glanced around to see if there were any trolls. Suddenly a female voice coming from the rear of the house pleaded. "Please don't."

Overcomer started toward the back where the voice came from.

A young woman named Millie grabbed her by the arm and whispered. "Don't go back there. You and your friend get out of here while you still can."

Overcomer stepped back and laughed as if she had been told something funny, then leaned toward Millie and whispered, "We're not here to stay. We're here to get you out."

Overcomer approached a back room and walked up to the door. She heard a gruff voice say, "This will teach you a lesson!"

She opened the door and spotted a troll raising a belt over his head as if he was about to whip the young girl. Startled at the sight of

Overcomer, the troll gasped and then froze. Just as he was about to yell out, Overcomer quickly raised her Book, then leveled two hard blows to the troll's head with her Sword, knocking him out.

The young girl, whose name was Myra looked frightened. "What have you done? Do you realize how much trouble we're both in now?"

Overcomer whispered, "Help me move this troll into that closet. We're going to get you out of here."

They dragged the troll into the closet then barred the door.

Overcomer said, "Wait back here until you hear the battle begin outside."

Myra still looked frightened, but something about Overcomer's demeanor reassured her that everything was going to be okay.

Overcomer left the room and joined the other girls out front. Speaking loud enough for the trolls outside to hear, she said, "This is a lovely house. I'm sure Esther and I are going to love staying here."

The other girls looked at her curiously as she walked back outside.

When Overcomer rejoined Esther, Bekar said, "Well since you've had a little tour, what do you think?"

Overcomer giggled. "I didn't see my friend, but I think we're going to love it here."

Bekar stepped closer to Overcomer, grinning an evil grin. "You two come on inside. Balek will show you to your room, and then we have just the right thing to help get you ready for the party we're planning this evening."

Overcomer smiled and glanced at the ground as if she was shy, slowly inching her hand toward her satchel. "If it's okay with you we'd like to start this party outside."

Bekar squinted and glanced toward the other trolls.

Seeing she had caught him off guard, Overcomer pulled out her Book and raised it until it became a Sword. Bekar reached behind him for his spear, but he was too late. Overcomer slashed him on his shoulder and then followed with a blow to the side of his leg, bringing him to the ground. Esther ran toward Overcomer and raised her Shield just in time to intercept a spear thrown by Bomar.

"Thanks," said Overcomer, as she whirled around and took a defensive stance.

The other trolls grabbed their spears and raced toward Esther and Overcomer, but they were suddenly startled when they heard loud shouting behind them. Joseph and the rest of the youth group came charging from behind a small patch of trees.

Bekar raised to his knees. "Jamik! You were supposed to make sure they never got this close! You will suffer for this!"

Overcomer motioned for Susan to come beside her, and Michelle lined up behind Esther.

Jamik lifted his spear into the air. "I will make up for my mistake Bekar. Not only will we defeat them, but we will add new girls to our house."

Esther rushed toward Jamik. "I don't think so. By the time we're done here, you will have fewer girls, not more."

Jamik thrust his spear toward Ester's stomach, but she lifted her Shield, and the weapon glanced off. Esther then landed a blow with her Sword on the troll's shoulder. Michelle moved around to the side and swung her Sword at Jamik's arm. As he pulled away to avoid her attack, Esther stabbed him in the gut with her Sword and then smashed her Shield into his face.

Bekar was now back on his feet, and Overcomer faced him while Susan circled in behind.

Bekar snarled at Overcomer. "I will have to get rid of you. But this younger one, she will make a fine addition to our house."

Overcomer held up her Sword. "Do not be afraid. His threats are worthless. We were not brought this far to fail."

Susan stood tall, tightly grasping her Sword and Shield. As Bekar shifted to locate her, Overcomer pounced. She connected with her Sword—a strike to his neck. Bekar yelled and thrust his spear toward Overcomer's head. When she ducked out of the way, Susan lunged at him from behind and struck him on the back with her Sword. Overcomer then pierced him in the chest, and Susan stepped closer and swatted him on the back of the head with her Shield.

Bekar swung his spear behind him to move Susan back, then raised it with both hands, preparing to plunge it into Overcomer as hard as he could. But Susan recovered much more quickly than he anticipated, and she charged in and clipped him on the back of his knees with her Sword. Bekar fell forward, and Overcomer quickly brought her Sword down on top of his head. Bekar fell flat on his face and lay unconscious on the ground.

Jamik was still trying to hold off Esther and Michelle. He jabbed at Esther with his spear, but she stepped back and sliced the spear in two with her Sword. Jamik stood dumbfounded, holding a piece of his spear in each hand. Michelle swung her Sword from the side and connected with Jamik's stomach. As he doubled over, Esther plunged her Sword into the back of his neck, knocking him out.

Haley had been occupied by a mean troll who kept taunting her as he jabbed at her head with his spear. She dodged side to side as the spear whistled past her ears. Timing the troll's attacks, she thrust her Shield to the side of her head and knocked the spear out of his hand. She then charged her enemy and swung her Shield upward catching the troll under the chin. She followed up by whacking him on the side of his head with her Sword. The troll wobbled and struggled to stay on his feet. Haley then jumped into the air and kicked out with her Shoes, landing a perfect blow to his gut. The troll tumbled backward and hit his head on a rock. He groaned for a moment, then lay unconscious.

At the same time, two large trolls had been bearing down on Joseph and Mike. Working as a team, they backed each troll up against the other, then finished them off with a flurry of blows.

As both trolls fell to the ground, Joseph held up his fist and said, "Now that's teamwork."

Mike smiled. "Yes it is."

Sean and the others fought valiantly as well, battling the other trolls until they were all knocked out.

Before they could celebrate, Susan pointed toward the house and yelled, "Bekar!"

They turned to see that Bekar had regained his footing and was running into the house. At once, he reappeared at the door holding one of the girls named Melinda. He had one arm around her neck and pointed at them with his index finger. "So you came here to save these girls, did you? Well throw down your Swords immediately and leave, or I'll snap her neck."

Overcomer had slipped around and picked up one of the spears. She hurled it so that it landed just to the left of Bekar and stuck in the wall.

Bekar laughed and reached out to grab the spear with his free hand. "Looks like you missed."

Suddenly another spear sailed through the air and pinned Bekar's right arm to the wall.

Overcomer rubbed her hands together. "I didn't miss."

Bekar winced in pain. He let go of Melinda and reached out with his left hand to pull the spear out of his arm. When he did, Overcomer pounced on him and landed successive blows to his arms and legs. Bekar fell out of the doorway and onto the ground. She then finished him off with a blow to his temple. Bekar lay face down on the ground.

Joseph located some rope, and they began tying up all the trolls. By now, several girls who had been trapped in the house stood at the door, but even with their captors lying on the ground defeated, the girls were hesitant to come outside. Joseph motioned for all the guys to step back, as Haley, Overcomer, Esther, Susan, and Michelle stepped forward.

Overcomer held out her hands. "I've been where you are. There is hope, and there is freedom."

Millie shook her head. "You don't understand. We've been told that if we go out this door without permission, then we're going to be severely beaten. We've seen it happen, and it's frightening."

Esther took a step toward her. "God has sent us here with a message." Taking out her Book, she read, "For I know the thoughts that I think toward you, says the LORD, thoughts of well-being and not of misery, to give you a future and a hope."

Myra stepped into the doorway. "Doesn't God know what we've been doing in this place? How could He want us?"

Overcomer said, "God knows you've been trapped here and forced to do things against your will."

Millie shook her head, "But I chose to do many sinful things before I ever came to this house."

Susan crept forward. She hesitated at first but then began to speak. "All of us are sinful before God. The message of the Gospel is that even while we were sinful, Christ died for us. None of us deserves that kind of love. If you will repent of all of your sins and accept what Christ did on the cross, then you can be washed clean and completely forgiven."

Millie began to cry, "I feel so dirty on the inside. Can I really be clean?"

Overcomer read, "Come and let us reason together says the LORD, for even though your sins are like scarlet, they shall be white as snow. Even as they are red like crimson, they shall be white like wool."

Overcomer motioned toward the house. "I was once trapped in a place just like this. God took me with all of my sins and washed me white as snow. Because of Christ's perfect sacrifice, God can look on us as not only clean but as if we've always done what was pleasing in His sight."

Millie took a step out of the house, and the others gasped. Walking down the steps, tears flowed down her face. A minute later, Myra and Melinda followed, and then one by one, others stepped out of the house as well.

But not all wanted to leave. Another girl named Tracy shook her finger at Esther and Overcomer. "You do-gooders, take yourselves and your Books on out of here. I don't need anyone to save me. This might not be the best place, but it beats what I had. This house isn't so bad if you just follow the rules."

Millie reached out toward her. "Please come with us. How many times have you been beaten? You know what's going to happen as soon as the sun sets. There's not much time left."

Tracy shook her head. "I only get beat when I deserve it. You all think you're getting freedom? I can do whatever I want here and never have to worry about someone judging me. That's real freedom."

Overcomer had met others like Tracy, and she knew there was nothing else that could be done. Taking Millie's arm, she said, "It's time to go."

Bekar regained consciousness as they started walking off. He raised his head up and shouted at them. "You girls think you can leave me! You'll be back, and you'll beg me to let you stay here again."

Millie suddenly whipped around. "I will not be back! If Jesus loved me enough to die for me, then I will spend the rest of my life living for Him!"

Eight girls left that day, while four decided to remain behind. After traveling for an hour, they came upon a Building of Reflection.

The youth group waited at the bottom of the Hill of Calvary as each lost girl made their way through the building. The girls in the youth group along with Esther and Overcomer accompanied them up the hill. They each bowed at the cross, repenting of their sins and asking Jesus to come into their hearts and save them.

A large bright cloud overshadowed the hill, and a Great Voice boomed from the center. "You are a new creation. What was before is no longer. You are now daughters of the King!"

Millie lifted her hands toward heaven. "I feel so clean now, and I feel completely alive for the first time ever."

Esther gave Millie a hug, and right there at the Hill of Calvary, the whole group began to sing:

Amazing Grace, how sweet the sound,
That saved a wretch like me.
I once was lost, but now I'm found,
Was blind, but now, I see.

After a time of rejoicing, Joseph motioned for everyone to sit down as he took out his Book. The girls who had been rescued each sat next to one of the other girls so they could share their Books. Joseph read the story of Jesus approaching the Samaritan woman at the well. Millie and the other girls listened intently as this woman with a troubled past was given a new beginning. They were startled to learn that not only did Jesus save her, but He immediately used her to spread His message to others. When Joseph was finished, there was a time of prayer, and then the whole group started off.

They found a place to camp for the night, and they gathered around the fire, singing songs of praise. The next day their paths led them to a trail they hadn't seen before. To their surprise, it led them back to their village just as the sun was beginning to set. Tents were set up for all the girls that were rescued, and the next day a service was held at the House of Instruction. When the meeting was over the Pastor announced that there would be a baptismal service and then a picnic right afterward.

All the girls were baptized that day, and the next day the townspeople began to build a shelter for them to stay in. Some stayed for a few weeks and then went back to their families, but others had no place to go and stayed in the shelter as their new home. Those that remained joined the youth group and began to grow in their walk with God. Esther and Overcomer stayed for two weeks to help minister to the young women, and then they saw that their paths were leading away.

As they prepared to leave, members of the youth group, and all of the young women who were rescued gathered around to tell them goodbye.

Joseph extended his hand to Overcomer. "Thanks for everything. I don't know what would have happened to us if you and Esther hadn't come along."

Shaking his hand, Overcomer said, "God sent us to help, but you were already equipped and ready for what He had planned. You thought those previous few days were a disaster, but God was doing something in each one of you to get you ready."

Haley gave Esther and Overcomer hugs. "We're going to miss you."

Millie walked up to them with tears in her eyes. "Someday I want to be known as an overcomer."

Embracing her, Esther said, "You already are."

Overcomer and Esther wiped away tears as they departed.

After turning around to wave one last time, Esther said, "That youth group is going to do great things for God."

"Yes, they are," said Overcomer. "I can't wait to hear about their adventures."

18

BRINGING IN THE SHEAVES

As the days went by Esther and Overcomer became closer, and they encouraged one another in their relationship with Christ. One day as they were traveling, they saw a skinny young man with a straw hat and dirty overalls plowing in a field. He didn't appear to be a day over sixteen, and it was obvious he was struggling with the mule.

When they came closer, a younger girl, not more than ten, ran out of a small log cabin. She pointed toward them, as she hopped up and down and called to the weary youth behind the plow. He pulled back on the reins and brought the mule to a stop. Esther and Overcomer waved to them. The young man took off his hat and wiped the sweat from his brow.

A woman came out of the cabin and hurried toward the field. The weariness in her eyes suggested she had struggled through many things in life, yet at the same time, judging from her appearance, the years had been kind to her. Her hair was neatly piled on top of her head and fastened with a comb. She wore a blue dress, neatly pressed, and a snow-white apron. As she strolled up next to the young girl, she dusted flour from her hands.

"Hello there," she called out.

"Hello," said Overcomer.

The young girl grasped the woman around the waist, and the young man left the field and stepped in front of the two as if to protect them.

Esther eased her pack from her shoulder. "We don't mean to intrude, but we've been traveling for days, and our paths have led us in this direction."

"Well, welcome to our little farm. My name is Cassandra. This is my son Jim, and my daughter Katie."

"It's so nice to meet all of you. I'm Esther, and this is Overcomer."

Cassandra smiled and held out her hand. "Why don't you two come in and sit down for a little bit. We don't get many passersby, and we'd enjoy having some company."

"Thank you so much for the offer," said Overcomer. "We'd love to join you for a little while."

After going inside, Cassandra showed them to a table and then brought out five glasses and a large pitcher of lemonade. Katie buzzed around helping her mother and snatching peeks at their guests, but Jim sat silently, keeping a watchful eye on the newcomers.

Cassandra handed a glass to Esther and to Overcomer. "As I said, we don't see many people passing by this way, but I don't know if I've ever seen two young women traveling together by themselves."

Esther took a small sip of her lemonade. "We met about a month ago, and we've been traveling together since."

"Yes," said Overcomer. "We feel God has brought us together for a purpose."

Jim rolled his eyes and turned sideways.

Cassandra paused and peered through a window. "I've always believed God has a plan and purpose for everything."

Jim suddenly stood up and put on his hat. "Yeah, just like God had a plan for Dad, and for this farm, and for us. I don't have time to sit around and talk about God. He's not the one that's going to get that field plowed in time for planting."

Jim stormed out of the house and returned to the field. Cassandra wiped a tear from her eye, and Katie stared down at the table, as a look of sadness came on her face.

Cassandra took a seat next to her and rubbed her arm. "You'll have to excuse Jim," she said to Esther and Overcomer. "The last year has been tough on him. It's been tough on all of us."

"We don't want to pry," said Overcomer, "but if there's something you'd like to share, we'd be glad to listen."

Tears welled up in Katie's eyes. "Our dad died from pneumonia, and Jim's been angry ever since."

Cassandra hugged Katie and stroked her hair. "Frank worked so hard around the farm, and sometimes he didn't take care of himself the way he should. He'd work long hours and be out in all kinds of weather. Last winter he came down with a terrible flu, but he kept working anyway. Then it turned into pneumonia, and he never recovered."

Esther placed her hand on Cassandra's arm. "I'm so sorry."

"Thank you," said Cassandra. "He loved God, and I know he's in heaven, but I do wish he was still here."

"I'm so glad to hear he was a Christian," said Esther. Turning to Katie, she said, "But I understand it was still a terrible thing to go through."

Cassandra nodded. "You try to trust in God, but it's hard. Katie seems to have handled it as well as she could, but Jim became angry and bitter. He feels like all of the responsibility of the farm is on him now. Sometimes I think the best thing to do is move into a town or village. I could try to find a job sewing or cleaning houses, but Jim wants to see if we can make it here. It's the only thing he has left from his father."

"I don't want to leave either," said Katie.

"I don't know a lot about farming," said Esther. "What all has to be done for you to make it?"

Cassandra stood and filled their glasses with some more lemonade. "Frank had already purchased the seed we needed for this year, and Jim's been working as hard as he can to get the field plowed in time for planting season. One good crop would be enough to pay for next year's seed and everything else we'd need to get us through until the following harvest."

Esther said, "I understand why Jim feels so much pressure then."

Cassandra nodded. "Pulling a plow behind a mule is tough for a grown man, but it's even more challenging for a young man his size."

Katie pulled on her mother's arm. "Mom, can they stay for dinner and maybe even overnight?"

Cassandra smiled. "That would be a great idea. We have a spare room with two cots."

Overcomer glanced toward Esther who gave her an approving grin. "We'd love to stay with you, but you have to give us something to do so we can help out."

Katie jumped from her chair. "There's always lots to do—laundry and fetching water, milking the cow, feeding the chickens and gathering the eggs in the morning."

Cassandra said, "Now Katie, it was nice of our guests to offer, but they're guests."

Overcomer went to Katie's side and rested a hand on her shoulder. "We'd feel much better if we could help. Besides, it would give us more time to spend with each of you. Why don't I go with Katie to draw some water, and Esther can help you here."

Cassandra leaned forward. "Are you sure? I mean we'd love to have some company as we go about our chores, but you both have been traveling for awhile. Aren't you tired?"

Esther picked up their empty glasses and headed to the kitchen. "We're just fine. This lemonade has helped us feel refreshed already."

Katie started toward the door. "Come on. I'll show you where we keep the buckets and then I'll take you to the well."

As Overcomer and Katie left, Cassandra and Esther finished clearing the table.

"Do you ever get to leave the farm and see other people?" Esther asked.

Cassandra paused for a moment. "We go to a nearby village once a month to get any supplies we need, but we're not there long enough to talk to anyone too long."

"And that's it?"

"We used to go into the village once a week to attend services at their House of Instruction, but we haven't gone since Frank died. The people there were real nice and helped us with the funeral, but afterward, it was so hard to make the trip. It was something that Frank and I always did together, and I was afraid I would break down if I went by myself." She stared toward the field. "Jim said he wasn't going even if Katie and I went."

Esther picked up a towel to dry, and Cassandra poured water from the stove into the wash basin to wash the dishes. "I understand it must be hard, but it would seem like being around other Christians would be just the thing you all need right now."

"I know," said Cassandra, "and I think Katie misses it as much as I do."

"When is the next service?"

"In two days."

Cassandra rinsed off the last dish and handed it to Esther to dry.

When she finished, she put it in the proper cupboard. "I don't want to sound pushy, but what if we stayed and helped you for a few days, and then we could all go to the service together?"

Cassandra stood quietly for a moment. "I would like that, and I think Katie would too."

****

Katie had run out the door so fast that Overcomer could barely keep up with her. For a moment, Katie disappeared into a small shed and then dashed back out with two buckets, one bigger than the other. "Let's go."

Overcomer followed as Katie skipped through a small patch of woods and into a small clearing. A large rock sat on top of a flat piece of wood covering a well. They removed the covering and tied the smaller bucket to a long rope.

Lowering the bucket into the well, Katie said, "I like getting the water. Sometimes as I'm going through those woods, I pretend I'm going off on an adventure. I imagine there's a big castle on the other side of those trees, and I'm going there to rescue someone in trouble."

Overcomer grabbed the rope to help steady the bucket as it descended. "That sounds exciting."

"Have you ever been on an adventure?" asked Katie.

"Yes I have, and I'm sure you'll go on many adventures someday too."

"I hope so," said Katie as she started pulling the bucket back up.

When it reached the top, Katie poured it into the larger bucket. "I usually have to make two or three trips to get all the water we need, but with your help, I think we can do it in one trip."

"You must be a lot of help to your mom. I'm sure she appreciates all you do."

"I try," said Katie. "I used to come out with my dad and get water every day, so I'm good at it." She paused as if she was thinking back to another time. She then lowered the bucket into the well again. "After Dad died, Mom was so sad. I was sad too, but I tried to help her feel better. Jim and I told her that we could keep the farm going."

Grabbing the rope once again, Overcomer said, "You and your brother are hard workers."

After filling both buckets, they started back toward the house, talking all along the way. When they arrived at the cabin with the water, Esther and Cassandra had just finished sweeping the floors.

"Look Mom. We've got both buckets in one trip."

Reaching out to take the large bucket, Cassandra said, "I can see that. Thank you. And thank you, Overcomer, for helping."

Overcomer put her arm around Katie. "It was fun, and we had our own little adventure."

Cassandra set the brooms back in a closet. "What kind of adventure was that?"

Katie made a motion as if she was waving a Sword. "We talked about how we can use God's word to fight off feelings of sadness."

"That's very good," said Cassandra. "I think I need to do that too. Can you tell me what you learned?"

Katie beamed with excitement. "We use verses from the Book. Like this one: 'Rejoice in the Lord always: and again I say, Rejoice.' "

"That's a wonderful verse," said Cassandra as she reached over and hugged her.

Stepping back and clapping her hands, Katie said, "Oh Mom, do you remember when we would have picnics after service, and all the children would sing that song?"

"I do."

Katie started to sway in time to the tune in her head. "All the boys would form a circle and sing it as loud as they could, and then all us girls would get in a circle too, and we'd try to sing it louder. That was so fun."

"How would you like to go to service the day after tomorrow?" asked Cassandra.

"I'd love to!" said Katie, grinning from ear to ear. "Can Esther and Overcomer come too?"

Esther smiled. "I've already talked it over with your mom, and we can't wait to go with you."

Overcomer put her arm around Katie's shoulders. "Just in case they sing this song, why don't you help us learn it?"

Katie motioned for everyone to get in a circle, and then she started singing.

Rejoice in the Lord always and again I say rejoice,
Rejoice in the Lord always and again I say rejoice!
Rejoice, rejoice, and again I say rejoice,
Rejoice, rejoice, and again I say rejoice!

Everyone joined in and repeated the simple chorus.

As everyone was singing and laughing, Jim walked in.

Katie grabbed him by the arm. "Come on Jim, sing with us. Remember how you and the other guys used to always win when you tried your hardest?"

"I don't have anything to sing about." He headed for the kitchen to get a drink of lemonade, then marched back outside.

Throughout the afternoon, Esther and Overcomer helped with the chores, and then when evening came, they helped prepare dinner. Ever since their time of singing and rejoicing, it felt as if a heaviness had lifted from the house. Throughout the afternoon and during the dinner preparation, they all continued laughing and enjoying their time together.

That is, everyone except Jim. He kept quiet and stayed to himself, but even he seemed to notice a difference in the atmosphere. Although he didn't join in on any of the conversations, he at least didn't interrupt them.

After dinner, everyone retired to the living room and sat down.

Esther took out her Book. "How would you like it if I read some Scriptures? Or we could read them together."

Katie ran to her room and got her Book. When she returned, she took a seat next to her mom. "It will be just like when Dad was here. We always used to read from our Books together."

Jim stood up. "It's been a long day, and I think I'll get a head start on getting some sleep. I'll see everyone tomorrow." He gave his mom a quick kiss on the cheek, then left for his room.

Katie opened her Book. "Where should we start?"

Esther turned a few pages. "I think we should continue to talk about joy. Here is one of my favorites: 'This is the day which the LORD hath made; we will rejoice and be glad in it.'"

"This is one of mine," said Overcomer. "For ye shall go out with joy, and be led forth with peace: the mountains and the hills shall break forth before you into singing, and all the trees of the field shall clap their hands."

Cassandra took her Book from a shelf and slowly turned the pages. "Right after Frank died I used to read this at night. 'For though His anger is only for a moment, His favor is for a lifetime. Weeping may last through the night, but joy comes in the morning.'"

Setting her Book in her lap, Cassandra dabbed at a tear with the edge of her apron.

Katie took her hand. "It's okay Mom. Don't cry."

Cassandra wiped her eyes. "I'm not crying because I'm sad. For the first time in a long time, I feel like my sadness is finally leaving. I've missed God's word. I don't know why I shut myself off like I did." She then rubbed Katie's hand. "I'm sorry I haven't been the mother I should have been. I should have continued to read God's word to both of you and continued the devotions and prayer time that your dad led."

"It's okay Mom," Katie repeated as she leaned over and hugged her. "I know this has been tough. I know you still love God, and I know that God knows it too."

Cassandra smiled, pulling her daughter closer. "There's been enough grieving around here. From now on there's going to be more joy."

They read more in their Books, then each one shared something they were thankful for. There were smiles all around, as they recalled the many times God had blessed them. After a time of prayer, everyone settled into their rooms to go to sleep.

As the others were leaving the living room, Jim scooted down in his bed and fixed his pillow. When everyone else had been discussing God's word, he had sat up in his bed listening. He wouldn't have admitted it at the time, but a small tear formed in his eyes as he prepared to go to sleep that night.

The next day was a joyous day, and Esther and Overcomer took over all the chores to give Cassandra an opportunity to catch up on some things she had wanted to do for months. After lunch, they had another time of singing and praising together, and when dinner was finished, they sat in the living room again and discussed God's word. Jim still didn't participate, but he certainly listened.

Katie talked and talked that evening, mostly about going back to the House of Instruction in the morning. She had missed the services and seeing all of her friends.

The next day everyone but Jim got ready to go to the service. Katie skipped into the living room wearing a cute lavender dress and a white hat. Cassandra seemed transformed as she strolled out of her room in a beautiful pink dress that she hadn't worn since her husband died.

Jim sat quietly at the kitchen table drinking a glass of orange juice.

Cassandra picked up her Book from the table, then leaned over to kiss Jim on the forehead. "I do wish you'd come."

"I know Mom, but I'm going to take it easy today and rest a little bit. I'll see you when you get back."

Katie gave Jim a hug, and then they all started out the door. When they arrived at the House of Instruction, many from the village welcomed Cassandra and Katie back and told them how good it was to see them again. Cassandra introduced her neighbors to Esther and Overcomer, and then they all went inside. The singing was beautiful, and Katie sang as loud as she could as if she was trying to make up for all the times she wasn't there.

When Pastor Davis stepped forward, he prayed and then asked everyone to take a seat. "I had a sermon all prepared for this week, and then two days ago I felt God was leading me to teach on something different. That doesn't happen often, but when it does, I know to listen. What I want to talk about today is how to trust in God during the hard times of our lives. You know, when everything is going good, it's easy to trust God, but it's when things get tough that we have to work to put our trust in Him."

Cassandra put her arm around Katie, knowing this message was for them.

Pastor Davis continued, "When you're a pastor for as many years as I've been, you see people go through all kinds of hardships. The one thing that is always the same is that they each have the same question: 'Why?' And I must tell you, that's one of the hardest questions I ever have to answer. Most times I just have to be honest and say, 'I don't know.' As we read God's word, sometimes we can see Him pull back the curtain and give us a glimpse of how He works. We see the story of Job, Joseph, Daniel, and many others, and we see how the difficult circumstances in their lives were turned for good. But sometimes in our own lives, we don't get to see that part, and all we see is the suffering and the tragedy."

Esther grasped Cassandra's hand.

"I wish I could give all of you a better answer," said Pastor Davis, "but sometimes there is no answer other than to say, God is working all things out for our good. If you're like me, there are occasions when you don't want to hear that. I know there's been days when I've said, 'God, instead of having to make all these bad things turn out for good, wouldn't it be a lot easier if we just started out with some good, to begin with?' "

Some of the members chuckled.

Pastor Davis smiled as he looked out at the congregation. "I guess it all boils down to the fact that when challenging circumstances come into our lives, we can either get mad at God for something we wish He had done, or we can praise Him for what He's already done. There's nothing more tragic than the perfect Son of God having to die an awful and painful death on a cross for something that wasn't His fault. Because of our sins, He was mocked, beaten, tortured, and then hung up like a common criminal for all to see. He did that for us because of how much He loves us. He wanted to spend eternity with us and give us an everlasting joy that is unspeakable and full of glory. When I think about all that He's done for me, all I can do is agree with Job, 'Though He slay me, yet will I trust in Him.' "

An elderly lady, two rows in front of Esther, dabbed at her eyes.

Pastor Davis turned in his Book. "As we close here today, I want to read a couple of Scriptures. The first is in Isaiah. 'Therefore the redeemed of the LORD shall return, and come with singing unto Zion; and everlasting joy shall be upon their head: they shall obtain gladness and joy; and sorrow and mourning shall flee away.' "

Pastor Davis turned over a few more pages. "And the next verse is in the Psalms. 'They that sow in tears shall reap in joy. He that goeth forth and weepeth, bearing precious seed, shall doubtless come again with rejoicing, bringing his sheaves with him.' "

Pastor Davis closed his Book. "Would everyone rise as we sing a song of praise to our Lord."

Just then Cassandra felt a hand on her shoulder. Glancing back, she saw it was Jim.

****

After his family and their guests had left, Jim sat in the living room by himself. The idea of them going to a House of Instruction where they would praise God was almost more than he could stand. He was angry at God and wanted answers. He paced around the living room telling God exactly how he felt, letting Him know just how unfair it was that such a good man as his dad had to die.

Jim stopped and looked upward. Then he shouted, "Why!"

He shouted it again and then again. He went to his knees, crying while still shouting, "Why?"

At that moment something broke inside of him. He didn't feel God was answering his question, but what he did feel was that God was right there with him. Jim also knew he had a choice. He could either go on with life apart from God, or he could surrender his life to God. He took a deep breath, then got up off his knees. Overcome with a sense of the Holy Spirit's presence, he darted into his room to get his Book and then sprinted out the door.

Jim hadn't made it to the service on time, but he had arrived just as Pastor Davis started his message. He had listened intently from the beginning to the end and knew God was speaking directly to him. As they stood at the end of the sermon, Jim moved up a couple of rows and placed his hand on his mother's shoulder.

When Cassandra saw him, she cried tears of joy and motioned for him to come forward. Esther scooted over, and he took a place next to his mom. Cassandra embraced him, and Katie reached over and hugged them both.

Pastor Davis held out his hand. "Isn't it a wonderful promise that even though we may sow in tears, we can reap in joy. There are times when we go forth with weeping, but we know there'll be another time when we will come again with rejoicing, bringing in a harvest of sheaves."

The choir director came forward and led everyone in a song.

Sowing in the morning, sowing seeds of kindness,

Sowing in the noontide and the dewy eve;
Waiting for the harvest, and the time of reaping,
We shall come rejoicing, bringing in the sheaves.
Bringing in the sheaves, bringing in the sheaves,
We shall come rejoicing, bringing in the sheaves,
Bringing in the sheaves, bringing in the sheaves,
We shall come rejoicing…, bringing in the sheaves.

Pastor Davis bowed his head and prayed for a blessing over the congregation. When he finished, he looked up and said, "We invite everyone to stay with us today for a picnic as we continue to fellowship and celebrate our time together in the Lord."

Katie grabbed her mom's arm in excitement. Following the others in the congregation, they filed outside and joined them for the picnic. It was a great afternoon, and both Katie and Jim reconnected with many of their old friends. And yes, Katie made sure they had the contest to see whether the boys or the girls could sing the loudest. They had a great time, although there may have been a slight disagreement about who won.

As everyone prepared to return home, Cassandra assured the other members of the congregation that they would be back that next week.

Walking home, Jim opened up about what happened after everyone left, and for the first time in a long time, Cassandra felt like they were a close family once again.

Esther and Overcomer stayed one more day, and then they started back on their path.

A few years later Cassandra would send them a letter to let them know what all had transpired since the time they last saw each other. Not long after they left, Jim finished plowing the field, and then Katie and Cassandra helped plant the seed. At harvest time, they had one of the best yields they had ever had. Many from the village came to help, and after they sold the excess at the market, they had more than enough money for the following year. They were even able to start a small savings fund.

Two years later an older single man named John moved into the village and started attending services. He spent several weeks getting to know Cassandra, Jim, and Katie, then asked if he could walk with them to services. Not too long afterward John and Cassandra married. The following year Jim went off to attend a House of Knowledge, and after graduation, he felt God was calling him to be a traveling minister.

He assured his mom and sister that he would be back from time to time, and then he started out on his journey. It turned out that God seemed to use him on many occasions to minister to those who were going through tough times in their lives. Jim shared his life-story and always emphasized the love that God showed him during his own time of tragedy. Katie grew up to be a strong woman of God, and just like Overcomer had said, she would go on many adventures.

19

A NEW MISSION

Esther and Overcomer's next few days of travel were peaceful and relaxing. One evening as the sun was about to set, they came upon an inn. They approached the front desk and paid for a night's stay. After receiving their key, a friendly young lady not much older than Esther showed them to their room. They were both tired, and after getting ready for bed, they immediately fell asleep.

The next morning rays of sunlight streamed through their window, and the sound of a rooster crowing echoed in their ears. To Overcomer and Esther's delight, this particular inn provided a bathhouse. While traveling and camping they had to make do with whatever water source they came upon for bathing, but the opportunity to soak in a nice warm bath was something neither of them could pass up.

The owners of the inn had water piped in from a nearby river and then heated it near a fire. Each person had their own private area and could soak for as long as they wanted. When Overcomer and Esther finished bathing, they felt clean and refreshed. As soon as they were dressed, they returned to their room to prepare for breakfast. Downstairs, small tables sprinkled the dining area. They scanned the room, then chose a table next to a window with a wonderful view of the countryside.

As they were eating, an older couple sat down at a table nearby. A waitress took their order then soon brought them some coffee, waffles, and toast.

In a high-pitched voice, the wife said, "What are we going to do?"

The husband took a drink of coffee and shook his head. "I don't know. Ever since we got the letter, I've been thinking about what we possibly could do, and I'm still not sure."

The wife tore off a piece of toast and put a little butter on it. "I just wish we had known sooner. Maybe we could have done something before it got this bad."

"I know," said the husband. "I've thought that too. But God is in control, and if He would have wanted us to know sooner, then we would have."

"Sometimes I wonder where God was when this all started."

The husband reached out to take his wife's hand. "We all wonder those kinds of things. We still have another day's journey, so maybe we'll have more of a plan before we get there."

"I hope so," replied his wife.

The couple finished their breakfast and then went back to their room.

Esther looked over her shoulder as the couple left. "I don't like to be nosey, but it does seem that couple is upset about something."

"I know," said Overcomer. "Whatever it is, I pray God will give them the wisdom they need."

"Amen," said Esther.

After going back to their room for a time of reading and praying, Esther and Overcomer decided to go outside for a walk. The scent of fresh flowers filled the air. A gentle breeze off the nearby river cooled them, and large trees, spaced throughout the property, provided intermittent shade, so they were never in direct sunlight for more than a minute at a time. The weather seemed as perfect as could be on this present earth.

As they strolled along, Esther noticed that the couple they had seen at breakfast was seated on a bench up ahead. She nudged Overcomer. "Let's go over and introduce ourselves."

As they approached, the couple talked in low tones, worry lines noticeable around their pinched mouths. A twig snapped under Esther's foot, and the couple looked up. They smiled and stood to greet them.

"Hello. Lovely day, isn't it? My name is James, and this is my wife, Clara."

"Nice to meet you. I'm Esther, and this is Overcomer."

"Overcomer?" said Clara. "Now that is a good name to have."

Feeling as if this was God's opening for her to share some of her testimony, Overcomer gave them a brief summary of her life and how God had saved her by His grace.

"My, my," said Clara, "you are indeed an Overcomer." Turning toward her husband, she said, "Should we get her input on the situation we're heading into?"

James lowered his voice. "I don't know. I don't want to burden others with our problems."

Esther motioned toward the bench. "We'd love to sit and talk with you. If there's something we can help you with, please tell us."

The couple scooted over to the far end of the bench and made room for them to sit down.

After Overcomer and Esther took a seat, Clara glanced at her husband, then started. "Our son and daughter-in-law moved to a new area about five months ago. They felt God had called them to start a ministry for those who struggled with different kinds of addiction. Soon afterward, God connected them with another couple who also felt called to the same kind of ministry."

Esther said, "That type of outreach can do a lot of good."

"Yes, that's what we thought too," said James. "We received a letter every few weeks from them. At first, they were excited because God was leading many people to their ministry to receive help. For the first two months, each letter we received from our son was upbeat and full of optimism. Then a month ago, the tone of the letters changed, and he wrote about how little progress they were seeing. He sounded discouraged, and in this last letter, I got the feeling they were ready to give up and move back to our village."

"What happened?" asked Overcomer.

Clara shook her head. "We don't know exactly. They mentioned some kind of opposition, but they never came right out and said what it was. After this last letter, James and I felt we should go visit them and see for ourselves."

Overcomer said, "During my time of wandering in sin, I had my own struggles with addictions. I ran into many others who did as well. People with addictions have learned how to be manipulative. They've convinced themselves that they don't have any major problems, and what problems they do have are someone else's fault."

Clara sat up and put her hand on Overcomer's shoulder. "As I was listening to you share your story, I thought you might have some insight into what we may be heading into."

Overcomer nodded. "The type of ministry they're engaged in can be challenging. Sometimes there's a fine line between trying to help people and trying to do it for them. When someone with an addiction senses that another person feels the need to fix them, they may latch onto that individual to get whatever they can, and the results usually aren't good for either party."

James sighed. "I guess I just wish our son had chosen a different kind of ministry. I know he felt this was what God called him to do, but it seems he's in over his head and doesn't know how to get out."

Overcomer tapped Esther on the arm, and Esther knew what she was thinking.

Overcomer said, "We would like to pray and ask God if we should come with you. Is that okay?"

Clara smiled and grabbed James' hand. "That would be wonderful. We plan to leave in the morning, and we should be there by sundown. We'll see you two at breakfast, and you can let us know what you've decided."

Overcomer stood up. "We'll be praying for the rest of the day, then we'll see you first thing tomorrow." When they had walked off a little ways, Overcomer said, "I hope you didn't feel put on the spot."

Esther glanced back at the couple. "Oh no, I knew what you were thinking, and I agree."

They spent the rest of the day getting to know some of the other guests, and after dinner, they took a walk along the banks of the river. They prayed about the situation with James and Clara throughout the day, and then just before going to sleep, they prayed about it once again together. As soon as they awoke the next morning and got dressed, Esther and Overcomer met the couple, walked outside with them, and saw that their paths were lined up together. They enjoyed a quick breakfast together, and then they all set off.

They made good time, and just before sunset, they came upon a large and mostly flat area of land. The soil appeared dark and fertile, and a small brook ran through the middle of a large clearing. There were two smaller homes on one end, and a little further away was a much larger home. As they drew near to the first house, a young woman pulled a sheet from a laundry basket and spread it across a clothesline. As she stooped to grab her last bit of washing, she spotted them approaching and shouted toward the home. "Mitchell, we've got company!"

A tall man with brown hair and a mustache emerged from the house. "Mom! Dad! What are you doing here?"

Giving his son and daughter-in-law a hug, James said, "After we got your last letter, we felt we had to come."

Mitchell smiled. "It's great to see you, but I didn't mean to get you so upset that you felt you had to come all this way. Sometimes it's been nice just to sit down and write about all the things I've been feeling. It helps to know someone is out there listening and praying."

Clara hugged her son and then stepped back. "I want you to meet our two new friends, Esther and Overcomer. We met them at an inn yesterday, and they've been great traveling companions." She smiled at the girls. "And this is my son Mitchell and his lovely wife, Sandra."

"It's so nice to meet both of you," said Overcomer. "Your parents have told us about the ministry God has called you to. It's an important work, and there are many people who need this kind of help."

Putting his arm around his wife, Mitchell said, "We know it's important, and we both want to serve God, but it seems like the harder we try to help people, the more difficult things become."

Sandra said, "Let's go inside and have some tea. I know you all must be worn out from the journey."

After they finished a snack of pound cake served with their tea, Overcomer said, "I have some experience dealing with addictions myself. May I ask what kind of problems you've been having?"

Mitchell put his hand on Sandra's. "At first we were a typical bright-eyed couple new to ministry. We were going to set the world on fire and minister to thousands. We met another couple who had a similar vision, and we just knew we were destined for success. When God began sending travelers our way who needed the kind of help we wanted to provide, we felt like everything was lining up."

Sandra said, "God sent three young men here in our first week, and with their help, we built that big home you saw. It can house at least fifteen. Our goal was to build more houses and open up shelters for women and children as well."

"That's a great start," said Esther.

Mitchell said, "That's what we thought. During the time we were ministering to these first three men, five more showed up. Soon word began to spread that this was a place for people to receive help for addictions, and over the next six weeks seven more men showed up." He paused and glanced at Sandra. "Then about two months later the problems started."

Clara said, "That's when we noticed a change in the tone of your letters."

"Yes," said Mitchell. "At first I didn't realize how much it was affecting me, but you've always known me so well that I'm sure it showed through in my letters whether I intended for it to or not."

James shifted in his seat. "So what happened?"

Mitchell shook his head. "I don't know. We started to get some guys who said they wanted help, but when we would try to help them, they said that we were judging them and not understanding their problems. This attitude seemed to spread, and it has been harder and harder to make any progress with these men. I'm starting to wonder if we're cut out for this sort of thing."

Overcomer nodded. "That happens. Sometimes people want to relieve their guilt, but they don't want to change their behavior."

Sandra said, "We and the other couple certainly feel exhausted by the process."

Overcomer responded, "It's difficult to know when it's time to confront someone, but there comes a point when you have to."

Mitchell sighed. "It seems they already think we're not understanding enough, so we've felt the caring thing to do was to keep showing them God's love."

"They need God's love," said Overcomer, "but they also need God's truth."

Overcomer took out her Book. "God's word says that Jesus came with grace and truth."

Clara smiled at her. "As soon as I heard your testimony, I knew God could use you in this situation."

Mitchell nodded. "This has been helpful. I do feel like there are some who are really trying, but I'm not so sure about a few others. It's almost as if the ones who don't want help are more of an influence than those who do."

Esther turned in her Book. "That reminds me of a verse: 'Don't be deceived. Bad company corrupts good behavior.' "

Mitchell pushed his chair back from the table. "I want to involve Don and Susan, our partners in the ministry, in this discussion. I know they've been just as frustrated as we have."

Mitchell left, and within minutes he returned with the couple. They spent the next hour discussing the issues the ministry was facing. When they finished, the group agreed that James, Clara, Overcomer, and Esther would accompany them the next morning to meet with all the men currently living in the ministry house. Everyone said goodnight, then went to bed.

Esther and Overcomer woke to the smell of fresh coffee and freshly baked Danish rolls. When they had dressed, they headed to the dining area where Clara and Sandra were setting the food on the table.

Overcomer pulled up a chair. "This smells great."

"Yes it does, and it looks delicious," said Esther, taking a seat next to her.

Pouring each of them a cup of coffee, Sandra said, "James and Mitchell went over to let all the guys know there will be a meeting before they start working in the garden."

"There's a garden?" asked Esther.

"Yes, it's been a great way to support the ministry," said Sandra. "The men grow vegetables and sell them to those passing by. It turns out that there are a lot of people who travel through this area."

Clara said, "That's a great way to help the men learn a useful set of skills, and it provides for all your needs as well."

Sandra sat down next to Clara. "It is, but…it seems like the garden was producing a lot more at first. Lately, we've barely been getting by."

As they began to eat, Mitchell and James walked in.

James kissed his wife. "This smells wonderful. Mitchell, do we have time for a quick breakfast before the meeting?"

"Sure," said Mitchell as he took a seat next to Sandra. "The men will be busy fixing their own breakfast and then cleaning up, so we've got some time. I told Don and Susan we'll be starting in about thirty minutes."

Everyone enjoyed a nice breakfast together, and then they met with the other couple. Together they headed over to the ministry house. When they arrived, ten men sat waiting in the living room. Mitchell pointed toward a row of seats that had been set up in the front, and they all sat down.

Don opened the meeting with prayer.

Mitchell then addressed the men. "As I shared with you this morning, some guests have arrived, and I've asked them to attend our morning meeting." Turning to his right, he said, "These are my parents, James and Clara, and these are their traveling companions, Overcomer and Esther. I'd like to start this meeting like we have all the others. I want you to feel like you can share anything that's on your mind."

A man named Richard, who had long sideburns, curly black hair, and a styled mustache, raised his hand.

Mitchell gestured to the lanky man. "Yes, Richard. What would you like to say?"

Richard, who looked like he could be in his late forties, placed his hands together and leaned forward. "Following up on our meeting last night, I just want to say that I still think you're not understanding what it is we're going through."

Some of the other men slightly nodded.

Richard continued, "You see, when you haven't struggled with addiction, it's hard to know what it's like. You keep telling us what we need to do, but you're not listening to how hard it is to do it."

Mitchell shook his head. "Richard, it seems like this is all we've been talking about for the last four weeks. We keep trying to get around to a solution, and you keep telling us we're not understanding your problem."

Richard glanced at the other men. "Exactly. We aren't connecting."

Sensing Mitchell's exasperation, Don interrupted. "We've been talking about the same problems for almost a month, and it isn't getting us anywhere. I feel like we've tried to be patient and listen, but it seems like we're going in circles."

"That's part of the process," said Richard. "It's taken years for most of us to get into these circumstances, and you can't expect us to get out of them in a few weeks."

Mitchell responded, "We're not expecting complete victory in weeks, but we're just looking for progress." Glancing around the room, he said, "Does anyone else want to share anything?"

A younger man, whose name was Billy, raised his hand. "I understand what you're saying Mitchell, and we appreciate you all opening up this ministry for us to get help. I do feel like Richard sometimes though, and I wonder if you understand how hard this is for us."

Some of the other men shared as well, but no one suggested a way to change things. After another hour of discussion, Mitchell dismissed the meeting, and the men went outside to begin work. As Richard passed Overcomer on the way out the door, she thought she noticed a slight grin on his face.

Mitchell led the group back to his house for further discussion. Once they had gathered in the living room, he said, "Now do you see what we're going through?"

"I do," said Clara. "That seemed like wading through a swamp with a hundred pounds on your back."

"I know," said Sandra. "Usually Susan and I only attend the weekly meetings, but most of the time that's how the discussion seems to go."

Clara placed her hand on Overcomer's shoulder. "What do you think about all of this? You've been quiet ever since the meeting."

"I've been pondering the situation and praying," said Overcomer. "Something isn't right about Richard. I don't see any evidence of someone who wants help. I've met people like him before. I do sense that others in the group want to change, but right now they seem to be following his lead."

Don nodded, "We've talked about this several times before, but we're concerned that if we confront Richard too hard, he'll walk away and several others will go with him."

"It's almost like we're trapped," said Mitchell, shaking his head.

Susan leaned forward. "I've got an idea. What if Overcomer shared her testimony at the meeting tonight? Maybe they need to hear from someone who's been where they're at and has come through it successfully."

Mitchell turned toward Overcomer. "How do you feel about that? I think it's time to do something different."

Overcomer rubbed her cheek. "I always enjoy giving my testimony, but I'm going to need some time to pray and prepare."

"We'll be praying for you," said Sandra.

20

LIVING WITH THE ENEMY

As the others left to go about their day, Esther and Overcomer went back to their room to pray together.

"Do you know what you're going to say?" asked Esther.

"I don't really. Please be praying for me. There's something that's not right about this whole thing."

"What do you mean?"

Overcomer looked out a window toward the ministry house. "I don't know yet."

Esther helped Sandra and Clara around the house, and all of them kept Overcomer in their prayers throughout the day. When evening came, they all gathered back at the ministry house.

Mitchell stood. "We're going to do something a little different tonight. I've asked Overcomer to share some of her experiences with addiction and what God has done in her life."

Everyone gave Overcomer their attention.

Glancing nervously around the room, she began. "First of all, I want to say that I admire each one of you for coming here and seeking help. That's the first step to solving any problem. There are many out there with worse problems than you who aren't willing to admit their struggle with addiction."

Some of the men had appeared stiff and rigid at first, but after hearing this, they seemed to relax.

Overcomer continued. "When I came to God, I came just as I was. There were some things that He instantly delivered me from, and there were other things that took time."

She turned a few pages in her Book. "Here is a verse that God used to minister to me right after I started on this Quest. 'I beseech you, therefore, brethren, by the mercies of God, that you present your bodies a living sacrifice, holy, acceptable to God, which is your spiritual worship.'"

Richard slightly grunted as he looked around at the other men.

Not letting anything distract her, Overcomer said, "When we come to God, we are completely dependent on His grace to save us, and afterward we are still dependent on this same grace to live out our Christian lives. But while we owe all of our effort and all of the results to grace, there is still a part for us to play. God initiates, but we must cooperate."

Richard squirmed in his chair and huffed as if to show the others how uncomfortable he was with what Overcomer was saying.

Keeping her focus on the men who showed interest, Overcomer continued. "Cooperating with the grace of God means that we surrender and offer our lives as a continuous living sacrifice. We give up the right to live as we choose because we recognize that we are bought with the precious blood of Christ. As a result, we seek to live in a way that is pleasing to Him."

She glanced over at Clara who was smiling and nodding. Overcomer held up a finger. "One thing I had to learn was not to make excuses or blame others for my problems."

Richard started shaking his head and tried to make eye contact with the men near him.

Overcomer closed her Book. "Others can either be a hindrance or a support in your life, but I had to come to grips with the reality that I alone determined whether or not I would surrender to God and turn from my sin."

There was a moment of silence as most of the men were thoughtfully pondering what Overcomer said.

Suddenly Richard raised his hand and then started talking before anyone called on him. "Well that's all nice and everything for you to come in here and lecture us, but maybe it's not that easy—"

Mitchell interrupted. "You know, Richard, I think you've talked enough. I think it's time to hear from someone else."

Billy slowly raised his hand. "I appreciate what was said here today. It's what I needed to hear. I've wanted help, but at the same time, I've also wanted someone to blame. I guess it became easy to blame those who were trying to help us. I'm sorry about that, Mitchell, Don, Sandra, and Susan."

Several men nodded, and they began to share how they too needed to start taking more responsibility for their problems. Richard sat quietly with his arms folded, rolling his eyes at some of the comments. At the end of the meeting, there was a time of prayer, and several men took the opportunity to confess their shortcomings and struggles to God.

When the meeting dismissed, most of the men approached Overcomer to shake her hand or thank her for what she said, while others approached Mitchell to repeat how sorry they were. At last Mitchell, Sandra, and the others said goodnight and left. When they were outside, they each hugged Overcomer and thanked her for sharing.

Don said, "That was exactly what we needed."

"I agree," said Mitchell.

Overcomer glanced back at the ministry house. "I'm so glad God could use me. It felt like I was in a wrestling match the whole time though."

"I know," said Sandra. "I could feel it too."

Sandra took Mitchell's arm as they strolled toward their house. "Richard wasn't too happy, but maybe he'll get the breakthrough he needs as well."

After returning to Mitchell's and Sandra's, Esther and Overcomer settled into their room. As they lay down to go to sleep, Overcomer thought she heard something coming from the direction of the ministry house. She jumped out of bed and peered through the window.

Sitting up, Esther said, "What is it?"

Overcomer pressed her face closer to the window. "It looks like someone is leaving the house, and I think it's Richard."

"Why would someone be going out at this time of night? Does he have his backpack? Is he running off?"

"No, he isn't carrying anything." Overcomer ducked down. "He keeps glancing around as if he's making sure no one is watching." After a moment she inched higher and peered out again. "Now he's heading toward the woods. Hold on. Someone is just outside that wooded area and appears to be waiting for him."

She backed away from the window and grabbed her clothes off the dresser.

"What are you doing?" asked Esther.

"Something hasn't been right since the first time I heard him speak. I want to find out what's going on."

"That could be dangerous," said Esther. She sat up and swung her feet on the floor. "But if you're going, then I'm going with you. Can we get close and stay out of sight?"

Overcomer quickly buttoned up her blouse. "I believe so. We only have to get close enough to hear what they're saying."

Esther and Overcomer got ready and then crept outside and around the back of the house. They snuck down a bank, keeping out of sight until they were close enough to hear.

Someone with a gruff, angry voice said, "What's been going on?"

Richard replied, "Everything was going fine until today. I've been able to keep things off track since I arrived, and I could sense the ones doing the ministering were frustrated with me."

"So what happened?"

"Some new people came in last night," said Richard, "and there was this young woman who shared her testimony. She directed the men to focus on their responsibility for their addiction rather than blaming others, and some of the men were affected."

"You let a girl get in your way!" said the rough, angry voice.

Richard held up his hand. "Now hold on. It was just one meeting. I can still do what I've always done. These men aren't that far along, and one night of victory isn't going to be enough. Give me a day or two, and I'll get things off track again."

"You better," said the gruff voice. "We paid you a lot of money to stop this ministry. We can reveal ourselves and go on the attack, but it's far better if we can destroy it from within."

"I'll take care of it," said Richard.

"You better. You know how the Master feels about failure."

Richard sneaked back to the ministry house, and the other figure disappeared into the woods.

Overcomer and Esther waited a few more minutes to make sure they were alone, then crept back to their room.

"Can you believe that?" exclaimed Esther.

Overcomer shook her head. "I knew something was up, but that surprised even me. The enemy must see this ministry as a significant threat."

"We have to tell everyone about this."

Overcomer took off her shoes. "Yes we do. First thing in the morning."

As soon as everyone was awake and stirring, Overcomer asked Mitchell if he would invite Don and Susan over so she and Esther could share some important information with them. When everyone was gathered at the kitchen table, Esther and Overcomer told them what happened the night before.

After listening to the account, Don slapped the table. "How could we not have seen this?"

"I should have known something wasn't right," Mitchell said as he stood up and paced around.

"It's okay," said Sandra. "We were all trying our best to be loving and caring. Sometimes that's the price you pay when you make yourself vulnerable."

Mitchell took a deep breath. "That's true, but we've got to learn how to continue to be loving and caring without allowing people like Richard to take advantage of us. It isn't just us who were affected. It was all those other men who really do want help."

Don stood up and grabbed his hat. "I know what I want to do now."

Mitchell loudly exhaled. "I think we're thinking the same thing. We're about to have one less occupant of our ministry house." He put his hand on Sandra's shoulder. "Pray for us. We know what has to be done, but something like this is never easy."

When Mitchell and Don arrived at the house, the men had just finished their morning chores. Mitchell gathered them and explained what Overcomer and Esther overheard the night before. All the other men stared angrily at Richard.

"What is this?" said Richard, throwing up his hands. "I've been here all this time, working hard and doing everything I could to help everyone else. Just because I don't always agree with Mitchell and Don is that any reason to bring in these new people to lie about me?"

Billy sat up. "I don't think you've been working all that hard. In fact, I've seen you do some things that are hurting our vegetable crop. I hadn't wanted to say anything because I thought it could be an accident, but now everything is making sense."

"What are you talking about?" said Richard. "I'm always the first one out to the garden and the last one to leave."

"That's true," said another man named Todd, "but I've seen you putting something in the seed buckets when I've gotten out there almost as early as you, and once or twice I looked out after I left, and I thought I saw you kicking around at the tomato vines."

Richard stood up. "These are all lies. You're letting that girl affect your thinking."

"That will be enough," said Mitchell as he faced Richard. "You need to pack up your stuff and get out."

Richard stormed upstairs and quickly gathered his belongings. As he was about to leave the house, he turned and gave everyone an evil look. "Have it your way. I was actually protecting all of you. You're going to be stopped one way or the other. By the time this day is over you're going to wish those girls hadn't heard a thing."

Richard slammed the door and marched toward the woods.

Don glanced over at Mitchell. "What do you think he means."

Mitchell pointed outside. "I think someone out there is planning to attack."

"Most of the men here are not battle-tested. Can we get them ready in time?" asked Don.

"We're going to have to."

The majority of the men were new to the Quest, and although they had received their armor, most had never used it in a major battle with the enemy. Mitchell and Don spent all that morning training them on the use of their Sword and Shield. After training until noon, they took a short break for lunch. While they were eating, three men were assigned to keep watch outside the ministry house at all times.

Overcomer and Esther ate lunch with James and Clara while Mitchell, Don and their wives ate lunch with the men.

Clara finished a bite of her sandwich. "What do you think this battle is going to be like Overcomer?"

"I don't know for sure. The men who are receiving ministry will need to fight for their freedom, but we will be there to support them.

It will be difficult, but they can do it."

James took a drink of tea. "I'm sure that's what Mitchell and Don are preparing them for."

After finishing their lunch, they headed toward the ministry house to join the others.

Mitchell addressed the assembled men on the practice field in front of the house. "I must take responsibility for allowing Richard to disrupt our ministry the way he has. I thought I was being loving and caring, but I was really being selfish. Truly caring about people is being willing to tell them what they need to hear even if it risks their disapproval."

"I think I fell into that way of thinking too," said Don. "We want to show you God's love and compassion, but we also want to help you see the problems in your life so you can take them to God and find answers."

Billy raised his hand. "We all have some responsibility in this. We didn't have to follow Richard's lead, but we did because it was a convenient way to avoid dealing with our sin."

Suddenly, the crackling of sticks emanated from the woods. Believing it to be enemy attackers, Mitchell instructed all of the men to line up, then he and Don took their positions in front. Overcomer, Esther, and Mitchell's parents spread out behind the men.

A burly figure emerged from the woods. The creature had the shape of a man, but the face was like a bulldog. It also had a large tail that swung back and forth.

Overcomer pointed toward the creature. "That is a Mythos. They linger around people trapped in addiction."

"Why haven't I seen one of them before?" asked Todd.

"Because," said Overcomer, "they don't show themselves until you're ready to fight for your freedom."

The muscular Mythos strode toward them carrying a tall cup. He took a long drink, then said, "Hello gentleman. It's a nice time for a drink, wouldn't you say?" After gulping down the rest of his beverage, the Mythos continued, "Now let me explain what's about to happen, so you understand your options. There's a lot more of my kind just inside those woods, and in a few minutes, things are going to get very ugly. However, if you join us, there's a large table set up on the other side of those woods with as much ale as you can drink.

Now, what sounds better? Do you want to enjoy some nice, relaxing . . . refreshments, or do you want to be beaten and bruised, then watch us tear down your little house."

Billy shouted at the Mythos, "I'm done with that kind of life. I came here to get free!"

"Ah, well, it's just the same to us," said the Mythos. "We rather enjoy handing out the beatings anyway. We've beat on all of you at one point or another. You were just too drunk or too high to realize what was happening."

The Mythos put his finger to his lips and whistled. At once ten more just like him stepped out of the woods, all carrying wooden beams four feet long and six inches around. One of them came up to their leader and handed him his weapon.

Throwing down his cup and grabbing the thick club, the leader said, "Well, let's get started."

The Mythos spread out, and Mitchell directed the men to do the same. Then the leader threw his hand forward, signaling for the attack to begin.

Mitchell shouted, "Raise up your Shields and get ready men!"

The Mythos stalked forward. Two of them targeted Mitchell, and two others attacked Don. Each of the other men were locked in a battle with one of the Mythos. Sandra and Susan joined their husbands, and all around wood crashed against Shields, and Swords struck the Mythos.

Clara shouted to Overcomer. "Should we help?"

Overcomer kept a close watch on the battle. "Not yet. This is their fight. If we have a role to play, God will show us when it's time."

The Mythos pressed the attack. They taunted the men, bringing up all their failures. Some of the men looked discouraged and began fighting defensively.

Overcomer yelled out, "If you have confessed your sins and turned toward God in repentance, then He has forgiven and cleansed you from all the filth that went with that sin. Do not allow your enemy to bring up what God has forgotten."

Fighting harder, the men swung their Swords more forcefully. The leader of the Mythos stood back and watched. After thirty minutes of fighting, the Mythos were clearly losing. Mitchell and Sandra finished off both Mythos that had attacked them, and Don and Susan had knocked theirs out as well. Seeing that the battle was not going well, the leader skirted the battlefield and approached Mitchell from the left.

Sandra yelled, "Watch out!"

Mitchell ducked just as a wooden beam sliced over his head.

Growling, the leader said, "If you want a job done right, sometimes you have to do it yourself."

Mitchell gestured for Sandra to step back, and he motioned for Billy to draw in closer. Fresh off his victory over one of the other creatures, Billy stepped forward.

The massive Mythos smirked. "Oh, so you want to send in a boy to do a man's job. I'm okay with that. He needs to learn early in life that there are some things that can't be beaten."

Again and again, the leader swung his stick at them—the force of the blows rattling their Shields.

The Mythos jabbed at Mitchell, driving him back several feet and then turned toward Billy. "You can't beat me. You know you want a drink right now. You want it so bad you can taste it. There's still time to join me."

Raising his Sword, Billy shouted, "I will stand fast in the freedom in which Christ has made me free!"

Billy's Sword sliced through the air and landed on the leader's shoulder.

The creature grabbed his wounded arm. "You'll pay for that!" He cocked his arm and swung his club at Billy's head.

Billy ducked, then came up swinging. He struck the leader on his right arm, then connected with another blow to his stomach.

Doubling over in pain, the leader glared at Billy with contempt. Mitchell dashed into the fight and brought his Sword down on the Mythos' neck. The leader went to his knees and dropped his club. Billy slammed his Shield into his forehead and knocked him out.

By this time, the other men had defeated all the other Mythos, and the creatures lay unconscious on the ground.

Mitchell shouted to the men, "Let's get some rope and some poles. We'll tie these creatures up and carry them to the other side of those woods. I'm anxious to see what's out there."

After they had all the Mythos tied up and stretched out on the poles, the men carried them through the woods. As they emerged on the other side, they saw long tables set up with tall pitchers of ale. Billy, Todd, and the other men began smashing the tables and the pitchers. The men whooped in victory, and everyone was giving each other high fives.

Off to the side, where they'd left him, the leader of the Mythos began to awake. Still groggy and trying to free himself from the ropes, he snarled, "You think this is over. It's only beginning." He raised his head and shouted, "UNLEASH THE KRAKEN!"

About a hundred feet away was a large mountain with a tall rocky cliff. The rock wall suddenly began to break away from the mountainside, and it took shape as if it was coming alive. A large creature in the form of a giant gorilla emerged. As it stepped out, it let out a terrible yell and beat its chest with its rock fists.

Clara grabbed Overcomer's arm as the creature started toward the men. "Do you know what that is?"

Overcomer held her Sword and Shield tight. "Yes, it's the Kraken of Addiction. Before someone can live in victory over their cravings, they must defeat this enemy."

"But how?" said Esther. "It's solid rock."

"If it cannot dominate you," said Overcomer, "then you've defeated it in your life. There will be smaller battles still ahead, but once you stand up to the Kraken and refuse to be dominated, you can live in victory."

Overcomer moved forward. "Men, consider yourselves to be dead to this sin of addiction. Your old man has been crucified with Christ with all of its passions and lusts. Since you have been raised to a new life in Christ, sin can no longer dominate you if you choose to resist it."

The men from the ministry house took their places facing the mountain, and Overcomer and the others stood back. The ground shook as the Kraken approached.

"What do we do," yelled Billy. "That thing is too big to fight."

Overcomer yelled back, "Having done all to stand, Stand! Sometimes it's not about how hard we fight, but how firmly we resist. Plant your Shoes of the Gospel firmly into the ground, knowing it's by grace through faith that you stand. And hold up the Shield of

Faith, placing your hope in God's strength and not your own."

The men dug in with their Shoes and held up their Shields. The Kraken screamed a frightening scream as it brought its massive rock fists down on top of them. Their knees buckled, but they held steady. Again, the Kraken raised its fists and beat down on the men. Thrusting out their Shields, they once again held off the blows from the Kraken.

Billy yelled, "Don't give up men! No matter how fierce addiction presses down on top of you, resist with all your might, knowing that God is fighting with you."

Again and again, the Kraken tried to break through their Shields, but they would not give up.

Seeing that the men were resisting to the point of exhaustion, Overcomer called to Mitchell. "Now is the time for us to join them. We can't fight someone's addiction for them, but sometimes they need others to stand with them during difficult times of temptation."

Esther, Mitchell, Sandra, and the rest joined Overcomer and stood with raised Shields next to the men. Each time the Kraken landed a blow, it appeared some of its rocky exterior chipped off. After letting out a terrible scream and beating down on them one more time, the Kraken retreated toward the side of the mountain, then disappeared into the rock wall once again.

All the men collapsed onto the ground.

Mitchell grabbed Billy's arm. "I'm proud of you." He looked around at all the other men. "I'm proud of all of you. Saying you want help is one thing, but being willing to stand firm against the toughest moments of temptation is what beats this enemy. In that quiet moment when you simply refuse to take that drink, you are winning a mighty battle."

Billy gathered himself and marched over to the leader of the Mythos. "I guess you don't have much to say anymore do you?"

The leader let out a grunt. Mitchell gave the order to roll all of the Mythos into a deep pit.

"Will that end them?" asked Billy.

"I don't think so," said Mitchell, "but it will certainly give them a painful ride to the bottom."

Both laughed. Next, they picked up the poles holding the other Mythos and rolled them into the pit.

That evening they had a special time of celebration to give glory to God. One by one, the men talked about the freedom they felt, and the boldness they now had to face their addictions. Everyone felt they'd experienced a breakthrough. They lay down to sleep that night with a sense that the ministry had just reached an important turning point.

The next morning as Esther and Overcomer prepared to leave, Clara took them by the hand. "I'm so glad we met you two. Thanks for all you've done."

Overcomer smiled. "I'm thankful that God was able to use us to help. I know this is going to be a successful ministry."

James put his arms around his son and daughter-in-law. "We'll stay on a few more days, and then we'll head back home. We expect to keep getting letters of course."

Mitchell laughed. "Of course, and I expect the tone to be much better now. It's never going to be easy, but we're going to stay on top of things rather than allowing them to push down on top of us."

After Esther and Overcomer had said goodbye to everyone, they started out on their path once again. They traveled and camped for two days, then came upon a mountain trail. They trekked up the steep passageway for a mile, then it wound around a bend and stopped.

Suddenly, Esther's eyes widened, and she pointed in front of her. Frightened and alarmed, they stared at a giant spider web blocking their path.

Esther reached for her Book, as an icy wave washed over her. "Please tell me we don't have to face the spider that created that thing!"

21

THE WEB OF DECEIT

Esther pointed toward the giant web, which hovered a few feet above the ground. Thick pine trees anchored it at each corner. The weave was flat and spread out over a hundred feet like a large trampoline. "Have you ever seen anything like it?"

Overcomer took a step forward. "I don't think I have, but like you, I'm concerned about how big the spider is that built it."

The faint sound of whimpering came from the middle of the web. Esther and Overcomer cautiously approached. When they came to the edge of the web, they saw a deathly pale young woman rolled up in the web from her feet to her neck. She was unable to move, and a look of hopelessness peered from her eyes.

Overcomer quickly glanced around and surveyed the area. Not seeing any enemies, she stared at the woman ensnared by the webbing. "How did you get trapped here?"

"I'm Lucy," she said, though talking was clearly a struggle. "I was traveling alone, and one day I got off my path. I tried to find it again, but somehow I got tangled up in this web. You two need to get out of here. The Tarok will be back soon, and you don't want to meet her."

"What is a Tarok?" asked Esther.

A deep fear gripped Lucy's eyes. "The giant spider that built this web. Get out of here now while you still can."

Overcomer shook her head. "We're not going to leave you here."

She started to climb up on the web, but Esther reached out and grabbed her arm. "Won't we be trapped just like she is?"

"No," said Overcomer. "Our shoes will allow us to walk on the web without getting stuck, and the rest of our armor will protect us as well."

She stepped up on the web, and Esther followed. They made their way toward Lucy and knelt to examine the wrapping that was all around her. Suddenly, a humming sound vibrated through the air, and the giant web quivered.

"Run!" exclaimed Lucy.

Overcomer glanced around. "There's nowhere to hide. Grab some of this webbing, and let's roll ourselves up like we've been caught."

"Won't we be easy prey for this enemy?" said Esther.

"No, the spider lets the web do all of its work. As long as it feels we're bound up and can't move, it won't see us as a threat. And like I said, our armor will keep us from getting stuck."

As the humming grew louder, a giant spider sprang around the corner and came straight toward them. The Tarok's body was bright red while its face and legs were black. Long fangs protruded from the spider's mouth, and it hummed and skipped along the web as it approached. It was bigger than they had imagined—even bigger than all three of them put together.

Pausing to look at its new prisoners, the Tarok said, "Well what do we have here. Fresh food I see. I've only been gone an hour, and I come back to find not one, but two more tasty morsels wrapped up in my little web. I do hope I can space you two a few days apart though. I'm trying to watch my figure, and I fear eating both of you on the same day would just ruin my diet."

Creeping over a little closer to Esther and Overcomer, the Tarok's fangs swished back and forth, and an evil smile came on its face. "Would you two like to introduce yourselves?"

They stayed silent.

The Tarok said, "That's okay. Soon you'll want to tell me everything. You'll tell me your names, your parent's names, and just about everything you've ever done, all in an attempt to convince me to let you go. Of course, it won't work, but when someone is desperate, they'll try anything. Take Lucy here for example. She was quiet at first, but now I think I know her whole life story."

Lucy faintly whimpered, "Please let us go."

"Oh dearie, you know I can't do that, but what's truly a shame is that you haven't even admitted how you got trapped here in the first place. I bet you told your two new friends that you just wandered in here. Now we both know that isn't what happened, don't we? Oh, what a tangled web we weave, when we decide to deceive." The Tarok raised one of its legs to its chin. "Or at least I think the saying goes something like that. It's not like I actually read it out of a book. Whoever heard of a spider that reads? What a silly notion."

"But please, I'll do anything," said Lucy.

"It's too late for all that. You just settle down. By the looks of your skin I'd say you'll be gone by tomorrow, and then you'll make a nice meal."

Turning toward Esther and Overcomer, the Tarok said, "I'll have to wait on you two for a few days. I don't eat my food while it's still moving. It gives me indigestion something awful. If you'll pardon me, I need to go put the finishing touches on my latest web. This isn't the only one I have, you know, and there are many other travelers who need to be trapped. Don't you worry though, I'll be back soon to wrap you up even tighter."

When the Tarok crawled off and was out of sight, Esther and Overcomer threw off the webbing and stood to their feet.

"We've got to find a way to save her," said Esther. "Can't we just cut her loose?"

Overcomer poked around with her Sword at the outside of the webbing that held Lucy. "I don't think so. This is wound so tight we'll first need to loosen it at least a little."

Esther put her hand on Lucy's forehead. "We're going to find a way to help you."

"I don't think you can," said Lucy. "You heard the Tarok. I've only got one more day left. I'm so weak there's nothing I can do to help."

Overcomer stared into her eyes. "What did that spider mean by implying you haven't been honest about how you got here?"

Lucy sighed. "I guess I've always known, but I haven't wanted to admit it. It started with one lie and then another and another."

"What did you lie about?" asked Esther.

"I lied about everything, but it started out with small things. When I turned thirteen, I lied to my parents about where I was going and who I was staying with. My parents suspected something wasn't right, and after catching me in a few lies, they started confronting me about my behavior."

"That was the caring thing for them to do," said Overcomer. "It's much easier for parents to ignore those kinds of problems so they can keep their children's approval."

"I know that now," said Lucy. "But at the time I was angry at them. When I turned sixteen, I ran away. I wandered around from place to place and anytime someone would ask me why I was living on my own, I told them that my parents kicked me out for no reason. At first, this worked, and I received lots of sympathy, but soon I got caught lying to the people that were helping me. They too confronted me, and I ran off again."

Overcomer sat down at Lucy's feet. "I think I'm starting to see the pattern. I spent years of my life trying to deceive others so I could get my way, but what I found out later was that the person I deceived the most was myself."

Lucy sniffed back tears. "I know that now. I wish I could go back and do it all over. I miss my parents. I'd give anything to see them one last time to tell them I love them, and that it wasn't their fault."

Esther put her hand on Lucy's cocooned body. "It's not too late. As long as you have breath, you have the opportunity to repent."

Lucy used what little strength she had left to force out her words. "I don't know. I've told so many lies. I've even lied to God, though I understood that He knows all things."

Overcomer opened her Book and read, "LORD, who will abide in your tabernacle? Who will dwell on Your holy hill? The one that walks uprightly, practicing righteousness, and who speaks the truth in their heart."

Overcomer said, "The first person we have to be honest with is ourselves. When we're willing to speak the truth in our own hearts, then we can come before God and be truthful with Him as well. Let us pray with you."

"Okay," said Lucy. "If this is my last day, then I want to tell God how sorry I am for everything."

Overcomer reached over and put her hand next to Esther's on Lucy's forehead. "Dear Lord, you forgave me of so many things. You said in Your word that if anyone is caught up in a fault, those of us who are living by your Spirit should seek to restore them. You said that we should do this with an attitude of humility knowing that we too are subject to the same temptations. It is only by your grace that I am not caught up in this same web."

Lucy struggled for breath and prayed. "Oh Lord Jesus, I have sinned against you. You shed Your blood for the forgiveness of my sins, and instead of living in thankfulness for what You did, I only cared about living to myself. Please forgive me and cleanse me."

As soon as Lucy finished praying, a loud ripping sound echoed around them. The webbing surrounding Lucy had started to come apart, starting at her feet.

Overcomer raised her Book. "Let's get her out of this!"

Using their Swords, Esther and Overcomer cut away the rest of the webbing material from around Lucy's body until she was completely freed. Still being weak from all the time she had been wrapped up, Lucy could barely move. Esther and Overcomer knelt down beside her and helped her sit up.

"I feel free!" said Lucy in the loudest voice she could muster.

Slowly she raised her hands, giving praise to God. While they were rejoicing the web suddenly began to shake.

"Oh no," said Lucy. "She's back, and I don't have enough strength to run away with you."

Overcomer put her hand on Lucy's shoulder. "We're not leaving without you. Begin reciting every verse from God's word that you know and pray for strength as we fight this Tarok."

Esther and Overcomer stood up and held out their Swords and Shields.

The giant spider appeared around the corner of the web, then came to a sudden stop when it spotted them. "What's this! You escaped? But how?" Then the Tarok noticed that Lucy was also free. "Treachery! You two must have helped her. She was so bound up in her own lies that she should never have been able to get free."

Overcomer thrust out her Shield. "Anyone who is willing to take responsibility for their sins can be set free!"

"I see," said the Tarok. "Well, being free of that web and being free from my fangs are not the same things. I shall have my revenge on all of you, and then I will wrap you up in my web and watch you slowly melt away."

The Tarok raised its front legs and simultaneously attacked Esther and Overcomer. They held up their Shields to block the sharp edges of the spider's legs, but the Tarok kept the pressure up so that they couldn't move out from behind their Shields. By thrusting out its fangs, the Tarok drove them backwards. It crept closer, positioning itself to inject them with its poisonous venom.

Esther retreated further. "If we don't do something soon, we're going to be flat on our backs."

Overcomer blocked another thrust of the Tarok's giant legs. "I know. We're going to have to take a risk."

Ducking as one of the spider's legs swept toward her head, Esther said, "I should have known you were going to say something like that."

As the Tarok launched another barrage of blows, Esther and Overcomer closed ranks and pushed toward the spider's head. In tandem, they struck with their Swords, finally landing blows on their enemy.

Stunned, the Tarok staggered back a step. "You dare to strike at me! My bite shall be even worse now!"

Esther and Overcomer pressed forward, making themselves even more vulnerable. The Tarok raised its hairy front legs high and then drove them straight down toward their heads. Esther and Overcomer both rolled out of the way seconds before the ends of the spider's sharp legs drilled down beside them.

The attack left the Tarok exposed, and Overcomer launched a counterattack with her Sword, slashing the bright red body of the spider. The Tarok rose in fury and bore down toward her with its fangs. Esther jumped into action to protect her friend and lunged at the face of the Tarok with her Sword. Just as the spider's fangs were about to slice through Overcomer, Esther's Sword struck it in the mouth.

Wounded and in pain, the Tarok was livid and determined to get revenge. With both of its targets close, the spider poked at them and searched for an opening. Esther and Overcomer swatted at its legs, but the giant spider patiently circled.

Suddenly one of the spider's legs swept Esther off her feet. Smiling an evil and vicious grin, the Tarok thrust its fangs toward her while keeping Overcomer at bay with its legs.

Overcomer yelled, "Get out of the way!"

The Tarok's fangs drove toward Esther's neck, but before they reached her skin, the giant spider jumped back. A Sword had seemingly come out of nowhere and pierced its body. The Tarok looked shocked as it stared at Lucy still holding the Sword. Overcomer glanced over her shoulder and saw Lucy let go of the Sword, then collapse in exhaustion. The spider moaned in anguish and stumbled backwards.

Determined to finish off their enemy, Esther and Overcomer quickly jumped up and thrust their Swords into the Tarok's head. The spider let out a shrill scream then fell back and closed its eyes.

Esther darted across the web and gave Lucy a hug. "Thank you, but how did you do that?"

Lucy gasped for breath, but she slowly recovered. "As I watched you two battle the Tarok, I prayed and asked God to give me the strength to help. I quoted every verse I learned as a child, and slowly I felt my strength returning. At the last place I stayed, a kind grandmother placed a Book in my backpack just before I left, so once I had enough strength to roll off the web, I searched for it. When I found it, I raised it until it became a Sword. I saw Esther was in trouble, so I lunged at the Tarok with all the strength I had."

Kneeling down beside Lucy and hugging her, Overcomer said, "Thank you. You are destined to be a mighty warrior. Do not let your past mistakes define you. Today is a new day, and you will be different from this point forward."

Overcomer and Esther crept closer to the Tarok's body to make sure there was no more danger. Convinced it was dead, they signaled to Lucy that she could safely retrieve her Sword. At once she pulled it out of the spider's corpse.

She stared at the web. "I can't believe I didn't see this before. When I was first approaching, I didn't see anything until I was too caught up in it to move."

Overcomer nodded. "That's because you can't see the web of destruction that deceit is weaving until it's too late. Now that your eyes are open and you're no longer practicing deception, you can see the danger that's in front of you."

Lucy took a step forward and began slicing at the giant web with her Sword. "Lying lips are disgusting before the LORD, but those who speak truthfully are His delight."

Forcefully swinging her Sword, Overcomer shouted, "Therefore, putting away lying, let each one of you speak the truth with his neighbor."

Esther joined them, slicing through the web with her Sword. "Do not lie or speak falsehood to another, for you have put off the old man and its sinful practices."

After they completely destroyed the giant web, they shouted and praised God. Overcomer glanced at the ground and saw that all of their paths were leading in the same direction. Together they started forward, and after traveling for a few miles, Lucy recognized that they were heading in the direction of her parents' home.

Esther and Overcomer accompanied her and watched the tearful reunion between the parents and their daughter. After repenting to her parents and talking for hours, she went into her room to see all the pieces of her armor laid out on her bed. She immediately put them back on, starting with the Belt of Truth.

Overcomer and Esther stayed with the family through that evening and most of the next morning. When they stepped outside with Lucy, they saw that their paths were leading away.

As they prepared to leave, Lucy gave them another hug. "Thanks for everything."

22

MS. CRANDLE

Esther and Overcomer resumed their journey, and soon they came upon a large, two-story home. When they stopped to admire the architecture, they heard someone singing. They peeked around the corner to see who it was. An older lady with a cheerful smile sang as she tended some flowers.

The girls glanced at each other, then stepped into the yard. "Hello."

At the sound of their voices, the lady turned toward them. "Hello. I'm Ms. Crandle."

Overcomer reached out her hand. "This is Esther, and I'm Overcomer."

Ms. Crandle shook their hands. "Did you come by to see Teacher?"

"Who is that?" asked Overcomer.

"I don't believe I've met anyone by that name either," said Esther.

"Most people who come this way are looking for him because he has so many wonderful things to show those who are on this Quest. He's not here at the moment, but he'll be back in a day or two. All the women who stop by stay at my home while they're visiting him, so you're welcome to stay with me until he comes back."

Esther nodded toward Overcomer and said, "We'd love to stay with you. May we help you with your work?"

Ms. Crandle smiled. "Sure you can. I have just a few things left to do, and then we can go to my house for some cold cider."

After helping Ms. Crandle weed some more flowerbeds, they all headed to her house—a lovely place decorated with lots of antiques and fine pottery. All of the curtains were hand-made, and on the backs of the furniture were pieces of crocheted fabric with verses from the Book woven in the pattern.

Ms. Crandle led them into the kitchen. Once they were seated, she poured them each a glass of apple cider. "I always enjoy hearing about the adventures of others on this Quest. I'm sure both of you have encountered many things on your journey so far."

Taking turns, Esther and Overcomer shared all of the exciting events they had experienced on their Quest. Ms. Crandle listened and smiled, seeing the hand of God on each of their lives.

When they were finished, Ms. Crandle shook her head in awe. "I must say, you've already had enough adventure for an entire lifetime. I can only imagine what else God has in store for you." She glanced over her shoulder, then quickly stood. "Why don't we go into the backyard. I have something I'd like to show you."

Following Ms. Crandle, the two girls went out back where a beautiful vegetable garden grew. The soil was a dark, rich brown, and there were rows of lettuce, peas, cucumbers, and onions. Each row looked like it had been freshly hoed and weeded, and all of the plants looked green and healthy.

"What a lovely garden," said Esther.

"Thank you," said Ms. Crandle. "It takes a lot of work though, and that's what I'd like to show you. What you're about to see is moving pictures that will look as if something is really happening, but it's not. However, the lessons you learn from these images are important."

She led them to the edge of the garden, where they saw two tomato plants growing in a separate patch of soil. One had bright green leaves with thick plump vines and was one of the finest plants they had ever seen. A few feet away another tomato plant grew beside it, but its leaves were yellow, the vines were thin, and it was wilted and bent over.

Soon they saw a gardener come by. He knelt next to the unhealthy tomato plant and began to prune some of the worst leaves. He then pulled out all the weeds from around it, mixed in a little fertilizer, and then carefully watered the soil. Finding a stake, he drove it into the ground next to the plant. Then he tied the vines to the stake so that the plant stood upright.

Ms. Crandle leaned over and whispered to the girls. "It will seem as if time is passing rapidly."

Soon it appeared as if the sun set and then almost as quickly rose again. The gardener came back and continued to work with the unhealthy plant. This happened several more times, but they noticed that while the gardener was paying special attention to the unhealthy plant, he was not doing anything to the one that originally looked so firm and vigorous.

The scene repeated several more times. Eventually what once had been a wilted and yellowed tomato plant was now healthy with lush green leaves and fat vines. But next to it, the plant that had at first been very pleasant was now brown and shriveled up. Time appeared to return to normal, and Overcomer and Esther were amazed at what they had seen.

Ms. Crandle held out her hand. "Let's go over and have a closer look."

They bent down and examined the plants. The one that had looked so unhealthy when they first came out was now producing firm red tomatoes.

Ms. Crandle reached out to touch the beautiful tomato plant. "Do you understand what you've observed?"

Esther nodded. "The plant that received the most care is the one that produced the fruit."

"That's right," said Ms. Crandle as she stood up. "In our spiritual lives, we must daily dig up the weeds of sin and surrender the unhealthy parts of our character to be pruned and removed. We must also receive a daily supply of nourishment from God's word. No matter where a Christian is in their walk with God, if they will do these things, then they will produce much fruit."

Esther dropped to her knees beside the tomato plant that had wilted. "After I graduated from a House of Knowledge, I was much like this plant at its beginning. I appeared to have it all together, but over time I neglected the hard work of staying vulnerable before God and allowing His word to prune me. I didn't think I needed that much work. I became over-confident, and then I was blindsided when the traps of the enemy came along. By the time I left the Camp of Sin, I looked a lot like this shriveled plant."

Ms. Crandle put her arm on her shoulder. "But you didn't stay in that condition."

Esther glanced up and smiled. "No, I didn't." She turned toward the bright green tomato plant. "I allowed the Holy Spirit to work in me and remove the weeds of self-righteousness and pride. It took time, but through God's grace I became a fruit-bearing plant again."

Ms. Crandle motioned for them to go back inside. When they sat back down at the kitchen table, Overcomer asked her about some of the different items in her house. Ms. Crandle seemed delighted to share the stories attached to her antiques. After a few minutes, she noticed that Esther was staring straight ahead and appeared to be deep in thought."

"You look like something is on your mind," said Ms. Crandle, reaching out to pat her hand.

"Oh," said Esther, shifting her gaze toward her. "Seeing all the hard work that the gardener was doing with the tomato plant, reminded me of how much work is involved in the Christian life." She appeared to drift off in her thoughts again.

"And...?" said Ms. Crandle.

Esther took out her Book and turned over a few pages. "I must admit that I've struggled with a particular passage where it seems like Jesus is saying that after all of our efforts, we are looked upon as just servants who've done our duty and nothing more." She read Luke 17:7-10.

Ms. Crandle turned to the same place in her Book. "Yes, that last verse does seem troubling, doesn't it. 'Even so, you also, when you have done all the things you've been commanded to do, say, we are unprofitable servants who have done only what is our duty to do.' "

Ms. Crandle gently squeezed Esther's hand. "This passage is not meant to show us how God looks at our efforts, but it's meant to show us how *we* should view our own efforts. We are not to see our works as gaining us favor with God. We only have favor with Him through His grace."

"That's helpful," said Esther. "Thank you."

"You're welcome. If we focus on our works, we'll either become discouraged when we feel they don't measure up, or we'll become prideful when we think they do. In either case, we're focusing on the wrong thing."

Ms. Crandle turned in her Book and read, "But by the grace of

God I am what I am, and His grace toward me was not in vain; but I labored more abundantly than they all, yet not I, but the grace of God which was with me."

Esther rested a finger on the side of her forehead. "So Paul worked hard, but yet he recognized that it was the grace of God that was actually accomplishing the work."

Ms. Crandle smiled and nodded. "That's right. All glory belongs to God. We should only boast in Him." Grasping her Book, she said, "If we tried to earn God's acceptance based on our works then none of us would be acceptable." She turned over a few pages and read, "But God, being rich in mercy, because of His great love with which He loved us, even while we were dead in transgressions and sins, made us alive together in union with Christ (for by grace you have been saved)."

They spent the rest of the afternoon helping Ms. Crandle with her garden, and then they had a wonderful supper together. Afterward, they spent time reading in their Books before going off to bed.

The next morning, they had a delightful breakfast of assorted fruits and cream toppings, while they chatted about gardening. Then they toured the property together, observing the surrounding fields and meadows along with the different animals that lived in this area.

When they stopped underneath a gnarled old oak tree to rest, Esther said, "Ms. Crandle, sometimes I wonder why we fall for sin. What makes it so attractive?"

Ms. Crandle motioned for them to sit down. "That's the kind of question we all ought to be asking. The most powerful allure of sin is the promise that we can be gods. This is what Satan and the fallen angels told themselves when they rebelled. Satan said that he would be like the Most High."

"I can't imagine how an angel living a perfect existence in heaven could make that choice," said Overcomer.

"It wasn't just angels who made that kind of a choice," said Ms. Crandle. "When God created man, He put him in a perfect paradise on earth. Satan knew that the most powerful temptation he could offer Adam and Eve was the same thing with which he himself had been tempted. Satan told them that if they would eat of the Tree of the Knowledge of Good and Evil, then they would be just like God."

Esther shook her head. "I don't understand. Satan must have

known he could not be like God, and Adam and Eve must have known even more that they could not be anywhere near equal to the Almighty God. What made them think they could?"

Ms. Crandle nodded. "That's true, but that's not what Satan was offering. When Satan said he would ascend to his own throne and be like the Most High, he was not trying to be bigger or more powerful than God. What he was attempting to do was establish his independence from God's authority."

"That's interesting, please go on," said Overcomer.

"When Satan asked Eve if God had told them not to eat of every tree in the garden, he was not questioning whether or not God had actually said these words. What he was doing was asking Eve to think about why God said them in the first place. He was poking and prodding to see how Eve would respond to the reminder that God had established certain limits and she couldn't do as she pleased. Satan was baiting his hook in order to tempt them to establish their independence from God's authority."

"I don't think I've heard that before," said Esther.

"Let me give you an example you can relate to. What if you had lived next to a wide rushing river as a small child, and for your own safety your parents wouldn't let you go out of your yard. Then one day as you grew older, a neighbor child came by and made fun of you and said, 'Did your parents really say that you can't go out of your yard?' And you replied that not only could you not go out of your yard, but you weren't even allowed to go beyond your front porch."

Esther said, "That sounds like a child who is resentful of their parents and wants to make them sound more strict and austere than what they really are."

"Yes, and what would cause that kind of attitude?" asked Ms. Crandle.

"Rebellion," said Overcomer.

Esther quickly flipped over in her Book to read the account of Satan's temptation of Eve in the garden. When she finished, she looked up and said, "Ah, now I see what you're getting at. When Satan asked Eve what God had said about eating from the trees, Eve answered that not only had God said they should not eat from the forbidden tree, but they couldn't even touch it, or they would die. God never said anything about not touching any of the trees. Eve added that."

Ms. Crandle smiled. "That's correct. When Eve gave that answer, Satan knew he had her. Satan was appealing to the very same rebellious attitude that he had when he fell. He wanted to be independent from God, sitting on his own throne and being his own boss. You see the knowledge of good and evil was not the ability to tell right from wrong. Adam and Eve were highly intelligent beings who understood morality. The knowledge of good and evil was the ability to decide for themselves what was right and what was wrong."

"That makes sense," said Esther, "because Satan told Eve that when they ate from the tree, they would be like God knowing good and evil. No longer would God be able to tell them what tree they could eat from or not eat from, and no longer would He be able to set limits for them."

Ms. Crandle nodded in agreement. "But there is something that Satan left out. Declaring independence from God has terrible consequences. It produces spiritual and physical death."

Esther leaned back against the tree, deep in thought. "So that's why sin is so appealing. It offers us independence instead of being subject to God's rule."

Ms. Crandle said, "Rebellion is so deceptive. It promises us independence and freedom, but all it delivers is slavery."

"Thank you for sharing that," said Overcomer.

"You're quite welcome." Ms. Crandle took a deep breath and seemed to enjoy the nice cool breeze sweeping across the property.

When they had rested for a few more minutes, they continued their tour of the grounds. As they walked back toward the house, the sound of humming echoed in the distance. Soon they saw an elderly man walking merrily along and humming loudly.

Ms. Crandle hurried toward him, waving Esther and Overcomer to follow her. Calling out to him, she said, "Hello Teacher. Did you have a wonderful trip?"

"Yes I did, and I see that you have guests."

"This is Esther and Overcomer. They've been staying with me since yesterday. I told them that you would be back soon and that you could show them all the amazing things in your house."

"Sure, I would love to. We'll start first thing tomorrow."

Esther and Overcomer spent another night with Ms. Crandle, and then the next morning she walked them over to Teacher's house. They learned many wonderful lessons over the next two days, and on the third day, Teacher and Ms. Crandle accompanied them to Mount Sinai. After observing those trying to climb the mountain, Esther and Overcomer made their way through the Valley of Humility. They traveled on, discussing the many things they had learned over the last few days.

When they passed through a small wooded area, they emerged to see a vast open field. Standing in the center was a huge knight who must have been fifteen feet tall. The knight was covered from head to toe in dark grey armor, and he held a large staff at his right side. At the entrance to the field was a sign which read, "The Field of Dreams."

23

THE FIELD OF DREAMS

Staring with alarm at the giant knight, Esther said, "I don't know why this would be called the Field of Dreams."

"I don't either," said Overcomer.

Taking a closer look at the sign, they saw another, smaller line which read, "With God all Things are Possible."

They surveyed the area and observed that the field was in a gorge with high cliffs on both sides. The only way to continue on their paths was to go straight through the field.

Glancing to her left, Overcomer pointed out two tents that were set up at the far end. "Let's go introduce ourselves to the ones who are already here. Maybe they know more about this place."

Careful to avoid the knight, Esther and Overcomer made their way around the outside of the field, to the area where the others were camping. Two couples sat and talked together, but when Esther and Overcomer approached, the couples stood up.

A cheerful looking young couple walked toward them. The man wore glasses, and his clothes were neatly pressed. He placed his arm around the petite woman at his side and said, "Hello, my name is Nicholas, and this is my wife, Pam."

The second couple, both middle-aged and well dressed stepped forward. "And my name is Scott, and this is my wife, Julie."

Esther set her backpack down. "Nice to meet all of you. I'm Esther, and this is Overcomer. How long have you been camping here?"

Nicholas glanced at the others. "Pam and I have been here for three days, and Scott and Julie arrived two days ago."

Esther pointed toward the field. "Do any of you know what this field represents and why there's a giant knight standing in the middle of it?"

"That's what we've been talking about for two days now," said Pam. "We're not sure. All we know is that this is where God has brought us, and if we are to follow our paths, we must cross that field."

"Have you tried?" asked Overcomer.

"Yes," said Scott. "We tried yesterday. We marched out to the field and circled around the knight thinking all of us together could defeat him. But as soon as any of us came within reach, he struck out with his long staff and kept us from getting any closer. Even when we tried to approach from different angles at the same exact time, he was so fast that he knocked us all back within a matter of seconds."

Overcomer held out her Sword. "We've faced some powerful enemies along the way. I know that God would not have brought us here unless He intended for us to defeat this knight."

Julie nodded. "We all agree. We've been talking about the different enemies we've faced during our Quest, and God has been faithful each and every time. But what we've concluded is that God needs to do something within us before we can face this enemy. That's what we were talking about when you arrived."

Overcomer placed her Sword at her side until it became a Book. "It makes sense to have a plan before you attack."

Nicholas motioned toward their campsite. "Why don't you two join us? It looks as though God has brought you here for the same reason He brought us."

A fire pit had been set up outside the two tents. Esther sat on a log facing the field and said, "If this is a Field of Dreams, and we are being reminded that all things are possible with God, then what does this knight represent?"

"We don't know," said Pam, sitting down beside Nicholas. "When we tried to attack it, the knight didn't say anything. He just stood in one place and swung his staff."

Overcomer opened her Book and silently read some verses. "You said that when you fought him, he was too fast for any of you to successfully attack. What if this knight represents the impossible?"

Nicholas removed the spectacles he wore and took a handkerchief from his pocket to clean them. "That could be. There didn't appear to be any weakness that we could take advantage of. Nothing we tried, worked."

Pam sat forward. "So what do you do when you encounter the impossible?"

"Nothing is impossible," said Overcomer. "It just looks that way. If God has called us to do something that looks impossible, then we must expand our vision."

Esther said, "I think I understand what you're saying. We limit God by thinking according to how things look from our perspective."

Overcomer nodded. "We are used to limiting our dreams according to what we believe is possible, but what if we defined what was possible according to what we could dream?"

Esther flipped open her Book and read, "Behold, I am the LORD, the God of all mankind. Is anything too difficult for me?"

Julie snapped her fingers. "When Sarah laughed because God told Abraham that she would bare a son in her old age, God's answer was, is anything too hard for the LORD?"

Scott rested his chin on his folded hands. "With God all things are possible? I want to believe that, but it's difficult when I see something directly in front of me that looks insurmountable."

"Like that knight?" said Pam.

"Yes, exactly."

Nicholas sighed. "I want to believe all things are possible too, but when I see something like this knight, I think in terms of my inabilities and not God's abilities."

"I think that's something we all wrestle with," said Overcomer.

Julie, appearing to struggle, picked up a stick and threw it on the fire. "My problem is not that I don't believe God can do all things, but I don't know if He will do them for me. How do we know that our dreams are from God and not just something that we've imagined on our own?"

"That's a good point," said Overcomer, balancing her book on her knees. "It's easy to get into presumption instead of faith. Presumption is when we expect God to bless our dreams, but faith is when we expect God to bless His dreams for us."

Pam said, "I guess one of the challenges is figuring out which one it is."

Esther turned to another page in her Book. "Paul wrote to the Romans that as our minds are renewed, we are able to know what the will of the Lord is for us. It does seem that the more time I've spent in God's word, the better I am at distinguishing between God's will and my own."

Overcomer motioned toward the two couples. "What dreams do you feel God has given you?"

Nicholas grasped Pam's hand. "Well, we've dreamed about opening an orphanage someday."

Julie sat upright, her eyes widening. "Us too!"

"What's stopping you?" asked Overcomer.

Nicholas shook his head. "There's a lot involved. You have to have resources, then you have to build buildings, and then you have to make contacts with those who can refer children to you. After that, you have to hire more staff. I'm not sure we'd even know where to begin."

"I know," said Scott, tucking his handkerchief back in his pocket. "We've thought about all those things too. It seems like so much."

Pam raised her hand. "But what's stopping us from starting? It looks like God has brought our paths together for a reason."

"Yes," said Julie, "God has given us the dream in our heart, but we have to take the steps to bring that dream into reality."

Julie pulled out her Book. "Listen to this. 'And when you turn to the right hand, and when you turn to the left, your ears will hear a voice behind you, saying, This is the way. Walk in it.' " Setting her Book down, she said, "What if God has given us the vision for what we're to do, and He'll give us more guidance once we act on what He's already said?"

Scott nodded toward Nicholas. "You know, they're right. There's nothing stopping us from taking the first steps toward our goal."

Nicholas stood up and surveyed the field. "Now that we know why God brought us here, we just have to get by that knight so we can move forward."

Overcomer stood. "I believe we need to go face this enemy, and as we move toward it, let's expect more guidance on how to defeat it."

All six of them tapped their chest to reveal their armor, then raised their Books until they became Swords. They slowly marched toward the field. Nicholas and Pam stayed close together, as did Scott and Julie. Overcomer and Esther spread out on opposite sides. As they came close to the knight, he thrust out his staff toward each of them so fast his movement was a blur. They pulled up just short of where the knight's staff could reach.

Overcomer slid to her right, and her foot hit something in the ground. She stooped to see what it was and discovered a pole of some kind lying half-buried in the dirt.

"Come over here, everyone!" she shouted.

Gathering around, they examined what Overcomer had found. When they dug into the dirt, they discovered that the pole was long and slender.

Overcomer grasped one end. "I have an idea. It's impossible for us to get close enough to attack that knight from the ground, but what about from the air?"

"What are you thinking?" said Esther. "I hope it's not what I think you're thinking."

Overcomer smiled. "You're starting to get to know me."

"Someone let us know," said Scott.

Holding out the long pole in front of her, Overcomer said, "I'm going to take a running start toward that knight, and when I get to the extent of his reach, I'm going to stick this pole in the ground and vault myself into the air. Hopefully, I can land on that knight's head, and if I do, then you should be able to get close enough to attack."

"That sounds risky," said Julie.

Esther chuckled. "Welcome to what it's like to travel with Overcomer."

Esther and the two couples took places just outside the knight's range while Overcomer retreated several feet to give herself enough space to run up to her launching point. Holding out the pole, she sprinted toward the knight. Just as she was within range, she stuck the pole into the ground and launched herself upward. The knight tried to thrust his staff toward her, but Overcomer was just out of reach. Sailing upward, she released the pole when it came to an upright position. She then flew through the air and landed on the neck of the knight.

The knight shook himself, trying to knock her off, but she held on tight. Seeing that their enemy was occupied, the others raced forward, Swords in hand. Recognizing he was under attack, the knight swung his staff toward them, but they were closer now, and he was not able to attack with the same speed.

Lunging forward with his Sword, Nicholas shouted, "Oh Lord, I know that you can do all things, and nothing that you plan can be stopped."

Pam struck the knight on the back of its knee. "With God nothing is impossible!"

Jumping into the air to strike the knight in its side, Scott proclaimed, "Jesus said that all things are possible to those who believe."

Circling around beside Scott, Julie blocked the knight's staff while readying her Sword. "We serve the Lord our God! It is He who has made the heavens and the earth by His great power and mighty outstretched arm! Nothing is too difficult for Him."

As they continued to land blow after blow, the knight began to wobble.

Overcomer clung to her enemy with one arm while holding out her Sword with the other. She shouted, "If God is for us, who can stand against us!" She then plunged her Sword deep into the back of the knight's neck."

The knight threw down his staff and reached behind his head in an effort to grasp Overcomer. As he did, she withdrew her Sword and jumped down to the ground.

Now that the knight could no longer wield his staff, the others pressed the attack even harder, at last bringing the knight to its knees. They landed several more strikes with their Swords until their enemy crumpled to the ground. The knight twitched and bucked, then broke into several pieces. To all of their surprise, nothing was inside the armor.

Nicholas kicked at the breastplate. "That's odd. What was giving this thing its life?"

Picking up the empty helmet, Pam said, "I think it was us. Maybe God is showing us that we are the only ones that stand in the way of His plans for our lives. Once we are determined to go forward without letting anything get in our way, then there's nothing that can stop us."

Scott opened his Book and read, "Declaring the end from the beginning and from ancient times the things still yet to be done, saying, My counsel shall stand, and I will accomplish everything that I have purposed."

Julie rested a hand on Scott's arm. "God is going to bring to pass whatever He wills. The only question is, will we surrender as vessels to be used to help Him accomplish it."

"Amen," said Esther.

Everyone returned to the campsite together and packed up. Both couples saw that their paths were going in the same direction.

Julie said, "I guess it shouldn't come as a surprise that we'll be traveling together."

"No, it shouldn't," said Pam, smiling. She turned to Overcomer. "Where will you two go?"

Overcomer studied her path. "I'm not sure, but it appears we're going in a different direction."

Esther gave Pam and Julie a hug. "We'll be praying for you and the ministry God has called you to."

Nicholas replied, "We'll keep you two in our prayers as well."

The couples waved goodbye to them, as they started out on their paths.

When they had crossed the field, Esther turned to Overcomer. "What are your dreams?"

Overcomer chuckled. "A little house, with a little fence, with a few little ones playing out in the yard."

Esther stopped and gave her a look of surprise. "Really?"

"Yes, why do you seem so shocked? Do I not look like the mom type?" Overcomer said with a grin on her face.

Esther shook her head and smiled. "No, I think you would make a great mother. I just didn't take you for the little white-picket-fence type of girl. I see you traveling around the world, climbing volcanoes, scaling mountains, taking on giants, that sort of thing."

"I can still do some of that, but one day I want to have a family."

"You do realize that requires settling down and finding a husband, right?"

Overcomer laughed. "Yes, I do. What about you? What do you dream about?"

Esther gazed into the distance. "I want the same thing. I want to meet the man God has for me and raise a family together."

As they started forward again, Overcomer said, "That reminds me. I met a man that I think would be perfect for you."

Esther's eyes widened. "Really, who?"

"I met him when I fought the Giant of Shame. His name is Disciple."

"Disciple?" said Esther. "That's an interesting name."

24

DOWN BY THE RIVERSIDE

The next day Esther and Overcomer followed their paths through a meadow and into a grove of trees. Soon, they heard the loud sound of rushing water. When they emerged from the grove, they saw a wide river flowing with fast currents.

"How are we going to get across?" asked Esther.

Overcomer surveyed the river in both directions. "I don't know. This is where our path brought us, but there's no way we can cross here. Let's walk a little further downstream and see if we come across anything that will help."

They hiked down the bank of the river, and soon they heard voices. When they rounded the next bend, they came upon an inlet where a family of four were loading a raft.

As Esther and Overcomer drew closer, the mother called out to them. "Hello, which way are you traveling?"

Overcomer said, "We're not sure. Our path has brought us to this river, but we don't see any way to cross."

"That's because there is no way," said the father. "My name is Luke, and this is my wife, Katelyn. This little boy is our son John, and this little girl attached to my leg is Teresa. We're heading down the river on our raft, and you're welcome to join us."

Nodding toward Overcomer, Esther said, "Thank you."

After helping the family finish loading the raft, they climbed aboard. John and Teresa clung to their mom and dad, as the raft made its way down the rushing river.

When the current eased up a little, Overcomer turned toward Katelyn. "Where are you traveling?"

Katelyn stroked Teresa's reddish-blond hair. The little girl was just starting to relax now that the raft was not moving as fast. "We're going to a place Luke found a few months ago that he believes would be perfect to build an inn."

Guiding the raft with a long pole, Luke looked over his shoulder. "That's right. It's been our dream for some time to open up an inn for those traveling on this Quest so they would have a place to rest and be refreshed on their journey. Katelyn is the best cook ever, and we know that we can build one of the finest inns in the whole country."

"That sounds like a great idea," said Esther. "Camping can be fun and adventurous, but sometimes you just want to eat a home-cooked meal and sleep in a warm bed."

"That's true," said Katelyn. "And while Luke brags on my food, the truth is he is a great teacher of God's word. Our vision is to provide a place of comfort and rest while also ministering to the ones who stay there."

"Thank you, Katelyn," said Luke. "I've always wanted to teach from the Book, but I wasn't sure what my calling was. One day I was traveling to a job to build a house, and I came across this great area near the river that looked like a perfect place to build an inn. I asked around and found out that it was owned by a retired pastor. After I visited him and shared my vision, he said I was welcome to build an inn there. So I took the money I made from the job and ordered a bunch of lumber from a nearby mill."

Katelyn reached out to touch his arm. "I got a letter from Luke not long after that telling me that he had found the perfect place for our dreams to come true and that he was coming back to get me and the children. So as soon as he returned, we loaded everything up, purchased this raft, and prepared to set off."

"It seems it would take a lot of work to build an inn."

Luke nodded. "A few men who live nearby are going to help. We have enough saved up to live off of while we're finishing the construction, and just enough to pay the men who will help with the building."

The raft continued to move steadily downstream, and the further they went the wider the river seemed to become. After another thirty minutes, they came to a large dock.

"This is it," said Luke as he guided the raft toward the pier.

When he had secured the raft, they unloaded everything onto the nearby bank.

"Please let us help you carry some of these supplies," said Esther. She whisked to little John's side and helped him lift a basket filled with blankets and other bedding.

"That would be great if you don't mind," said Katelyn.

After they finished unloading everything, Luke assembled a large cart for transporting the heavier items, and Katelyn, Esther, and Overcomer carried the rest. John and Teresa followed close in behind holding their own little bags. The clearing where they planned to build the inn wasn't far, and within three trips they had everything at the site.

Katelyn surveyed the area. "Now we just need to get our tents set up, so we have someplace to keep our belongings dry in case it rains."

Luke unloaded the cart, then examined a pile of lumber that sat on the edge of the clearing. "This wood looks to be of great quality. I can't wait to get started building."

Esther glanced around the area. Her path and Overcomer's had led from the bank of the river to this spot, but now it stopped. "Overcomer," she called. She pointed to the ground.

Overcomer nodded. "It looks like we're supposed to stay here for now. I don't know how much help we can be, but we'll do whatever we can."

Katelyn picked up one of the bags. "You're welcome to stay for as long as you like."

After moving the heavier items into a large storage tent, Luke said, "I'm going on over to the place where I got the lumber and look up the men who are going to help. I'll let them know I'll be ready to start first thing in the morning."

Esther and Overcomer helped Katelyn sort out all their belongings, while also helping to keep an eye on the children. After that, they placed everything into different storage tents. By the time they were done, Luke returned, but instead of the excited spring in his step that he'd had when he left, he trudged toward them with his head down.

Katelyn slipped next to him and placed her hand on his shoulder.

"What's wrong?"

Luke sighed. "The three men who were going to help said they weren't coming near here."

"Why not?" asked Overcomer.

"They said there were weird sounds coming from near the river."

"What sounds?" asked Katelyn.

"I don't know," said Luke, shaking his head. "They said it sounded like high pitched wailing."

"Do you think it was wolves or some kind of animal they were hearing?" asked Esther.

"I don't think so," said Luke. "What they described didn't sound like any animal I've ever heard of."

Teresa and John came up next to their mother and grabbed onto each leg.

Putting her arms around the children, Katelyn said, "Is it safe to be staying here at night?"

Luke glanced around. "I believe this is where God called us, and I'm not going to be run off. If it turns out to be nothing, then I'll go back tomorrow and let the men know there isn't anything to be concerned about. If it really is something, then I know God will give us the strength to deal with it."

Overcomer stepped forward. "We're going to be staying here too."

With everything sorted out and put in its place, Katelyn started preparing the evening meal. Esther, Overcomer, and Teresa helped while Luke took John to gather plenty of wood to keep a fire going through the night. When their meal was ready, they sat down to eat. The sun was just starting to set, and by the time they were finished eating, darkness had descended over the whole area.

All six of them pitched in to do the cleanup. Suddenly, they heard loud splashing in the nearby river. Soon a high-pitched wailing drifted toward them from that direction. Katelyn quickly scooted John and Teresa into their tent, then the adults readied their Swords and Shields.

From the small wooded area just beside the river, a green glow pulsed as if a thousand fireflies were all flying together. Then a figure taller than Luke and as big as a bear emerged. A bright green glow hovered around the creature, illuminating its lizard face and long spiked tail. Within the wooded area, the trees rustled as if they were filled with the creatures, and high pitched wailing resonated from all around.

Thumping its large tail on the ground, the creature began to speak. "Consider yourself warned. You're trespassing on our territory. We will be back tomorrow night, and we expect all of you to be gone. If you're still here, then let's just say it will not be a pleasant experience for you."

The creature retreated into the woods, and by the sound of the rustling among the trees, all the others went with it. Soon a loud splashing sounded from the river, and then there was silence.

Grabbing Luke's arm, Katelyn said, "What are we going to do?"

Luke rubbed her hand. "I don't know yet. Let's get a good night's rest, and we'll talk about it in the morning."

"What if they come back?" said Katelyn.

"I don't think they're coming back tonight. If they wanted a fight, they could have had that already."

Everyone prepared for bed, but no one slept well that night. The next morning they all gathered for breakfast.

After they were seated, Katelyn said, "Luke, I don't want to leave either, and I know we have a lot of money invested in this project already, but we've got to think about the children too."

"I know," said Luke. "I've been thinking about it all night. We're going to take the rest of the morning to pray, and we'll make a decision by lunch."

"We'll pray as well," said Overcomer.

"Yes," said Esther. "I still feel like we were brought here with you for a purpose."

Overcomer stood and started toward the river.

Jumping to her feet, Esther said, "Where are you going?"

"I'd like to know where those creatures came from," said Overcomer, and she entered the woods.

Glancing toward Katelyn and Luke, Esther said, "She's got that look in her eyes. I'm going to go see what she's up to."

After catching up with Overcomer, Esther joined her investigation. At the edge of the river, Overcomer stooped to examine the ground. A large set of footprints came from the water, but there was no way anything could have crossed the river at that point. "It's as if all these creatures just appeared out of nowhere."

"We've seen a lot of strange things," said Esther, "but that creature we saw last night didn't look like its kind could live underwater."

"I know," said Overcomer. "That's why I wanted to come down here and explore. Are you ready for some adventure?"

Esther's eyes widened. "Oh no, what are you thinking?"

Overcomer smiled. "Let's go for a swim."

Before Esther could reply, Overcomer waded into the river, then dove underwater and out of sight. Esther quickly dove in as well, and soon they were both midways across the river. The sun was shining so brightly that they could easily see through the water. Within a few minutes, they spotted the opening to an immense cave.

Overcomer motioned for them to rise to the top for some air.

Surfacing, Esther said, "Did you see how big that cave is?"

"Yes, I did, and I've got a feeling that's the key to all of this."

"So now what?"

Overcomer grinned as she bobbed up and down, preparing to go back underneath. "Do you even have to ask?"

With a big gulp of air Overcomer dove underwater. Esther had no choice but to try to keep up. They swam toward the cave, and one at a time ducked through a narrow opening near the main entrance. Inside, the water leveled off about halfway to the ceiling. Esther and Overcomer stuck their heads up and breathed. They swam further into the cave, but the water receded. Soon they were wading, and by the time they were at the back of the cave, the water was barely up to their ankles.

They spotted another opening to the right. On the other side, a dark and dreary valley extended underground. Esther said, "What is this place?"

Overcomer stepped out of the cave. "I don't know, but I'm sure it's where those creatures came from."

They surveyed the area. No grass grew anywhere, but a few weeds sprang up here and there. Scattered throughout were several decayed tree trunks, and a rotten, sour smell permeated the air. A dim light illumined the surroundings, but it seemed to struggle to get through a dark mist hovering above, and if there was a sky in this land, it was not visible. Nothing they had seen in their world compared to this place.

Overcomer crept forward, and Esther stayed close behind. Soon voices drifted toward them from beyond a hill. Looking for a place to get out of sight, they quickly ducked into the base of a large hollowed out tree.

The voices drew closer and stopped not too far from where they were hiding. One said, "So do you think that group will have moved on by tonight?"

Another replied, "I don't know, but for their sake they better. We've kept watch over this area for a long time. Bandar has always said it would be a very strategic place. It's the perfect spot for those traveling the river to stop and cross to the other side. Bandar says one day they may have boats that can carry over a hundred people at once, all traveling down that river and looking for the perfect place to dock."

"I'm sure Bandar knows what he's talking about. Seems no one has discovered our little cave, so we can easily keep an eye on that place to make sure only those friendly to our cause can build there."

"Yeah, Bandar said it's the perfect place for a saloon. It could provide everything from drinking to gambling to prostitution, and just about anything else we want to offer."

"Let's just make sure nothing messes up our plans. That old pastor may not allow someone from our side to build there, but he won't be around that much longer, and we just have to keep it clear until he moves on. After that, we'll figure out a way to make sure it gets owned by the right person."

"Yes, that piece of land will always be just like this place, The Land of Darkness."

25

THE LAND OF DARKNESS

The lizard-like creatures departed, and soon their voices faded. Once Overcomer and Esther could no longer hear their footsteps, they emerged from the hollowed out tree.

Esther scanned the area. "I'm not sure what we can do about this. We are much too small a group to try and take on a whole army from another land."

Overcomer dusted herself off. "We can't fight them all, but maybe we can take away their access to the river. I have an idea, but we need to get back and talk to Luke and Katelyn. They're probably wondering what happened to us."

After swimming back to the other side, they told Luke and Katelyn everything they heard.

Luke stood. "When I asked the pastor for permission to build an inn here, I also asked him how he came to own this land. He said that when he retired he was looking through some old papers his grandpa left him and came across a deed for this area. He then moved and settled in an old house a few miles from here."

Overcomer nodded. "I don't like to speculate on these kinds of things, but I wonder if his grandpa was on the side of the enemy and never thought one of his grandchildren would become a Christian. He probably felt safe leaving it to him."

"That does make sense," said Esther, "and when these creatures found out it was now owned by one of their enemies, they decided to make sure it stayed clear until they could regain control of the property."

Katelyn joined her husband. "I don't like the sound of all this. If this land is that important, then they'll stop at nothing to keep us from building. I wonder why they just didn't attack us last night."

Overcomer glanced toward the woods. "I think they would like to keep people away without having to reveal themselves. In this instance though, they had no choice but to directly challenge us, but if they can scare us off without a fight, then that's in their best interest."

"But if we're still here tonight, then there will definitely be a fight," said Katelyn.

"So maybe we need to take care of this before tonight," said Overcomer.

Esther shook her head and smiled. "I should have known. What is it you're planning?"

Overcomer pointed toward the river. "If we can destroy that cave, then they can't come back and forth from their land to this spot."

Katelyn held out her hands. "But won't they just find another way?"

"Maybe," said Overcomer, "but I believe it's going to take them several months, if not years. By that time, you will have been operating your inn for quite awhile. That will be plenty of time for God to bring together many more people to help you."

"Reaching for her children, Katelyn said, "What about Teresa and John? They can't come along."

"Can they swim?" asked Overcomer.

"Yes, but–"

"Then they can come along. I know they're young, but they have armor too, and their angel will be with them."

Katelyn looked at Luke. "I don't know. This sounds dangerous."

Luke put his arm around Katelyn. "I believe God has a plan, and His plan will not be stopped." He grasped his wife's hand and turned to leave. "Let's all pray and read in our Books to get prepared, and then let's meet in an hour to talk about how we're going to do this."

Luke and Katelyn took the children and went into their tent.

Esther caught up to Overcomer. "Do you mind if I read and pray with you? I think we need to put our heads together on this one."

"I was thinking the same thing." Overcomer held up the tent flap, and they both went inside.

Taking a seat, Esther said, "I could tell you were uncomfortable on the other side of that cave."

"Weren't you?"

"Yes," said Esther, "but there was something different about your reaction."

Overcomer sighed. "You're right. I recognized that place."

"You've been there before?"

"Not exactly," said Overcomer. "I haven't actually seen it, but I've felt it. You became a Christian at an early age and grew up in a Christian home so you may never have felt what it was like to be under the control of the enemy. I lived in darkness for several years, and I still remember what it was like. When you are lost, The Land of Darkness is always around you, even if you can't see it. It's a place where there's no hope. You have to constantly convince yourself that everything is okay even though you know something isn't right."

Esther straightened. "I think I know what you're saying. When I looked into the eyes of the tavern girls, I saw despair and hopelessness. It was like they were trapped with no way out."

Overcomer nodded. "That's what it feels like. The only way to keep going is to try to escape the reality that surrounds you. Some people use addictions, while others pursue riches and success, and still, others just live day to day as if this temporary existence is all there will ever be."

"It's so sad that people are wandering around in darkness, and they don't even know it. There is an eternal existence that is available to them if they would just reach out and grasp it."

Overcomer opened her Book. "Jesus said, 'And this is the condemnation, that the light has come into the world, and men loved darkness rather than light because their deeds were evil. For everyone practicing evil hates the light and does not come to the light, lest his deeds should be exposed.' "

Esther replied, "So the Land of Darkness provides cover for their sin. As long as they can convince themselves that the light doesn't exist, then they are free to live as they choose."

"That's right," said Overcomer. "Not only is God light, but He's also an all-consuming fire. You cannot come to God unless you're willing to give up your sin. Satan wants to keep this area in darkness so that the light of the gospel will not shine through."

"How did these creatures get access to that cave, and how do we tear it down?"

Overcomer rested her index finger on her cheek. "I'm not sure, but I know there has to be an answer."

After an hour, they emerged from their tents, and soon Luke and Katelyn joined them.

Luke turned to Overcomer. "From what you've told us, we're going to have to find some way to destroy that cave."

Esther clasped her hands. "We agree, but we're not sure how to do it."

Katelyn noticed that all their paths were leading toward the river. "I think we need to head toward the cave and believe that God will give us more direction when we're there."

Luke said, "Let's pray together before we start out." Bowing his head, he prayed, "Dear Lord, we know that you are with us wherever we go. You were sent to this earth to give light to the ones sitting in darkness, the ones who are covered by the shadow of death. We want to be vessels through which the marvelous light of Your gospel may shine to all those who pass by. Give us the strength and wisdom to accomplish what You have already commanded."

Luke knelt in front of John and Teresa. "Do you remember the Psalm you learned from David?"

John nodded, "Yes father. 'For though we walk through the valley of the shadow of death we will fear no evil.' "

Teresa grabbed her father's hand. "For Thou art with us, Thy rod and Thy staff, they comfort us."

Katelyn hugged the children. "That's right. God is with us, therefore, we will not fear."

"Let's go," said Luke.

Everyone waded into the river and then dove under. Luke held onto John's hand while Katelyn held Teresa's. Overcomer and Esther led the way. When they reached the cave and waded toward the opening to the Land of Darkness, Luke and Katelyn saw firsthand what Overcomer had described. Only the faint glimmer of light filtered through the mist and everything in the land appeared as if it were only a shadow.

"Now what?" said Katelyn.

Overcomer glanced up at the ceiling. "There has to be a way to shut this down —"

Suddenly, loud voices erupted in the distance, along with the wailing sound they heard the night before.

Luke grabbed his Book, ready to raise it at any moment. "I didn't expect them to begin the attack until sunset."

"I didn't either," said Overcomer. "They must be preparing early."

Katelyn grabbed the children. "What do we do? There's nowhere to hide."

Luke stepped from the cave toward the voices. "We're not gonna hide."

Soon Bandar, and eight other creatures just like him, marched over a small hill, heading straight for the cave. When they saw Luke and the others at the entrance, they all stopped.

Bandar stepped a few feet closer. "I see you discovered our little passageway. It's been there for centuries, but knowing that isn't going to help you a whole lot now. You ignored our warnings, and even more foolishly you came here to our territory."

Holding out his Sword Luke said, "We are all children of light, and children of the day. We don't belong to the night, or to darkness."

"I see," said Bandar. "Well, whether you belong to us or not doesn't matter to me. We will give you a beating that you won't soon forget, and then you'll beg us to let you leave."

Bandar motioned toward the other creatures to spread out, then quickly flicked his long tail toward Luke. Seeing the threat barely in time, Luke jumped back. The tail snapped futilely in front of him.

Bandar snarled at Luke. "We are the Nuktos, warriors of the night. You cannot escape."

A loud wailing emanated from all the creatures as they prepared for battle.

Dropping to a knee beside the children, Katelyn said, "Stay here at the edge of this cave. Have your Sword ready and pray. God is going to get us all through this."

Overcomer, Esther, and Katelyn stepped out beside Luke. They fanned out in front of the cave entrance, determined that the Nuktos would not break through.

Bandar let out a loud wail, signaling for the rest of his group to charge. Two of the creatures headed straight for Luke and whipped at him with their tails. Quickly alternating back and forth, Luke blocked each swipe with his Shield, but he could hardly move to position himself to go on offense. Two Nuktos attacked Overcomer, two others came at Esther, and two headed toward Katelyn.

Overcomer searched for an opening, but just like Luke, she found that it was all she could do to block the constant whipping of the tails of the two Nuktos attacking her. Esther and Katelyn were having the same struggle.

Luke yelled out, "Stand your ground. Don't let them get by us."

"It's all I can do to keep their tails from cutting through me," said Katelyn.

Suddenly Luke spun around, kicking out with his spiked Shoes of the Gospel. As soon as he made contact, the Nuktos doubled over as if in intense pain. Luke shouted, "Use your Shoes as well as your Swords and Shields against these creatures."

Overcomer jumped as one of the tails came toward her legs. The next time the Nuktos whipped its tail toward her, she timed her jump so that she landed right on top of it, digging the spikes of her Shoes deep in the flesh of the tail. The creature groaned in pain and struggled to wriggle out from underneath Overcomer's Shoes. The other Nuktos frantically whipped its tail toward her in an attempt to rescue its partner, but Overcomer blocked every blow.

Seeing she had the creature trapped, Overcomer raised her Sword. "We are soldiers of the Light. For we were once darkness, but now we are light in the Lord." She plunged her Sword into the lizard's tail, and as soon as it made contact, the creature wailed in agonizing pain. She then struck it repeatedly until it fell over unconscious.

Overcomer had kept the other Nuktos at bay with her Shield, and now she turned her attention toward it. The Nuktos whipped its tail toward her head, but she ducked and lunged toward it with her Sword. The creature tried to move to the side, but her Sword pierced it through the shoulder. Overcomer then jumped into the air and kicked out with her Shoes knocking the Nuktos backwards. As it stumbled and hit the ground, she pounced and finished it off with a blow to the head.

Seeing Luke's and Overcomer's success, Esther and Katelyn went on the offense and pressed the attack against the Nuktos they were battling. Within a few minutes, they had rendered all of them unconscious.

Out of the corner of her eye, Katelyn noticed a shadow heading toward the cave. Bandar was charging toward the opening. She cried out, "Luke, the children!"

Hearing their mother scream, John and Teresa appeared at the opening of the cave. Bandar grinned an evil grin when he saw them, knowing their parents couldn't get there in time to save them. The children bravely held out their small Swords as they quoted the Psalm their parents taught them. Bandar stopped at the mouth of the cave, swishing his long tail back and forth, taunting the children and their parents who were running toward them.

Just as Bandar was set to release his tail at the children, a large golden Sword appeared in front of each child, glistening with an intense light. Bandar held his hands up to his eyes in an attempt to block the bright beams. Stepping back, he almost fell over.

At last, the adults made it to the entrance of the cave. Luke charged at Bandar. "You dared to attack my children!"

Katelyn gathered John and Teresa in her arms, hugging them tightly.

Regaining his balance and smirking at Luke, Bandar said, "Well, my plan was to get through that cave, but once I saw the little ones, I figured they would be an added bonus. You talk tough now that it's four on one."

Waving the others back, Luke said, "It will just be you and me."

Whipping his tail from side to side, Bandar smiled. "So be it."

"Be careful, Luke," shouted Katelyn.

Bandar shot his tail out at Luke trying to gauge the distance between them. Luke stepped to the side while keeping his Shield in front of him. Whenever he tried to take a step, Bandar would whip his tail at the ground just in front to keep him from coming any closer. Then all of a sudden, Bandar reached into a hidden pocket inside his shirt and pulled out a solid black stone. He tossed it on the ground in front of Luke. When it landed, a thick charcoal mist shot up around him.

Luke could barely see anything, but Bandar appeared to be able to see through the mist and locate exactly where Luke was. Bandar struck out with his tail and landed several strikes on Luke's legs.

Bandar laughed. "How did that feel? Those were easy blows compared to what's about to come."

Suddenly Luke heard the faint sound of buzzing coming toward his head. He raised his Shield just in time to deflect Bandar's tail from whipping him in the face.

Bandar laughed again. "You got lucky, but your luck will soon run out."

Realizing that Luke was in trouble, Katelyn gathered the others, including the children, to join hands and pray.

Luke tried to gauge where Bandar was by the sound of his voice, but the loud swishing of his tail made it difficult. Luke caught the faint glimpse of something coming toward him, and he quickly knelt behind his Shield in time to block another strike.

"I felt the metal of your Shield," said Bandar. "How long can you stay hidden before I finally land a fatal blow?"

Knowing he was in need of help, Luke prayed for wisdom. At once he knew what to do. Straightening, Luke shouted, "I have put away the works of darkness, and I have put on the Armor of Light!"

Suddenly, the mist vanished, and his armor began to glow. Bandar squinted and rubbed his eyes, but the reflection from Luke's Helmet and Shield almost blinded him. Realizing how vulnerable his enemy now was, Luke rushed toward him. Bandar caught a glimpse of his outline just in time to whip his tail toward his attacker, but Luke ducked and came up swinging his Sword. Bandar jumped back, but not before the weapon gashed his stomach.

Pulling back his Sword and readying for a fatal strike, Luke shouted, "I am a member of a chosen race, a royal priesthood, a holy nation, a person for God's own possession, so that I may proclaim the excellencies of Him who called me out of darkness and into His marvelous light!"

Luke plunged his Sword deep into his enemy's chest. A bright light spread from the blade throughout Bandar's body until he completely disintegrated. The other Nuktos had regained consciousness in time to see their leader defeated and immediately ran away, fearing they too would be vanquished.

Luke rejoined the others and embraced Katelyn and the children.

Esther scanned the inside of the cave. "This was a great victory, but if we don't find a way to close up this passageway, we're going to have to keep coming back and doing it all over again."

Holding his Sword up, Luke said, "As I was praying, I not only received wisdom about how to defeat Bandar but also about how we can shut down this cave as well. Everyone, take your Swords and hold them toward the ceiling."

Luke and Katelyn took the children in their arms so they too could hold their Swords toward the top of the cave.

Luke then shouted, "Oh God, you have called us to be vessels to open the eyes of those you send our way, in order to turn them from darkness to light, and from the power of Satan to the power of Your Kingdom, that they may receive forgiveness of sins and an inheritance among those who have been sanctified by faith in You."

The cave began to shake, and Luke shouted, "It's time to get out of here."

Everyone scrambled for the entrance and dove into the water. When they were clear, they looked back to see that the entire cave had collapsed. The passage to the Land of Darkness was completely sealed. As they rose toward the surface of the river, they all smiled and gave glory to God. After swimming back to shore, they returned to camp.

Once they had dried off and dressed in clean clothes, they gathered around a fire to warm themselves. Finally, Luke set off to inform the men that they could start building first thing tomorrow. While he was gone, Esther and Overcomer helped Katelyn get ready for what was going to be a big day come morning.

Theresa and John slipped from a tent carrying small boxes of supplies. Overcomer knelt in front of them. "You both were so brave today. I know your mom and dad are proud of you. I'm proud of you, too. You're going to be great warriors for God."

Theresa and John smiled and then took their boxes to their mom. After another hour of preparation, Katelyn thought they were ready for work to begin on the inn at daybreak.

Soon Luke returned, grinning from ear to ear. Grabbing Katelyn and hugging her, he said, "The men will be ready to go to work at sunrise. After I left them, I decided to go by and see the retired pastor and let him know what's been going on."

"What was his reaction?" asked Katelyn.

Luke pulled a large piece of paper out of his satchel. "He signed over the deed to us. He said he wanted to make sure this property was used for God's glory from now on."

Katelyn read over the paper and smiled. "That's wonderful!"

Esther and Overcomer gathered around and congratulated them. Hearing their father's voice, Theresa and John ran out from one of the tents and hugged his legs. He bent over and scooped them both into his arms.

Overcomer tapped Esther on the shoulder. She looked in the direction Overcomer pointed and saw that their paths were leading away.

"It looks like it's time for us to go," said Esther.

Katelyn gave them both a hug. "I'm so glad God sent you two."

"Yes," said Luke, "thank you for everything." He glanced over his shoulder. "If you continue in that direction, you're going to run into a beautiful inn. In fact, I stayed there a year ago, and it was during my time there that I felt God calling me to one day start my own inn. If you pass by it, you should definitely stay for a day or two."

"We'll do that," said Overcomer. "God bless all of you. I know this place is going to be a great success. Do you have a name for your inn yet?"

Luke placed his hand on his chin. "I believe we should name it … The Gospel Light."

Katelyn nodded. "That's a perfect name."

After hugging the children, Esther and Overcomer started back on their journey.

Luke and the men helping him made good time building the inn, and not long afterward, that stretch of river became a central hub for those making their way from one side to the other. Word spread that anytime a traveler came by that direction, he should always spend a night or two at *The Gospel Light*.

26

THE INN OF EXPERIENCE

Esther and Overcomer spent the day traveling due west and arrived at a beautiful inn right before sunset. The place was just as Luke had described, and they hoped their paths would stay there for a few days. After checking in, a courteous young lady showed them to a room and let them know that dinner would be served in half an hour.

They washed up, then came downstairs and made their way to the dining room. A gigantic table sat in the center of the strikingly elegant room, surrounded by beautiful paintings on the walls, each depicting a nature scene. The table looked as if it came out of a king's palace. A large antique china cabinet stood against the back wall, and old mahogany end tables, three feet tall and holding a custom piece of porcelain, occupied each corner of the room. The antique wood floors were freshly stained with a deep rich maple color. The ceiling towered twenty feet above them, and a large candle chandelier hung above the center of the table.

Baskets of fresh hot rolls were laid out on the table for all the guests, and soon the staff brought out large pots containing freshly roasted beef, along with big bowls of mashed potatoes and gravy, and individual servings of garden-fresh salad. Esther and Overcomer felt overwhelmed by all the sights and smells. As they ate, they listened to many of the different guests share stories about all the adventures they experienced while on their Quest.

When everyone finished eating, the staff cleared away their plates. As Overcomer and Esther waited for dessert to be served, an older gentleman called down to them. "Welcome to our inn, young ladies. I'm Elder Jenkins, and we always enjoy listening to our guests talk about some of the exciting events of their journey."

Esther and Overcomer shared all their thrilling adventures, both before and after traveling together.

When she finished, a stately older lady named Ms. Jones raised a finger. "Your name is Overcomer? Didn't we have a guest here sometime back who spoke about a young lady named Overcomer who put the Giant of Shame face down in the dirt?"

Elder Jenkins nodded. "You know, I believe we did. Doesn't seem that long ago either. Disciple was his name, I think."

Overcomer grasped Esther's hand. "That's the one I was telling you about."

Eager to hear more about him, Esther said, "Did he say which direction he was going?"

Ms. Jones smiled, recognizing from her younger days that Esther wasn't just asking out of curiosity. "He didn't say, but sometimes people's paths cross when they're least expecting it."

Esther blushed and glanced at the floor.

Elder Jenkins wiped his mouth with a napkin, then said, "I hope you're going to stay with us a couple of days. There's lots of property to explore, and we like to take the time to get to know the ones God brings here."

Overcomer replied, "I hope we'll get to stay for at least two days. It's so relaxing here, and I feel refreshed already."

After finishing their dessert, Ms. Jones invited them out back to sit in a large chair swing where they could enjoy the scenery and talk some more. The conversation was pleasant, and a nice cool breeze fanned them as they gently rocked the swing back and forth.

"Ms. Jones," said Esther, "how do you know when you find the one, I mean the one you're supposed to marry? I made a terrible mistake by trying to rush into a relationship that was not God's will, and I don't want to do that again."

Ms. Jones sighed. "Something similar happened to me when I was much younger. My parents and others tried to tell me the relationship I was in was a mistake, but I was so headstrong during those days. Thankfully, God intervened, and I was able to discover just in time that God's plan was not for me to pursue that relationship. Then one day I met Sam. He was a godly man who loved the Lord."

Esther put her hand on Ms. Jones arm. "Was it love at first sight?"

"I don't know, but something sure happened immediately. Each time I'd see him, I felt a little flutter in my stomach. Of course, I tried to hide it, not wanting to be too obvious, but what really caught my attention was how much he loved God. Being around him made me want to grow in my own relationship with the Lord. After I spoke with my mother, she said that was a good sign. A relationship can pull you away from God, or it can draw you closer to Him."

"I wish I had used that as a measuring stick myself," said Esther.

"We all learn and grow," said Ms. Jones. "The most important thing is to stay on your path. God is able to place the people He wants in your life at just the right time. If we will pursue God, He will cause all the additional things in our lives to appear when we need them, but if we leave our path to pursue those other things, we end up missing them and God."

Esther nodded. "I need to remember that."

What happened next?" asked Overcomer, as she pushed off with her foot to give the chair swing extra momentum.

"I went on to marry Sam, and we had a wonderful life together. We have four children, thirteen grandchildren, and at least thirty great-grandchildren so far."

"It sounds like you've lived a full life," said Overcomer.

"Yes, I have." Ms. Jones stared ahead for a minute then continued. "Sam died about five years ago." She paused as if she was reflecting on her late husband. After a moment of silence, she glanced at the girls and smiled. "A few years ago I went on a trip with my granddaughter, and we visited this inn. I felt drawn to stay, and after I accompanied my granddaughter back home, I saw that my path was leading back here." She glanced around the property and smiled. "So I came back, and I've been living here ever since."

"This is a wonderful place," said Esther.

Ms. Jones leaned back in the swing. "Indeed it is. Whenever my children and grandchildren come this way, they stop in to see me. Also from time to time, God brings young people like yourselves through here as well. Listening to their adventures reminds me of my own, and it gives me and the others who live here the opportunity to share with them the things we've learned along the way."

Overcomer sat forward. "What advice do you give to young

women like us?"

Ms. Jones thought about the question. "I most often advise them to be themselves. There are all kinds of pressures on young women to be a certain way, but all you have to be is what God has called you to be."

"So you're saying there are no limits?"

"That's right," said Ms. Jones. "There are only a couple of things that Scripture has reserved for men, but instead of focusing on those few things, we should think about all the things we can do."

Overcomer said, "I've seen God use women in lots of different ways. In fact, a little over a week ago we met a cheerful older lady named Ms. Crandle who taught us some wonderful lessons from God's word."

"God has used many women to accomplish some very important tasks throughout time," said Ms. Jones. "There was Ruth, Rahab, and Deborah from the Old Testament, and then we see that women were an important part of Jesus' ministry, as well as the Apostle Paul's in the New Testament."

As they continued to swing in the chair, Ms. Jones began to hum a tune. Overcomer and Esther enjoyed the peaceful melody, which seemed to harmonize with all the sounds of nature around them. The time was worshipful and relaxing.

After a few minutes, Esther said, "We both have talked about having families one day."

"Motherhood is a special and important calling," said Ms. Jones. "And children are a blessing from the Lord. We only get a few years with them, and then they grow up and go out on their own." She grasped each of their hands. "I believe you both will make wonderful wives and moms."

Overcomer said, "But having children does come with certain limitations, doesn't it?"

Ms. Jones smiled. "You may not have the same kinds of exploits while your children are young, but you'll find that being a mother comes with its own set of adventures. As their mother, God will use you to prepare your children to be future warriors for Him. Everything that you pour into their lives will have an impact on future generations."

Esther and Overcomer spent the rest of the evening relaxing and exploring the property with Ms. Jones. On the next day, they spent more time with her and some of the other older ladies. They both took in all the wisdom that came with the life experiences of these seasoned warriors.

That evening after dinner Overcomer, Esther, and Ms. Jones stepped out onto the back porch.

Within a few minutes, Elder Jenkins joined them. "Good evening, ladies."

"Good evening to you, too," said Ms. Jones. She took a seat in one of the rocking chairs and pointed toward Esther and Overcomer. "I've gotten to know these young women really well since they've been here, and I told them that if they got the chance, they should ask you a few questions."

Elder Jenkins took a seat in his customary rocking chair and started to rock back and forth. "Why I'd be glad to answer any I can." Nodding toward the girls, he said, "Is there something in particular on your mind?"

Esther glanced at Ms. Jones. "We've asked all of the women for their insights into many different topics, but they always said that when it comes to fighting sin, you would be a great person to talk to."

"That's right," said Overcomer. "We both have talked about how frustrated we get because we find ourselves battling with temptations that we wished we could just be rid of."

Elder Jenkins sat forward and leaned against his cane. "That's a good sign. If you didn't get frustrated at times, then that would mean you weren't trying. When you read of the Apostle Paul describing his own sinfulness in Romans 7, you find that he was frustrated too. He saw that his old nature was continuously trying to sin, and he wanted to be completely rid of it just like we all do."

Overcomer turned toward the countryside. "I wish we could feel less sinful sometimes."

"I know what you mean," said Elder Jenkins, "but being constantly aware of our sinfulness is what constantly drives us to the Throne Room of Grace."

Ms. Jones nodded. "That's right. Realizing the depth of our problem is what motivates us to seek an answer. Being aware of sin is not to beat ourselves up, but so that we might go to God and be lifted up by his grace."

Elder Jenkins stood up. "The Apostle Paul tells us in his letter to the Philippians that we are to work out our own salvation with fear and trembling, knowing that it is God that gives us both the desire and the ability to work according to His good pleasure."

Overcomer smoothed a wrinkle from her skirt. "That's so humbling."

"Yes, it is," said Elder Jenkins. "When you get right down to it, the only good that we can do is to admit that there's nothing good that we can do. Anything we accomplish which is pleasing to God is completely by his grace."

Esther shook her head. "It feels like a constant battle. I sometimes wish there could be a little bit of a break."

Walking to the railing beside Esther and Overcomer, Elder Jenkins said, "We all do, but sin never takes a break and neither can we. If we aren't killing sin, then you can be sure that sin is killing us."

"Sometimes it seems so insurmountable," said Overcomer.

Elder Jenkins nodded. "And if we had to fight the battle against sin through our own strength, it would be impossible, but we have a power within us that is much greater than our sin. Paul said that if we walk by the Spirit, we will not fulfill the lusts of the flesh. That doesn't mean there won't be a fight, but what it means is even though sin presses hard against us, if we surrender to the Holy Spirit then we will not act on the sinful desires of our old nature."

Ms. Jones stood and joined them. "It's also important to remember that we are the ones who determine whether or not we will submit to our old nature or the Holy Spirit. If we set our minds on the things of the flesh, then we will live according to the flesh, but if we set our minds on the things of the Spirit, then we will live according to the Spirit."

"That's right," said Elder Jenkins, grasping his cane. "We cannot commit sinful actions without first giving in to sinful thoughts. If we surrender to God's word in our life and allow His Spirit to work those words in us, then we will be transformed day by day. Over time, you learn to rejoice in the progress you've made rather than to be discouraged because of the progress you still need to make."

"Thank you," said Esther. "This is what I needed to hear."

Overcomer hugged Elder Jenkins. "Yes, thank you very much.

Sometimes in my battle against sin, I can feel so intense that I forget to rejoice in what God's already done for me."

Elder Jenkins smiled. "I'm glad I could be of help. Being too intense is a sign that we're trying to do the work of sanctification in our own strength rather than relying on the Holy Spirit."

Ms. Jones nodded. "That's right. Of course, no intensity means a person isn't engaging in the work of sanctification at all. It's a balance that we all have to learn."

Esther and Overcomer spent that evening once again sitting in the chair swing with Ms. Jones, talking and listening to more of her adventures and experiences. After breakfast the next morning, they walked out to see that their path was leading away. They went back inside to say goodbye to all those staying at the Inn of Experience. They gave Ms. Jones a special hug and wished her well. When they had packed everything, they started out on their paths once again.

By mid-morning Esther and Overcomer found themselves in a wide-open country with rolling hills covered by luscious green grass. An hour later, a large shadow darkened the ground in front of them. From behind, giant figures sailed toward them.

Esther turned around and pointed. "Look at those monstrous birds."

Reaching for her Sword, Overcomer said, "Those aren't birds. They're gargoyles, and we're easy prey out here in the open like this."

THE SOVEREIGNTY OF GOD

Esther looked concerned. "What's a gargoyle?"

"It's a fierce enemy that's as massive as a giant and can fly."

The vast wings of the gargoyles flapped back and forth as they zoomed toward them. Their enormous round faces were grotesque and monstrous. Their hairy feet and hands were clawed, and their entire bodies were midnight black. Smoke poured from their nostrils as they drew near.

"Are they coming for us?" shouted Esther.

"I can't think of any other reason they'd be flying in this direction," said Overcomer, raising her shield. "There's nowhere to run. We're going to have to fight."

Esther and Overcomer stood side by side with their Swords and Shields ready for battle. The gargoyles came closer and then began to circle.

"What are they doing?" asked Esther, peering into the sky.

Keeping an eye on their enemies, Overcomer said, "I think they're trying to figure out the best way to attack."

Soon the gargoyles dove toward them. They soared over their heads but stayed just out of reach of their Swords. The gargoyles then turned in mid-air, flapping their wings and hovering just a little ways away.

One of the creatures pointed toward them. "Our Master is tired of you two meddling in his affairs. We have come to take you to a place where you will not be so much trouble."

The gargoyles ascended into the sky, then dove straight toward them. This time they flew between Esther and Overcomer and knocked the girls several feet apart. The gargoyles circled around, then dove straight toward them again. One flew toward Esther while the other headed toward Overcomer.

Ducking in time to avoid the giant-sized claws of the gargoyle, Overcomer thrust her Shield at the creature. She whirled around to locate Esther, but she wasn't there.

From above she heard Esther cry, "Help!"

Overcomer glanced up to see her dangling from the claws of one of the gargoyles. The other one caught up and glided beside it, apparently content with only capturing one of them. Overcomer sprinted to catch up with them, but by the time she reached the spot beneath the gargoyles, the one that had Esther was twenty feet off the ground. She realized her only hope at this point was to let herself be captured and hopefully, she and Esther could defeat them together when they reached their destination. With her next step, she pretended to stumble and cried out as if she was in pain. The second gargoyle swung toward her and snatched her in its claws.

With powerful thrusts of its wings, the creature caught up with the one carrying Esther, and they flew side by side. Esther opened her mouth in dismay at the sight of Overcomer, but she put her finger to her lips, and the two remained silent. The gargoyles lifted higher and higher into the air. They flew for miles through the wide-open countryside. Soon they neared a towering mountain range.

Within minutes, Esther and Overcomer spotted a massive rock wall. Terror gripped them both as they wondered if their fate was to be crushed against this wall of granite. But soon the opening of a cave carved into the side of the mountain came into view. When they were almost to the entrance, the gargoyles started swinging them back and forth, and then at the opening, they let them go so that Esther and Overcomer flew through the air and rolled into the cave.

Shaken up at first, they lay still for a few minutes, as their eyes adjusted to the darkness of the cave. Then something toward the back shifted. A dark shape moved on the right, then another to their left. Fearful they were being surrounded, the girls backed into a cleft in the rock and grabbed their satchels, ready to draw their Swords.

"Don't be afraid," said a quiet voice.

In the dim light filtering from the cave opening, Overcomer saw a young woman in tattered clothing.

"I'm Malia."

Esther and Overcomer glanced around. Other young men and women appeared.

"What is this place?" asked Esther, still waiting for her eyes to fully adjust to the poor light.

"We don't know. We were picked up by the gargoyles and brought here, same as you."

"How long have you been here?" asked Overcomer, as she slipped from the crevice.

Malia reached out to guide her around a cluster of rocks. "After talking with everyone, it appears we've all been brought here within the last few days. We've been sharing what little bit of food and water we had in our backpacks, but we don't know what we're going to do."

Overcomer took a few steps toward the mouth of the cave. "I don't see any way out of here. We're far above the ground, and the side of this mountain is solid rock." She faced Malia. "Have you all talked about why you may have been brought here?"

A slender young man named Jordan stepped forward. "I've asked myself that question many times. I've been following my path, and although I'm not perfect, I've tried to live my life according to the teachings of my Book."

Others nodded.

Malia leaned against one of the boulders. "Just before the gargoyles caught me, I thought I heard one of them say that this would teach me a lesson."

Jordan said, "Come to think of it, I seem to remember them saying something to me as well, but I was so shocked at the moment that I don't remember what was said."

As the others shared their story, each one reported that they had been following their paths and achieving victories on their Quest.

Esther shook her head. "I don't understand. Why did God allow this to happen to all of us?"

Overcomer drifted toward the back of the cave and surveyed the walls. "There's always a plan. Nothing happens by mistake."

Esther recognized the tone of Overcomer's voice and followed her as she explored the cave. From time to time she put a hand on the wall and felt up and down. Within a few minutes, she came to a section of rock that slightly protruded outwards and pushed. At once she shouted, "Come here, everyone!"

All the others gathered around. Three of them put their shoulders to the wall and helped push that section. Slowly the rock scooted back, exposing a large doorway leading to a hidden room. The faint light was too weak for them to see more than the outline of the room, but to the left of the doorway, Jordan discovered a torch hanging from the wall with a piece of flint tied to it.

"Just what we need," said Malia.

Jordan struck the flint on the hard rock next to the torch. After a number of attempts, a spark caught, and the torch illuminated the room. Spaced along the wall were stores of dried fruits, nuts, and water—more than enough for all of them for several days.

"At least we have provisions," said Esther, "but that still doesn't help us get out of here. And what do we do when this food runs out?"

Overcomer took the torch and inspected the room. In one corner she discovered what looked to be a pile of sticks. At first, she thought it was wood for a fire, but after kneeling and examining them further, she changed her mind. The sticks were more like spears with ropes attached.

Holding up one of them, she said, "There has to be a purpose for these being placed here."

Malia knelt and touched the end of the spear. "That is extremely sharp. I think I have an idea what they might be for, but it's going to be risky."

Overcomer's eyes lit up.

Esther put her hand on Malia's arm. "Oh no, you've just said her favorite words."

Overcomer smiled and picked up one of the spears. I think I know what Malia is thinking. "The next time the gargoyles come to drop someone off, we can throw these spears at them and then hold on to the ropes that are attached."

"That's right," said Malia. "And look at the small hook toward the tip of the spear. This will ensure that once they sink into the gargoyle's flesh, the spears will hold firm and support our weight."

Esther said, "That may get us out of this cave, but the gargoyles can fly around and take us anywhere they want."

Jordan picked up a spear. "I don't think so. There are twenty-two spears, and there are twenty of us. That leaves two spears for whoever the new arrivals are. That's eleven people pulling on each gargoyle. Those creatures are huge, but the weight of that many people is going to pull them down. It might be a slow descent, but if we can hold on, we can ride them to the ground."

Overcomer held the rope attached to one of the spears. "I think I have an idea how we can get a better grip during our flight. We need to wrap the end of the rope around one hand and throw the spear with the other hand. As soon as the spear pierces their flesh, we then grab onto the rope with both hands and hold on."

Malia motioned for everyone to stand back, and then she hurled the spear toward the other side of the room into a dirt wall. "That's about the distance we're going to need to throw them. I think one person should keep a look-out in case the gargoyles return, and the rest of us should spend a little time practicing."

"I agree," said Overcomer.

Esther saw a shiny metal object lying on the other side of the room. She picked it up. "A telescope! We can use it to see when those gargoyles are returning."

For the next couple of hours, one person kept watch with the telescope while the rest practiced throwing the spears and then grasping the rope. When they felt like they were ready, they returned to the main part of the cave and sat in a circle.

Jordan took the torch and fixed it up against the wall. "I don't think they'll return before morning. Not many people are going to be out on their path to be swept up this time of night."

Malia glanced at Overcomer. "What made you think to search the cave?"

"There's a purpose for everything. Sometimes it isn't this easy to figure out, but the more I listened to everyone's story, the more I thought we were all being brought together in one place for a reason."

Esther said, "But what is God accomplishing with us here that He couldn't have done in some other place?"

"The gargoyles," said Overcomer. "Those creatures think they're bringing us here to hurt us and further the plans of their master, but in reality, God is the one orchestrating all of this to defeat them."

Esther excitedly took out her Book. "That reminds me of a passage I read the other day." Turning a few pages, she found the place and read, "For truly against your holy Servant Jesus, whom you anointed, both Herod and Pontius Pilate, along with the Gentiles and the people of Israel, were all gathered together to do whatever your hand and Your purpose determined beforehand to be done."

Closing her Book, she said, "Think about that. Satan thought he had organized the most masterful and ingenious plan in history. He motivated the Jewish rulers and the governor of a powerful kingdom to do what he desired, but actually God was the one orchestrating everything and had planned it before the foundation of the world."

Malia said, "It's hard to imagine how God planned every single little detail for thousands of years which led to the circumstances to bring about His ultimate plan for redemption."

Jordan placed his finger to the side of his head. "But...if God was the one causing all these events to happen, are the ones who played their part still responsible for their sin?"

Esther turned in her Book again. "This is what Jesus said about Judas Iscariot. 'The Son of Man indeed goes just as it is written of Him, but woe to that man by whom the Son of Man is betrayed! It would have been good for that man if he had never been born.' "

Overcomer nodded. "Even though everything was happening according to God's plan; Pilate, the Pharisees, Judas Iscariot, and all those who played a role in Christ's crucifixion were held accountable for their actions. God may have set up the circumstances knowing what choice they would make, but they still made that choice willingly and will not be able to argue otherwise at the future Judgment."

"That reminds me of another verse," said Malia. She started flipping pages in her Book. "In whom also we have been appointed an inheritance, having been predestined according to the purpose of Him who works all things according to the counsel of His own will."

A scholarly woman named Simone said, "I've always been curious about this verse." She opened her book and read, "Your eyes saw me when I was still unborn, and in Your book, all the days of my life were written before they ever happened, when as yet there was none of them." She looked up, "It's comforting to know that God has everything in control to that degree, but then I wonder if we're just puppets."

Esther said, "It's hard to understand how God can be in charge of all things, and yet man is still responsible for his choices, but that's exactly what is taught in our Books."

"Yes," said Overcomer, "It can appear somewhat like a mystery, but we know that God's word teaches that our choices have real meaning and carry real consequences, and yet it also teaches that God is entirely in control from beginning to end. We may not fully understand it, but knowing God is in complete control causes us to rest in the knowledge that everything will eventually work together for our good, because God is the one orchestrating all those things."

Standing up to blow out the torch, Jordan said, "I believe God's purpose for bringing us here goes even deeper than the defeat of those gargoyles. We have learned some important lessons this evening that will benefit us for the rest of our journey."

As twilight faded to night, they all settled in to get some sleep.

28

ABBADON

As the first rays of sunlight peeked through the cave, the group of captives rose up quickly.

They all had a quick breakfast, then Overcomer stood to address them. "Those gargoyles could come back at any time. We need to set up our watch again and continue practicing our attack."

For the next hour, everyone took turns hurling their spears against the walls in the hidden room. Afterward, they all gathered near the front of the cave to pray together.

When they finished, Esther raised her hand. "There is one thing that I'm still not sure about. You saw how disoriented we were when we first arrived. How are the two new people going to be able to quickly understand what's happening?"

"That's a good question," said Malia.

"I've been thinking about that too," said Overcomer. "When the gargoyles arrive, we need to get their attention, so they will stick around just long enough for a couple of you to alert the new arrivals as to what's going on. We'll put two spears in the back of the cave for them, and as soon as they're ready, bring them forward so we can launch the attack."

Esther shook her head and smiled. "Couldn't resist adding a little more riskiness to this plan could you?"

Malia laughed, "Is it always like this around you two?"

"Yes," said Esther, as she put her arm around Overcomer. "But you get used to it."

Just then Jordan shouted, "They're coming!"

Overcomer quickly organized the others, then turned to Esther.

"You and Jordan step toward the back to help the new arrivals."

Malia held out her hand. "So how do you plan to keep those gargoyles around? They've been throwing us into the cave and immediately flying off."

Stepping to the front, Overcomer said, "Follow my lead."

As the gargoyles flew closer, the group saw two stout young men flailing in their grasp.

Overcomer motioned for everyone to back up. "Let's give them room to drop them off, and then close up in front of them once they land."

The gargoyles flew closer and heaved the young men into the cave.

When they did, Overcomer put her hands to her eyes as if she were wiping away tears. "Please, you can't keep us here. We will die with no food or water."

One of the gargoyles laughed and nodded toward the other one as they hovered at the entrance of the cave. "That's the plan! You've all caused so much trouble that we decided to let you die a slow and agonizing death together."

Stepping forward and falling to her knees, Malia cried, "But I miss my sister and my family. Can't you spare us?"

"NO!" roared the gargoyles.

Overcomer was right in her calculation. The gargoyles enjoyed seeing the misery they had caused their captives, and this kept them from immediately leaving. In the meantime, the two young men who had just rolled into the cave landed near Jordan and Esther. They were brothers named James and John, and rather than being disoriented, they were quite angry and wanted to immediately jump up and launch themselves at the gargoyles. However, Jordan and Esther grabbed their arms and whispered the plan to them.

James quickly rose to his feet and wiped the dust off his pants. "Get word to the ones delaying the gargoyles that we're ready. I can't wait to see the looks on their faces as my spear sinks deep into them."

"I can't either," said John.

As Malia was about to say something else to beg for her release, Esther stepped forward and knelt beside her. Addressing the gargoyles, she said, "Can't you at least bring us a little food?" Esther put her head on Malia's shoulder while whispering, "They're ready." Pretending to cry even harder, she climbed to her feet and leaned on Overcomer's shoulder. Again she whispered the same message.

"Well this has been fun," said one of the gargoyles, "but there's more of you out there for us to catch, so we'll be on our way. Don't worry though. We'll soon be back with more."

All of a sudden, James and John sprinted to the mouth of the cave and hurled their spears at the gargoyles—each striking a different one. Both men were strong and pulled with all their might. The gargoyles were caught off guard, and this gave the others time to retrieve their spears from the side of the cave and launch them as well. One by one, the spears sailed through the air and dug into their enemies.

As the sharp tips of the spears penetrated their flesh, the gargoyles frantically flapped their wings in an attempt to get away. James and John pulled tighter to give the others more time to get a better grip. Now desperate, the gargoyles flapped their wings as hard as they could. Slowly they began to move away from the cave entrance, carrying all the warriors who were firmly maintaining their hold on the ropes attached to the spears.

As the gargoyles gathered momentum, they flew about a hundred feet away from the mountain and then turned around to go back toward it.

Esther shouted, "What are they doing? We're flying too low to land back in the cave."

"That's not their plan," yelled Overcomer. "They're going to try and crash us into the side of that rock wall."

Seeing what was happening, everyone began to pull down on their ropes causing the gargoyles to fly lower and lower. Desperate to get rid of their attackers, the creatures increased their speed, but they were carrying too much weight. Before they could get to the rock wall, they dropped so low the captives could touch the ground.

"Let go of the ropes and prepare for battle!" shouted Overcomer.

Rapidly unwinding the ropes from their hands, they readied their Swords and Shields. The gargoyles were weakened from all the spears attached to them, but they were so angry that they attacked anyway. Even their own arrogance and pride had been factored into God's plan, for it would have been far better for them to fly off and recover before beginning an attack.

James, John, and three others circled around one of the creatures who was called Gorgumoth.

The massive gargoyle slammed his fist into the ground and shook the earth. "I will smash you into powder!" He then slowly flapped his wings, ascending a few feet, and prepared to attack.

James sprinted toward Gorgumoth and leaped into the air. At the top of his jump, he grabbed one of the spears still sticking in Gorgumoth's chest and swung himself upward so that he was level with the gargoyle's head. He then thrust his Sword straight into Gorgumoth's neck. When James landed from his jump, the gargoyle fell to the ground and clutched at his throat. Immediately, John charged at the gargoyle and struck a flurry of blows to his midsection. Gorgumoth stumbled forward, and Jordan and Simone launched a furious attack at the gargoyle's legs until he toppled over. They then pummeled Gorgumoth until he lay still and lifeless.

At the same time, Overcomer, Esther, Malia, and the rest were surrounding the largest enemy who was called Gilgamar.

The fierce gargoyle widened his wings, and smoke shot from his nostrils. "May the Master break me into pieces if any of you are still standing after today."

Malia cocked her Sword arm. "I will be steadfast immovable, and always abounding in the work of the Lord."

Gilgamar slowly rose into the air, then circled overhead just out of reach. Suddenly, he swooped toward them, simultaneously punching out with his large fists toward Esther and Overcomer. They blocked the blows with their Shields, then landed a hard strike on each of his arms. Malia jumped toward Gilgamar and pulled one of the spears out of his flesh.

Overcomer shouted at the gargoyle, "Just as Christ defeated you on the cross when you thought you had won, God has orchestrated all the events that are about to lead to your destruction."

Gilgamar shook his fist at her. "You will never—"

All of a sudden, a spear—the spear Malia had retrieved—sailed through the air. It sunk into his forehead and knocked him out of the sky. He plunged to the ground with a thud and didn't move.

A loud cheer rose from the others, as both gargoyles lay lifeless on the ground. They celebrated together and gave praise to God.

Malia turned toward Esther and Overcomer. "We're all so thankful God brought you two into our lives."

"Where will you go next?" asked Esther.

Malia glanced at the group. "It looks like all of us will be traveling together from here. Instead of taking us off our paths, all the gargoyles accomplished was to join us with other warriors. Now we will be even stronger as a team."

Jordan had stepped up beside them while Malia was speaking. "What about you two?"

Overcomer studied her and Esther's path. "It appears we're going to be continuing on by ourselves, but I'm so glad we got to meet all of you."

Jordan held out the telescope to Overcomer. "I think you should keep this. We're all grateful that you arrived."

Before everyone departed, they prayed together and wished each other well. Esther and Overcomer gave Malia one more hug and then she and Esther started on their way. The day was bright and sunny, but suddenly the sky darkened as if dusk was upon them. Thinking at first that a cloud had temporarily blocked the sun, they both continued without a second thought. Suddenly a loud snorting sound burst out above them. They scanned the sky and saw a ferocious dragon flying overhead.

Fiercely beating his wings, the dragon spoke in a deep, growling voice. "I am Abbadon, Ruler of the Dark World, second in command to Satan himself. I'm tired of hearing about all your exploits." Turning to Esther, Abbadon said, "You should never have been able to get back on your path, but Michael failed. Just know that he paid for his failure." Snarling at Overcomer, he said, "And you, you should never have been able to start your Quest, to begin with. I sent legions after you since you were a small child. Well, today it all ends!"

Esther and Overcomer drew their Swords.

Abbadon breathed out a long breath of fire, and in a hideous voice roared. "Do you think you can fight me? I do not lose!"

"Neither do we!" said Overcomer as she thrust her Shield toward the flames.

Abbadon lifted into the air, his wings spread wide and glared down with contempt. "I've been fighting battles for thousands of years against your kind. You are nothing but children!"

Esther dug in with her Shoes. "We do not come at you today with our own strength, but with the strength of the LORD Almighty, Jesus Christ, the Commander of the Armies of God."

Overcomer defiantly stood with her Sword raised high. "Our Lord has already triumphed over you on the cross, and through His power, we will triumph over you as well."

A cruel hate-filled look flashed across Abbadon's face. Suddenly he bolted toward them at full speed. Esther and Overcomer crouched behind their Shields, but the sheer size and force of Abbadon's attack sent them sprawling in opposite directions. The dragon circled in the air, then dove toward Overcomer. Jumping to her feet, Esther sprinted to her friend and lunged at Abbadon with her Sword. Her aim was true, and her Sword punctured his side. Abbadon reared back and growled in anger.

Pivoting from Overcomer, Abbadon launched himself toward Esther, but as soon as he came near, Esther sliced his neck with her Sword. Wounded by another blow, the dragon swung his head in fury, as flames shot out his mouth. Overcomer bounded to her side, and Abbadon breathed out another inferno of flames toward them. They raised their Shields and absorbed the fire, but the air around them felt like it would melt their lungs.

Abbadon seized the opportunity and whipped his long sharp tail toward them from the side.

Overcomer yelled, "Watch out!"

The two of them jumped just in time to avoid the swipe.

Abbadon rose into the air laughing. "How long do you think you can hold out against me? It's only a matter of time."

Still refusing to give into fear, Overcomer shouted, "Thanks be to God who always causes us to triumph in Christ Jesus!"

Abbadon beat his wings together and ascended higher. He circled overhead then dove toward them, breathing a stream of fire.

Overcomer glanced at Esther with a look of determination. Knowing that she was signaling for them to take a stand, Esther nodded. They dug in with their Shoes and crouched low. As Abbadon drew near, they sprang forward and thrust out their Shields, slamming them into his head. The attack knocked Abbadon backwards and almost caused him to fall from the air.

Slowly flapping his wings to recover, Abbadon growled at them, then landed on the ground several feet away. "So you want a real fight? I'll show you what a real fight looks like."

Abbadon slapped his tail back and forth. He breathed out another fiery blast, then flapped his wings in front of them, as if he was preparing to smash them.

Taking her position on Overcomer's left, Esther proclaimed, "The Lord our God goes before us. It is He who fights for us and gives us the victory!"

Abbadon took a deep breath. When he released it, fire hurled toward them. As Overcomer pushed out her Shield to absorb the flames, once again the dragon swiped at them with his long jagged tail. But with Overcomer's Shield providing protection from the scorching blast, Esther jumped into action and sliced down on the dragon's tail with her Sword. Abbadon jumped back in pain while instinctively thrusting his tail at Esther again. She swung her Sword with all her might and struck the dragon's tail so hard that it was completely crippled.

As his long tail lay motionless, Abbadon lunged toward them. He flapped his wings, preparing to smash their heads together as his wings closed in on them.

Overcomer yelled, "Get back!"

They jumped back as the dragon's wings closed in front of them. They then attacked from opposite sides, striking each wing with their Swords. Startled and wounded, Abbadon retreated several feet, tilting his head up and breathing out fire.

Abbadon appeared desperate now. He thrust his head forward and shot out large balls of fire. Esther and Overcomer ducked behind their Shields, and the fiery blasts bounced off. They darted to one side and landed a vicious attack on top of his head with their Swords.

Recoiling in defeat, Abbadon slowly rose into the air. "I'm not finished with you two. I will see you again."

As their enemy flew off, Overcomer yelled out, "God is not finished with you, Abbadon! Someday His mighty angels will throw you into the Lake that Burns Forever, and there you will remain for all of eternity!"

29

NEW BEGINNINGS

Exhausted from the battle, Esther and Overcomer collapsed to the ground and lay on their backs. They remained alert though, surveying the sky just in case Abbadon returned.

After a few minutes, Esther let out a deep sigh of relief. "That may have been our toughest battle yet."

"I agree," said Overcomer. "But I believe God has been preparing us to fight this enemy. Abbadon didn't attack us on his timing but on God's."

Esther sat up on her elbows. "I wonder what God has for us next?"

Sitting up, Overcomer said, "I'm not sure, but I can guarantee you it's going to be exciting."

They rested for another twenty minutes, then stood up and shouldered their backpacks. Seeing that their paths were heading in a new direction, they set off. On the second day's journey, they came to an inn. After inquiring about a room, they settled in, then headed to the bathhouse. They each soaked in a tub of warm water for an hour, then returned to their room just in time to get ready for dinner.

After the guests finished their meal, they all gathered in a large sitting room for a time of study and discussion. Overcomer and Esther felt refreshed by the uplifting time. When they awoke the next morning, their path had not moved, so they stayed another night. They had another relaxing day, and just before sunset went for a walk to explore the countryside.

As they passed a lovely cluster of apple trees, Esther turned to Overcomer. "I must say that my life has certainly been a lot more exciting since we started our journey together."

Overcomer chuckled. "I hope you mean that in a good way."

Smiling, Esther said, "I do, but I could certainly make do with a little less excitement for a few more days—weeks even."

Overcomer laughed, and they went back inside to enjoy a time of fellowship with the other guests. At bedtime, they returned to their room for another peaceful night's sleep.

The next morning Overcomer stepped outside to enjoy the fresh air and sunshine. She stretched her arms out wide and breathed in deeply while closing her eyes. When she opened them, she saw that their paths were moving away. After stepping back inside, she found Esther. "It looks like it's time to move on."

Feeling completely rejuvenated, Esther grinned. "Let's get started."

Brimming with anticipation, Esther and Overcomer set off from the inn. On their second day of traveling, they noticed they were moving further and further away from the paths of others. By the end of the next day, they found themselves in an area that was almost a wilderness. They set up camp and built a fire, then relaxed and enjoyed the sunset.

"I still think about the day we met at the Giant of Shame," said Esther.

Putting a stick on the fire and sitting down, Overcomer said, "I know. It seems so long ago. It's as if we've gone from being strangers to almost sisters. I never had a family, so you're the closest thing I've known to having a relative."

"I feel the same way," said Esther. "God has brought us together and formed a bond that I could never have predicted. I don't know what my future holds, but somehow I think you're going to be a part of it."

Nodding her head, Overcomer said, "I would like that. Can you imagine our children playing together someday? Having each other over for dinner? I do hope our husbands get along."

Esther laughed. "They better!"

After settling in for a good night's rest, they slept until sunrise. Wanting to get an early start, they had a quick breakfast and then headed out. Soon their paths took them to the top of a large hill.

Taking out her telescope and surveying the land, Overcomer saw what looked to be an extensive camp spread out in a valley. Excited that they were about to see others, she started to call to Esther, but her excitement quickly turned to alarm when she saw an ogre step out into the open. In fact, the whole valley was filled with ogres and giants. As she scanned the entire area, she spotted a small campsite with three tents set up away from the valley and to the far right.

She kept an eye on the smaller campsite waiting to see if the occupants would be friends or enemies. All of a sudden she placed the telescope back in her satchel and a big grin spread across her face.

Esther had been watching her. "What is it? Did you discover why we've been brought way out here?"

Still grinning, Overcomer said, "I know exactly why we've been brought here."

Esther reached toward Overcomer's satchel. "Let me see the telescope."

Taking a step back, Overcomer shook her head and smiled. "No, I think God wants you to see this up close for yourself."

Esther tilted her head to the side and put her hands on her hips. "You're acting awful strange." She then glanced at the ground and noticed their paths were going in different directions. "Why are our paths separating? After all this time, why would God split us up?"

Overcomer put her hand on Esther's shoulder. "I don't believe God is separating us. If you look way out into the distance, you can see that my path is starting to circle as it gets closer to that mountain. I'm sure that means that wherever I'm going, I will be back soon. You are meant to move ahead without me for just a little while, and soon you'll discover why. Don't worry about me. I know God will bring me back."

They prayed together and then Overcomer started off. When she was about fifty yards away, she turned and shouted, "When you get there, tell them that I'll be back soon, and I won't be alone."

Esther yelled out, "Tell who? Who am I about to meet? Do they know you?"

By now Overcomer was out of range. Wondering what lay ahead, Esther followed her path until it came to a small campsite. Keeping her hand near her Book in case she needed her Sword, Esther cautiously crept forward. As she drew closer, a man emerged from one of the tents. Esther was immediately struck by how handsome he was. He had a square jaw that exuded strength, and he carried himself with confidence. His eyes gleamed with kindness, and his smile made her feel safe and at ease. She had never seen him before, and yet somehow she felt as if she knew him.

As she drew closer, he held out his hand. "Hello, we haven't seen anyone coming this way in a while. It's nice to meet you. My name is Disciple."

Disciple! She could barely contain herself, but she gathered all of the self-control she could muster and extended her hand. "My name is Esther."

"I like that name. Esther is one of my favorite characters in the Book. She had such courage and poise in the midst of adversity."

Hearing the conversation, others began to come out of their tents.

A tall, athletic young man rambled up beside Disciple. "Welcome. My name is Peter."

She nodded. "Nice to meet you."

Disciple said, "This is Esther. Her path has led her here."

A young couple along with an energetic and good-natured German Shepherd joined them. "I see that someone else has arrived. I'm Jeremiah, and this is Zeal."

The dog barked.

"And this is Samson," said Jeremiah, reaching down to pat him on the head.

"You don't know how glad I am to see another female," said Zeal. "It's going to be nice having you around camp."

Esther smiled. "Hopefully soon, there will be another young woman arriving."

"How do you know she'll be joining us?" asked Zeal.

"I've been traveling with Overcomer for months, but moments ago her path took her in another direction. Before she left, she said to let all of you know that she would be returning soon and wouldn't be alone."

"Overcomer?" said Disciple, placing his hand on his chin. "Yes, I remember her. I met her at the Giant of Shame. After she defeated the giant, she said that she felt called to stay there and help others win their battle."

Esther held up her hand. "That's where I met her, too! We've been together ever since."

Disciple nodded. "So that's where she went. I came by that way with Peter a few months later, and a young woman named Elizabeth had taken her place."

Clasping her hands, Esther said, "Elizabeth! How is she doing? I've thought a lot about her since that day. Overcomer and I prayed for her on many occasions."

"She's doing great," said Disciple. "God is using her mightily to help others."

Zeal spoke up, "Elizabeth was the one who encouraged me when I battled the Giant of Shame."

After spending some time getting acquainted with one another, Jeremiah glanced over his shoulder. "I think someone should take Esther and show her what we're up against."

Zeal took a step toward her, but Disciple quickly said, "I'll do it."

Grinning, Zeal returned to Jeremiah's side.

After leading her to the edge of the valley, Disciple handed her his telescope and pointed below.

Esther peered at the vast camp of ogres and giants. "Overcomer didn't mention anything about this."

Disciple motioned for them to step back away from the edge. "I'm sure God is sending her to get re-enforcements."

They returned to the campsite, where the others were gathered.

Peter said, "I wonder how much longer it will be before God sends us into battle."

"Not long," said Disciple. "With the arrival of Esther, and soon Overcomer, I believe God is about to use us to launch an assault against His enemies."

Jeremiah grasped Zeal's hand. "I agree. We must all be prepared for what's ahead." He glanced toward the valley. "I believe it's going to be our greatest challenge yet."

****

Disciple and Jeremiah are right. Soon everything will be in place, and one of the most powerful teams ever assembled will be ready for battle. Their story will become legendary, and they will be known as The Warriors of God.

DON'T STOP READING:

Disciple's Quest IV: Warriors of God IS NOW AVAILABLE ON AMAZON!

Also available on Amazon:

Disciples Quest: The Adventure Begins

Disciples Quest 2: The Adventures of Jeremiah & Zeal

SCRIPTURE REFERENCES

Some of these quotes are only partial quotations from Scripture, and some are loose paraphrases designed to fit the dialogue.

Chapter 1

Esther took out her Book and turned to a comforting passage that she'd learned during the past year. "Do not fret or worry about anything, but in everything, continue to make your wants known to God, praying with definite requests and an attitude of thanksgiving. And God's peace, which transcends all understanding, will place a guard around your hearts and minds in Christ Jesus." (Philippians 4:6, 7)

Esther read these verses while staying at the inn: "He leads me in the paths of righteousness for His name's sake." (Psalms 23:3b NKJV) "Yes, even though I walk through the valley of the shadow of death, I will fear no evil, for You are with me; Your rod and Your staff, they comfort me." (Psalms 23: 4)

Chapter 3

Mr. Peterson preached from the following verses: "But seek first the kingdom of God and His righteousness, and all these things shall be added unto you." (Matthew 6:33 NKJV) "Therefore since you were raised up together with Christ, seek those things which are above, where Christ is sitting at the right hand of God. Continuously set your mind on things above, not on things on the earth. For you died, and your life has been hidden with Christ in God." (Colossians 3:1-3)

Chapter 9

Mrs. Johnson taught that it was the goodness of God that leads men to repentance. (Romans 2:4)

Mrs. Johnson read from Isaiah: "I, Yes I, am the One who wipes out and cancels your transgressions for My own sake, and I will not remember your sins." (Isaiah 43:25)

Mrs. Johnson read from her Book: "He has not dealt with us according to our sins, Nor punished us according to our iniquities." (Psalms 103:10 NKJV)

Mrs. Johnson taught that Jesus was our propitiation which means he bore all the wrath that was due our sins. (1 John 2:2)

Mrs. Johnson then read from another Psalm. "If You, Lord, kept account of and treated us according to our sins, who could stand? But with You there is forgiveness that You may be reverently feared and worshiped." (Psalms 130:3, 4)

When Mrs. Johnson read from Hebrews chapter 4, she was reading Hebrews 4:13.

Mrs. Johnson read, "For godly sorrow produces repentance leading to salvation, and leaves no regret, but worldly sorrow produces death." (2 Corinthians 7:10)

Mrs. Peterson said, "The moment you think you are standing, you should watch out lest you fall." (1 Corinthians 10:12)

Chapter 10

Esther read from Luke 7: 36-50

Esther read, "For I acknowledge my transgressions, and my sin remains continually before me. Against You, You only, have I sinned, and done this evil in Your sight, so that You may be justified when You give your sentence, and be blameless when You judge." (Psalms 51:3, 4)

Esther read, "For thus says the High and Exalted One, Who inhabits eternity and Whose name is Holy, I dwell in the high and holy place, with those who are thoroughly sorrowful for their sins and who are of a humble spirit, to revive the spirit of the humble, and to revive the hearts of the ones who are truly repentant for their sins." (Isaiah 57:15)

Esther taught that God gives grace to the humble. (Proverbs 3:34) And that we are invited to a Throne of Grace. (Hebrews 4:16) And in the presence of God there is fullness of joy. (Psalms 16:11)

Chapter 12

Esther read, "John says that when we abide in God, His love is perfected in us and this gives us confidence." (1 John 4:17a)

Esther read, "There is no fear in love, but perfect love casts out fear, because fear has to do with the dread of punishment. The one who fears has not been made perfect in love." (1 John 4:18)

Esther said, "God does not deal with me according to my sins but according to His mercy." (Psalms 103:10, 11)

Naomi remembered a verse she had been taught in Sunday school. "I have no strength of my own, but I am becoming strong in the Lord and in the power of His might." (Ephesians 6:10)

Esther said, "Our God has given us authority to trample on serpents, scorpions, and over all the power of the enemy, and nothing shall by any means hurt us. Today you will not taste our flesh, but you will taste our Swords!" (Psalms 91:13)(Luke 10:19 KJV)

Naomi said, "Through my God I shall do valiantly, for it is He who will tread down my enemies." (Psalms 108:13 NKJV)

Naomi said, "My Heavenly Father gives me so great a love that I can be called His very own child. That is why He fights for me!" (1 John 3:1)

Mrs. Green read, "Fear not, for I have redeemed you; I have called you by name, you are mine. When you pass through the waters, I will be with you; and through the rivers, they shall not overwhelm you; when you walk through fire you shall not be burned, and the flame shall not consume you. For I am the Lord your God, the Holy One of Israel, your Savior." (Isaiah 43:1b-3 NKJV)

Mrs. Green said, "That's why it's important to recognize that nothing can separate us from the love of Christ." (Romans 8:35)

Mrs. Green read from her Book, "But I am what I am by the grace of God, and His grace toward me was not wasted, for I worked harder than they all, yet it wasn't really me that was doing the work, but the grace of God in me." (1 Cor. 15:10)

Chapter 13

Pastor Jensen taught about the woman taken in adultery. (John 8:1-11)

A strong voice thundered, "From this point you shall be known as Overcomer! Your old life has passed away, and behold all things have become new." (2 Corinthians 5:17)

Chapter 14

Overcomer said, "You'll never feel good enough because you'll never be good enough. There is no one who is good. (Romans 3:12) Only God is good." (Luke 18:19)

Overcomer said, "All of the guilt and shame of our sin has been placed on Jesus at the cross. God is just waiting for us to come to Him and confess our sin so He can forgive us and cleanse us from its effects." (1 John 1:9)

The Holy Spirit reminded Elizabeth of the verse which said, "He has saved us, and called us with a holy calling, not according to our works, but according to His own purpose and grace, which He gave to us in Christ Jesus before the world began." (2 Timothy 1:9)

Elizabeth held out her Sword and took a step forward. "Even when I was nothing but sinful, God showed His unconditional love by sending His only Son to die for me." (Romans 5:8)

Elizabeth said, "For I have been persuaded that nothing is able to separate me from the love of God which is in Christ Jesus my Lord." (Romans 8:38, 39)

Elizabeth said, "God is my Father, and because I'm His daughter, He has sent forth His Spirit into my heart giving me the right and the privilege to call him ABBA FATHER!" (Galatians 4:6)

Elizabeth said, "It is my Heavenly Father that has qualified me and made me fit to share in the inheritance of all His children." (Colossians 1:12)

Elizabeth forcefully brought her Sword down on top of the giant's head. "I give praise to God's glorious grace, by which He has made me accepted among the beloved." (Ephesians 1:6)

The Holy Spirit reminded Esther of the Psalm, which assured her that God did not treat her according to her sins or reward her according to her iniquities. (Psalms 103:10)

Esther defiantly stared at the giant and raised her Sword. "If God kept a record of sins, no one could stand in His presence, but with Him, there is forgiveness that we might fear His name." (Psalms 130:3, 4)

Esther said, "God does not want my guilt offerings or else I would bring them. He only wishes that I bring him a truly repentant heart." (Psalms 51:16, 17)

Esther raised her Shield . "It was by grace through faith that I was saved, and not because of anything I could do." (Ephesians 2:8, 9)

Esther shouted, "The same grace by which I was saved, is the same grace in which I stand." (Romans 5:2)

Esther said, "As far as the east is from the west, this is how far He has removed my sins from me." (Psalms 103:12)

Esther readied her Sword for the final blow. "I know I'll fall short each and every day, but that's why I'll continuously come before the Throne of Grace for the mercy and forgiveness that I need." (Hebrews 4:16)

Chapter 15

Joseph turned a few pages in his Book and read, "Confess your faults to one another, and be praying for one another so that you may be healed." (James 5:16)

Chapter 16

Joseph took out his Book and read, "Make my joy complete by being like-minded, having the same love, being united in spirit, and being focused on one purpose." (Philippians 2:2)

Haley nodded and read from her Book. "I appeal to all of you, by the name of our Lord Jesus Christ, that you walk in harmony with one another, and that there be no divisions or rivalry among you. Be perfectly united together sharing the same understanding and judgment." (1 Corinthians 1:10)

Chapter 17

Esther took a step toward Millie. "God has sent us here with a message." Taking out her Book, she read, "For I know the thoughts that I think toward you, says the LORD, thoughts of well-being and not of misery, to give you a future and a hope." (Jeremiah 29:11)

Haley pointed toward heaven. "God wants to rescue you from the dominion of darkness, and transfer you into the kingdom of His beloved Son." (Colossians 1:13)

Overcomer read, "Come and let us reason together says the LORD, for even though your sins are like scarlet, they shall be white as snow. Even as they are red like crimson, they shall be white like wool." (Isaiah 1:18)

Joseph read about the Samaritan woman at the well.

Chapter 18

Katie beamed with excitement. "Rejoice in the Lord always: and again I say, Rejoice." (Philippians 4:4 KJV)

Esther turned a few pages. "I think we should continue to talk about joy. Here is one of my favorites, 'This is the day which the LORD hath made; we will rejoice and be glad in it.' " (Psalms 118:24 KJV)

"This is one of mine," said Overcomer. "For ye shall go out with joy, and be led forth with peace: the mountains and the hills shall break forth before you into singing, and all the trees of the field shall clap their hands." (Isaiah 55:12 KJV)

Cassandra took her Book in her hand and started to slowly turn the pages. "Right after Frank died I used to read this at night. 'For though His anger is only for a moment, His favor is for a lifetime. Weeping may last through the night, but joy comes in the morning.' " (Psalms 30:5)

Pastor Davis said, "When I think about all that He's done for me, all I can do is agree with Job, 'Though He slay me, yet will I trust in Him.' " (Job 13:15a KJV)

Pastor Davis turned in his Book. "As we close here today, I want to read a couple of Scriptures. The first is in Isaiah. 'Therefore the redeemed of the LORD shall return, and come with singing unto Zion; and everlasting joy shall be upon their head: they shall obtain gladness and joy; and sorrow and mourning shall flee away.' " (Isaiah 51:11 KJV)

Pastor Davis turned over a few more pages. "And the next verse is in the Psalms. 'They that sow in tears shall reap in joy. He that goeth forth and weepeth, bearing precious seed, shall doubtless come again with rejoicing, bringing his sheaves with him.' " (Psalms 126:5, 6 KJV)

Chapter 19

Overcomer took out her Book. "God's word says that Jesus came with grace and truth." (John 1:14, 17)

Esther turned in her Book. "That reminds me of a verse. 'Don't be deceived. Bad company corrupts good behavior.' " (1 Corinthians 15:33)

Chapter 20

Overcomer turned a few pages in her Book. "Here is a verse that God ministered to me right after I started on this Quest. 'I beseech you therefore, brethren, by the mercies of God, that you present your bodies a living sacrifice, holy, acceptable to God, which is your spiritual worship.' " (Romans 12:1)

The Mythos said, "We rather enjoy handing out the beatings anyway. We've beat on all of you at one point or another. You were just too drunk or too high to realize what was happening." (Proverbs 23:31-35)

Raising his Sword, Billy shouted, "I will stand fast in the freedom in which Christ has made me free!" (Galatians 5:1)

Overcomer moved forward. "Men, consider yourselves to be dead to this sin of addiction. Your old man has been crucified with Christ with all of its passions and lusts. Since you have been raised to a new life in Christ, sin can no longer dominate you if you choose to resist it." (Romans 6:1-13)

Overcomer yelled out, "Having done all to stand, Stand! (Eph. 6:13, 14)

Chapter 21

Overcomer opened up her Book and read. "LORD, who will abide in your tabernacle? Who will dwell on Your holy hill? The one that walks uprightly practicing righteousness, and who speaks the truth in their heart." (Psalms 15:1, 2)

Overcomer reached over and put her hand next to Esther's on the outer shell surrounding Lucy's body. "Dear Lord you forgave me of so many things. You said that if anyone was caught up in a fault that those of us who are living by your Spirit should seek to restore them. You said that we should do this with an attitude of humility knowing that we too are subject to the same temptations. It is only by your grace that I am not caught up in this same web." (Galatians 6:1)

Lucy stepped forward and began slicing at the giant web with her Sword. "Lying lips are disgusting before the LORD, but those who speak truthfully are His delight." (Proverbs 12:22)

Forcefully swinging her Sword, Overcomer shouted, "Therefore, putting away lying, let each one of you speak the truth with his neighbor." (Ephesians 4:25 NKJV)

Esther join them, slicing through the web with her Sword. "Do not lie or speak falsehood to another, for you have put off the old man and its sinful practices." (Colossians 3:9)

Chapter 22

Ms. Crandle said, "Yes, that last verse does seem troubling doesn't it. 'Even so you also, when you have done all the things you've been commanded to do, say, we are unprofitable servants who have done only what is our duty to do.' " (Luke 17:10)

Ms. Crandle turned in her Book and read, "But by the grace of God I am what I am, and His grace toward me was not in vain; but I labored more abundantly than they all, yet not I, but the grace of God which was with me." (1 Corinthians 15:10)

Ms. Crandle turned over a few pages and read, "But God, being rich in mercy, because of His great love with which He loved us, even while we were dead in transgressions and sins, made us alive together in union with Christ (for by grace you have been saved)." (Ephesians 2:4, 5)

Ms. Crandle motioned for them to sit down. "That's the kind of question we all ought to be asking. The most powerful allure of sin is the promise that we can be gods. This is what Satan and the fallen angels told themselves when they rebelled. Satan said that he would be like the Most High." (Isaiah 14:13, 14)

Esther quickly flipped over in her Book to read the account of Satan's temptation of Eve in the garden. (Genesis 3:1-5)

Chapter 23

Esther flipped over in her Book and read. "Behold, I am the LORD, the God of all mankind. Is anything too difficult for me?" (Jeremiah 32:27)

Julie said, "When Sarah laughed because God told Abraham that she would bare a son in her old age, God's answer was, is anything too hard for the LORD?" (Genesis 18:14)

Esther turned in her Book. "Paul wrote to the Romans that as our minds are renewed we are able to know what the will of the Lord is for us. (Romans 12:2)

Julie turned over in her Book. "Listen to this. 'And when you turn to the right hand, and when you turn to the left, your ears will hear a voice behind you, saying, This is the way. Walk in it.' " Setting her

Book down, she said, "What if God has given us the vision for what we're to do, and He'll give us more guidance once we act on what He's already said?" (Isaiah 30:21 WEB)

Nicholas shouted, "Oh Lord, I know that you can do all things, and nothing that you plan can be stopped." (Job 42:2)

Pam said, "With God nothing is impossible!" (Luke 1:37)

Scott proclaimed, "Jesus said that all things are possible to those who believe." (Mark 9:23)

Julie said, "We serve the Lord our God! It is He who has made the heavens and the earth by His great power and mighty outstretched arm! Nothing is too difficult for Him." (Jeremiah 32:17)

Overcomer shouted, "If God is for us, who can stand against us!" (Romans 8:31)

Scott opened up his Book. "Declaring the end from the beginning and from ancient times the things still yet to be done, saying, My counsel shall stand, and I will accomplish everything that I have purposed." (Isaiah 46:10)

Chapter 25

Overcomer opened up her Book. "Jesus said, 'And this is the condemnation, that the light has come into the world, and men loved darkness rather than light, because their deeds were evil. For everyone practicing evil hates the light and does not come to the light, lest his deeds should be exposed.' " (John 3:19, 20 NKJV)

Overcomer said, "Not only is God light, but He's also an all consuming fire." (Hebrews 12:29)

Luke prayed, "Dear Lord, we know that you are with us wherever we go. You were sent to this earth to give light to the ones sitting in darkness, the ones who are covered by the shadow of death. (Luke 1:79)

John nodded, "Yes father. 'For though we walk through the valley of the shadow of death we will fear no evil.' " (Psalms 23:4)

Teresa grabbed her father's hand. "For Thou art with us, Thy rod and Thy staff, they comfort us." (Psalms 23:4)

Luke said, "We are all children of light, and children of the day. We don't belong to the night, or to darkness." (1 Thessalonians 5:5)

Overcomer raised her Sword. "We are soldiers of the Light. For we were once darkness, but now we are light in the Lord." (Ephesians 5:8)

Luke shouted, "I have put away the works of darkness, and I have put on the Armor of Light!" (Romans 13:12)

Luke shouted, "I am a member of a chosen race, a royal priesthood, a holy nation, a person for God's own possession, so that I may proclaim the excellencies of Him who called me out of darkness and into his marvelous light!" (1 Peter 2:9)

Luke then shouted, "OH God, you have called us to be vessels to open the eyes of those you send our way, in order to turn them from darkness to light, and from the power of Satan to the power of Your Kingdom, that they may receive forgiveness of sins and an inheritance among those who have been sanctified by faith in You." (Acts 26:18)

Chapter 26

Elder Jenkins said, "The Apostle Paul tells us in his letter to the Philippians that we are to work out our own salvation with fear and trembling, knowing that it is God that gives us both the desire and the ability to work according to His good pleasure." (Philippians 2:12, 13)

Elder said, "And if we had to fight the battle against sin through our own strength it would be impossible, but we have a power within us that is much greater than our sin. Paul said that if we walk by the Spirit we will not fulfill the lusts of the flesh." (Galatians 5:16)

Ms. Jones stood up and joined them. "It's also important to remember that we are the ones that determine whether or not we will submit to our old nature or to the Holy Spirit. If we set our minds on things of the flesh then we will live according to the flesh, but if we set our minds on the things of the Spirit then we will live according to the Spirit." (Romans 8:5)

Chapter 27

Esther read, Esther turned in her Book again. "This is what Jesus said about Judas Iscariot. 'The Son of Man indeed goes just as it is written of Him, but woe to that man by whom the Son of Man is betrayed! It would have been good for that man if he had never been born.' " (Mark 14:21 NKJV)

Esther said that God had planned the events leading up to Christ's crucifixion before the foundation of the world. (Revelation 13:8)

Simone read, "Your eyes saw me when I was still unborn, and in Your book all the days of my life were written before they ever happened, when as yet there was none of them." (Psalms 139:16)

Esther said, "This is what Jesus said to Pilate. 'You would have no power at all against me, unless it were given to you from above. Therefore he who delivered me to you has greater sin.' " (John 19:11 WEB)

Malia read, "In whom also we have been appointed an inheritance, having been predestined according to the purpose of Him who works all things according to the counsel of His own will." (Ephesians 1:11)

"Yes," said Esther. "God is completely sovereign and working all things out according to His purpose and plan. We can rest knowing that everything will eventually work together for our good no matter what our circumstances look like at the time." (Romans 8:28)

Chapter 28

Esther dug in with her Shoes. "We do not come at you today with our own strength, but with the strength of the LORD Almighty, Jesus Christ, the Commander of the Armies of God." (1 Samuel 17:45)

Overcomer defiantly stood with her Sword raised high. "Our Lord has already triumphed over you on the cross, and through His power we will triumph over you as well." (Colossians 2:15)(Ephesians 3:10)

Overcomer shouted, "Thanks be to God who ALWAYS causes us to triumph in Christ Jesus!" (2 Corinthians 2:14)

Esther proclaimed, "The Lord our God goes before us. It is He who fights for us and gives us the victory!" (Deuteronomy 20:4)

As their enemy flew off, Overcomer yelled out, "God is not finished with you, Abbadon! Someday His mighty angels will throw you into the Lake that Burns Forever, and there you will remain for all of eternity!" (Matthew 25:41) (Revelation 20:10)

ABOUT THE AUTHOR

I have a passion for teaching God's word and making it relatable to anyone who wants to learn. I believe that understanding and applying the words of God is the key to success in all areas of life.

Walter Cantrell